Shadowflasher!

"Lass!" A stifled croak. "Behind you!"

She whirled to look.

All she saw at first was a white fog-whisp, crawling like a snake from inside the dungeon. In silent flight from it, Lord Archy skimmed past her. She saw the fog recoil, as if it had sensed some danger in her. Then the tip of it thickened, lifted, paused as if exploring.

She saw it change.

It took her dead mother's shape.

Darting at her, it struck like a snake.

THE QUEEN
OF THE LEGION

JACK WILLIAMSON

A TIMESCAPE BOOK
PUBLISHED BY POCKET BOOKS NEW YORK

Another *Original* publication of TIMESCAPE BOOKS

A Timescape Book published by
POCKET BOOKS, a Simon & Schuster division of
GULF & WESTERN CORPORATION
1230 Avenue of the Americas, New York, N.Y. 10020

ISBN: 0-671-82509-7

First Timescape Books printing January, 1983

10   9   8   7   6   5   4   3   2   1

For Blanche

THE QUEEN
OF THE LEGION

1

The legend of Jil Gyrel has an unlikely opening.

It finds her a lonely child.

A spindly little girl, big-eyed and generally grimed with red dust and mud, born in a shabby little town on a bare frontier world. She used to dream about the Legion, wishing she might grow up to be another of its storied heroes. But she was poor and isolated. Except for her old grandfather, nobody wanted her. She had no visible gifts, no visible promise of any great destiny.

True, fireballs had burned in the sky on the night she was born, but fireballs were common at Hawkshead Pass. Meteors rained out of the blazing nebular sky every winter night, and her mother hated them.

Nobody told her that she could ever grow up to write her name on the roll that men remember.

Yet she did.

Thanks to the nebula.

The Great Hawkshead Nebula on the star maps. It had been born when a small star cluster drifted into a larger galactic cloud. Gravity condensed gas and dust. New stars formed, some gigantic. The giant suns burned their mass, exploding into supernovas. A shockwave spread from the multiple explosions, searing the worlds of the older stars with nuclear fury.

A cosmic instant later, the dying shockwave met a faster-racing human explosion. Riding rockets and geodesic drives, men had srpead far from old Terra. The shockwave checked them. Cooler by then, grown too thin to see, it was still a deadly barrier to any craft under non-Newtonian propulsion.

Checked, the human wave refused to stop. Starmen hungered too hard for the worlds within the nebula. Those old planets were empty now, burned clean by the shockwave, all their strange wonders waiting to be reclaimed. It was Commander Ben Gyrel, on the *Legion Argo*, who found the way through the barrier wave.

The Gyrel Channel, as men came to call it, marked by the three Beacon Suns. Alpha, safely outside the nebula. Beta, at the channel mouth. Gamma, the first star inside. Beta itself had opened the channel. A hot blue star, flung from the nebula's exploding core by savage tidal forces, it had overtaken the dying wave to sweep a tunnel through it. Flying now at the wave's forefront, Beta and its single far planet were still wrapped in the hazardous clouds of meteor drift they had gathered.

Most men dreaded the nebula, even while its riches and mysteries allured them. It swallowed Jil's father. Her mother feared it and despised Hawkshead Pass. The Legion station there had been important once, but that cherished greatness had faded long before her birth.

The shining starships still went by, following the tachyonic flashers old Ben had set spinning to mark the channel, but most of them steered around Beta's meteor swarms. The Pass had little left but memory, yet Jil's childhood there began happily enough.

She loved the long winter nights, when she could see the nebula. Its splendid fire-wings burned green and scarlet beyond the black dust cloud that made the hook-beaked head. Even the meteor storms that terrified her mother were wild celebrations for her.

She used to stand outside until her mother screamed for her to come in, shivering to the frost and that blazing wonder. Sudden blades of white fire sliced the night, and bright explosions filled it with rumbling thunder. Sometimes rock fragments rattled down around her in a whiff of hot sulphur.

She felt born for the nebula, always somehow certain that it
would be her destiny. All her life she had known the hardy
people who ventured up the passage into its wonders and its
perils. She felt proud of her name, because the Gyrels had been
a Legion family. Some reckless prank had washed her grandfather out of the Legion Academy, but her father was a Legión
pilot, and she was determined to follow when she could.

"A space person?" The notion shocked her mother. "Baby
doll, you don't know what the Legion is. You'd have to live
with rough, foul-spoken men. You'd be a slave to silly regula-
tions. You'd be taught to fight—to destroy your own innocent
fellow beings. My darling baby doll, a butcher in the Legion!"

Her mother had her own plans for Jil.

"You hurt me, baby doll." Worry pinched her made-up
face. "You could be pretty. A proper little lady. If you would
keep out of the mud and comb your hair and learn the civilized
manners you'll need when we get out of this horrid hole and
back home to Terra."

Jil didn't mind the mud. She didn't want to be proper little
lady. Most of all, she didn't like being called baby doll. Her
grandfather never minded whether she combed her hair, and
he said she didn't need civilized airs here on the star frontier.

Sometimes she found it hard to like her mother. Her grandfather was the one she loved. A thin, frail old man when she
knew him, but very straight and spry. His eyes were blue and
bright, with a crinkly smile always around them, and he had
never been afraid of the nebula.

People called him Lucky Lyn. His luck had come from the
Gyrel gift. That was a special sense of space and energy and
mass and distance that the space medics had never entirely
understood, though they called it a space-adaptive mutation.
It made the Gyrel men master starpilots, able to perceive and
avoid the hazards of the nebula, at least as long as they were
lucky.

The gift had brought old Ben Gyrel up the channel into the
nebula. Lyn was his son, born with the gift. It had led him to
rich strikes on a dozen new planets while he was young, though
he had lost the gift and most of his luck long before she was
born.

She used to dream she might somehow inherit that rare
talent and pilot a craft of her own up Gyrel channel, but her

mother always told her that could never happen.

"Don't fool yourself, baby doll. Women can carry the mutant gene, but the gift itself is linked to sex. The medics say only males can display it." Her mother looked unhappy. "It broke your father's heart when you weren't born a boy."

If her father ever really felt that way, he had forgiven her long ago. He was a lean, quiet man with a gentle voice and sad blue eyes that seemed to be always looking for far-off stars. He limped a little from some old accident he didn't talk about. She never knew him really well, because he was nearly always gone on another endless voyage.

The commander of his ship was Captain Shon Macharn. The captain had no family, and he often came home with her father. He was stronger and taller, very straight, with shining Legion medals on his uniform. He liked to tell about the strange worlds where they had been. Sometimes he brought her little beads of fused metal and glass, relics of unknown creatures the shockwave had killed.

Fingering those odd beads, she wondered about those lost beings. Could they have been like men, perhaps as noble and brave as the old heroes of the Legion? Though the beads told her very little, a sense of tragedy haunted her. The wave must have been very dreadful, sweeping whole worlds and erasing everything.

Only the laser-diamonds had not been burned. Captain Macharn had told her about them before her father found one he brought back for her mother. It was a small black crystal, eight-sided like a natural diamond crystal, but different in every other way. The feel of it was queerly slick and cold, the color so black that it almost hurt her eyes. The laser light darted out of it in sudden stabbing arrows, red and green like the nebula itself.

Her father let her hold it in her hand, but he said he had to sell it because her mother needed the money. When Captain Macharn saw how much she wanted it, he paid her father for it and gave it to her to keep for her very own.

She loved him for the gift and for his deep rumbly laugh and because he loved her. After he and her father were gone back into the nebula, she kept the wonderful diamond in the bottom of the old space locker in her room, and one her grandfather had brought with him out to the nebula. Sometimes at night she took the diamond with her to bed, holding it in her hand

and wondering about the mystery of it till she fell asleep.

"Nobody knows," her grandfather said when she asked him what it was. "They've been found on a dozen planets deep inside the nebula. Somebody must have made them, back before the shockwave passed. Who? Why?" He shrugged, looking far away. "We can't even guess."

"I'll find out," she promised him. "When I grow up."

"Perhaps you can." His eyes came back to study her. "The nebula has a lot of mysteries men have never solved."

Even the laser flashes were something nobody could explain. Light was absorbed by that shining blackness, her grandfather said. Somehow it was stored and changed and flashed out again. When people split the diamonds, looking for the secret, all they got was graphite dust.

She used to hope her father and Captain Macharn might discover laser-makers still alive or, anyhow, learn how they had lived and died. Her grandfather thought they must have been in flight from the exploding stars in the core of the nebula when disaster overtook them, but he was afraid no evidence would ever be found.

The strange black diamonds were very hard to burn. That was why any were left. Slowly cooling, the shockwave had left air that men could breathe and such hardy plants as leather-weed on some of the outer planets, far enough from the nebula core, but nothing else alive.

Many of those burned worlds were still deadly traps, hot with killing radiation and wrapped in unknown danger, but they were all rich with precious heavy elements created in the supernovas. Her father's job, and Captain Macharn's, was to find those treasure planets and tame their dangers so humans could live there.

She loved her recollections of the times when they used to come home, nearly always together. Their space gear would have faint odors of the far worlds where they had been. Her father never talked much, but Captain Macharn would tell about their exciting flights and landings. Her mother would make good things to eat and open a bottle of bright-smelling Nebulon wine, and they were all happy together.

The captain and her father had been best friends since they first met at the Legion Academy, back on old Terra. They had known her mother there. Jil wondered once if her mother should have married the captain and kept him out of the nebula. Because she didn't really like the Legion, or anybody in it, or even the people coming up the channel.

"Scum of humanity," her mother called them. "Not one spark of culture in a shipload of them. Don't you ever speak to them, baby doll, or let them speak to you."

"Be nice to your mother," her grandfather told her once, when Jil was feeling hurt and angry. "We must try to understand. The trouble is, she doesn't belong. She was born too proud of her own people, and she's never learned to love the Gyrel name."

Her own people were the Ulnars. They claimed to be descended from the old space emperors, and her mother yearned for the time centuries ago when they had ruled Terra and all the other planets of Sol from their splendid Purple Hall.

Her name was really Tsara, but she had pronounced it Rara when she was small, and people still called her that. She was a slim little woman with a dimpled chin and bright yellow hair. Beautiful, Jil thought when she was happy. That wasn't often.

"Trapped herself." Lucky Lyn was wryly blunt about it. "When she heard about the Gyrel gift, she hoped your father would strike it rich here in the nebula. Rich enough to make her another Purple Empress."

Even the laser-diamonds left her disappointed. They had never led her father to the fine strike she longed for, and the few he found weren't worth much except to curious scientists. Interesting, maybe, but too queer and black and cold for jewels.

Jil was only seven when her father and Captain Macharn left on their last flight. They were taking a scientific expedition deep into the deadly heart of the nebula to look for the unknown birthplace of the laser-makers. Their starship was the *Iron Argo*. Tachyophone calls came back from Gamma II, where they took on reaction mass, and from Freeland IV, where they left a sick starman, but that was all.

Her grandfather kept promising that they could still get back safe, but her mother used to sit crying all day in the faint, stale perfume scents that clung to the Ulnar heirlooms she had brought with her from Terra. She wanted to take Jil back there, to her family and the world she still called home, but there was no money until her father's insurance could be paid. Waiting, they stayed on in her grandfather's old house at Hawkshead Pass.

"Baby doll, you don't know." Her voice was turning bitter now. "We're stuck way out here on the backside of nowhere. Nothing but mud and dust and brutalizing danger. No culture anywhere. We've got to get out before the nebula wrecks your life and makes a horrid hag of me."

The insurance took too long, because it had to wait for proof of presumption of death. Her grandfather said it had to be delayed because her father might come back, and Jil loved him for letting her hope. She used to talk to him in the tiny upstairs room he had kept for himself.

It was bare and very clean. She nearly always found him sitting at the window on a hard chair he liked, looking out across the starport. She would sit on the narrow cot where he slept, asking him about the Gyrel gift and the planets in the nebula and the old heroes of the Legion.

He was always very cheery, trying not to disappoint her, but of course Commander Kalam and Hal Samdu and the great John Star had all been men. Even old Giles Habibula, who was no hero at all. Though unknown planets were left in the nebula, most of them were too hot to be explored. Gently, he reminded her that she shouldn't keep hoping to inherit the gift.

She tried not to let that hurt.

Sometimes he let her walk with him down the hill to the Pass and on to the starport. Though he never drank much, he liked to sit in the Quasar Club or the Hawkshead House and sip one small glass of Nebulon wine. After she had promised not to tell her mother, he would let her come inside with him. She could have a plain synfruit ice, and they would listen to the dusters.

These were men and women on their way into the nebula or, now and then, coming back. Starpilots and spacemen in Legion green. Miners and traders and colonists with families. Some he used to talk to her about as they walked back home. Con men and gamblers and terraforming engineers. Sometimes people he thought were fugitive criminals or political exiles. People he called utopian reformers and missionary evangelists. People her mother despised, but they filled him with a wistful admiration.

"The breed I used to be!" His old eyes lit. "Out on their own, daring everything for one last chance at space and freedom and the style of life they want. If I were only young again—"

Sometimes when he paused he looked very solemnly at her. She thought he must be wishing she had been born a boy, though he was far too kind to say so.

"I saw the old worlds once," he told her. "When I went back to the Academy. I got one taste of what they call civilization. That little was too much. Too many people and too little freedom. Everybody smashed into the same hard mold, forced to live exactly like everybody else."

He stopped to frown at her.

"A thousand different social systems, all too much alike. They take your liberty away, always in the name of some high-sounding abstraction. They feed you—though not very well. They keep you busy at some dull job. While they're stifling your mind. Maybe they're what has to be, back on those hive-worlds. A lot of people seem content. The nebula was never meant for women. Anyhow, not for women like your mother."

"It's what I want." Jil squeezed his hand. "Even if I wasn't born a boy!"

The year she was nine, Captain Macharn got back from inside the nebula.

2

Jil went with her grandfather to see the captain in the hospital on the old Legion base. They found him sitting propped up in bed, staring at the window. He jumped in a frightened way when they spoke, and she saw he didn't know them.

She hardly knew him either, because something had changed him so dreadfully from the great laughing man she had loved so much. Something had shrunk him. His skin was bleached to a pale yellow color, and it hung loose on his big bones. His eyes had turned yellowish around the pupils, which looked huge and black and glassy. When they stared at her, she thought they were filled with a suffering and terror she couldn't understand. His lax lips twitched, as if he wanted to speak but couldn't. She crouched away from him, behind her grandfather.

"Shon—" Her grandfather's whisper was hoarse and broken. "Don't you know us?"

His gaunt head moved in a queer, jerky way. Those terrible eyes glared at her and back at her grandfather. His shriveled face twitched again.

"Who are you?" His voice was stronger than she expected,

yet stiff and strange as the way he moved. "What—you—want?"

"Don't you—don't you remember us?" Her grandfather leaned closer, speaking louder. "I'm Lyn Gyrel. Your pilot's father." He reached for Jil's arm, and she felt him trembling. "Don't you know Jil? Jef's daughter? The little imp you always tried to spoil?"

She tried to say hello, but no sound came. She had begun to smell a bad odor, like the burnt-sulphur reek of the meteor storms and more like the bogs down around Black Lake, where Terran fish couldn't live, but worse than either one. It made her feel queasy.

His gritty voice rasped again, "What's this—this place?"

"Hawkshead Pass." Looking pale, her grandfather reached to touch him. "Shon, what's hit you? And my son? What's become of my son?"

"Hawk? . . . Head?" Moving like a clumsy puppet, Macharn slapped her grandfather's hand away. He blinked around the room and back at them, whispering harsh, breathless words: "Am—still—in nebula?"

"You're almost—almost out." Her grandfather flinched from the slap and those wild yellow eyes. "Where's the *Argo*? Did you wreck—"

"Got to—" he grated. "Got to get—outside—"

A nurse at the door was beckoning, but her grandfather didn't move until she tiptoed in and touched his arm. White and trembling, he hurried Jil out of the hospital then and back to the old house on the hill, saying nothing at all.

That night she had a terrible dream. It was winter, with the nebula blazing green and red across the sky. Her father and Captain Macharn were walking on the ice across Black Lake. The ice was too thin. It crackled and broke. They sank into the bog, splashing the thick yellow mud. Somehow they couldn't scream for help, but she saw the terror in their staring eyes.

She waded out, trying to help them. The freezing mud had the hot-sulphur smell of the meteor storm. It tried to suck her under. Her father kept waving her back, but she slogged on until she couldn't move and the rotten bog stink took her breath. When she finally woke, shivering and cold, she was afraid to try to sleep again.

Morning came at last. Her grandfather was going back to the base to find out more about Macharn, and he let her come with him. The Legion scout ship that had brought the sick man out of the nebula was standing at the service dock. The corporal at the gate had no authority to admit civilians, but he said they could look for the ship's commander at the Hawks-head House.

They found him in the lounge, sitting alone at a corner table. He was Pilot-Major Kynan Star, a lean, straight man as tall as her father had been. He looked tired and grim, but his solemn brown eyes warmed when he saw her, as if he wanted to smile. He stood up when her grandfather told him who they were.

"I was hoping to meet you, sir, because I knew your son." He turned to Jil with a sad little bow. "Your father. He was my friend. A brave and able starman. I'm sorry we couldn't bring him back."

Her grandfather was asking about the *Iron Argo.*

"No news, sir." He looked distressed. "Sit down, and please forgive me"—he shook his head at the half-empty bottle on the table—"if I've had too much."

He held a chair for Jil as if she had been grown up, and they sat down.

"You must understand that search operations deep in the nebula are seldom possible." He looked at them both, making sure they understood. "It's too vast and too hostile for our little squadron. Macharn and your son had special orders for a flight far beyond our normal operating range. Too far for any search. Macharn's rescue now is sheer accident."

He reached for his drink, and she saw his hand quivering.

"We've seen him," her grandfather said. "I wish we hadn't."

"I wish I hadn't."

"What—what hurt him?"

Kynan Star squinted at his spilling glass and set it carefully back without drinking. "I'm afraid to guess."

They waited for him to say more.

"A hard thing to talk about." He looked at the bottle with a wry little shrug. "Or even to think about."

"The pilot was Jil's father," her grandfather reminded him. "We've got to know what happened to him."

"I've no idea." His tired eyes peering unhappily at Jil, he tried to explain. "The nebula has always swallowed starships and men. It seldom tells what happened. When they go inside, that's a risk you take. It gets greater as you approach the core.''

"But you did find Macharn," her grandfather said. "We need to know how and where."

"If you think that will help." He shrugged as if he knew it wouldn't. "We picked up a distress call. From Fuego IV. That's too far in for civilians. The Legion has it on the Red List, but that doesn't keep the dusters out. Not when they're striking it rich. They opened Thorium Lode a dozen years ago and shipped a lot of ore."

"Till the cliffdrillers struck."

"Drillers?" Her grandfather blinked. "I've heard the tales, but I never saw a driller."

"Nobody has—not really." The trouble lines in his face bit deeper. "They strike in the dark and hide again when they're through. But I saw what they did to Thorium Lode."

Jil wanted to ask him what the drillers were.

"Creatures." He had seen the question on her face. "There was life on these stars before the shockwave struck. Some of the toughest things survived, mostly on worlds still too hot for us."

His tired eyes went back to her grandfather.

"You don't find drillers in space labs or museums, because they don't get caught. Most of what we have is rumor—some of it I guess invented to discourage rival prospectors. But the drillers are said to be rock-eating moles with a special appetite for heavy metals and anything radioactive. Maybe able to migrate across space."

Her grandfather shook his head in a doubtful way, but he let Kynan Star go on.

"All I really know is what we found at Thorium Lode. Once a rich camp. Several hundred dusters working there, men and women tough enough to laugh at the risks—till the drillers hit. One midnight. No warning at all. The people who could got off into space. We found the rest huddled on a little hill a few kilometers from where the settlement had been.

"The camp itself was gone. Mine workers, ore mills, shipping docks, business street, dwellings—eaten! I walked across the site. Not a scrap of metal anywhere. Solid bedrock crumbled into the finest dust I ever saw where the drillers must have burst out and burrowed back.

"We took the survivors aboard. Not one had seen a driller,

because the creatures came from underneath. Ships and structures just sank into the ground. Fast, they said, in noise and dust that left them deaf and choking for breath."

He shook his head with a grim little smile.

"You've got to respect those dusters. Half-naked, most of them, because they'd had to run with what they could grab, but they got off the *Sunmark* at our first stop. Going back to Fuego, when they can, in spite of the drillers and everything else."

Sadly, he shrugged at Jil.

"That's about it."

"Not yet," her grandfather said. "Not till you tell us about Macharn."

"Staggered aboard with the rest." Kynan Star's worry marks bit deeper, as if he hated what he had to say. "In the rags of a Legion uniform. Collapsed on the deck. At the point of death, with a set of symptoms our medics had never seen."

"How had he got there?"

"Nobody knows." He was looking very solemnly at Jil. "He was too far gone to talk. I questioned the dusters, but none of them remembered seeing him around the mines or anywhere before the raid. They thought the drillers must have brought him, but I don't see how that could be."

He spread his empty hands.

"About my son?"

He shook his head at Jil.

"If you found Macharn, can't you—"

"We weren't searching." Kynan Star's voice turned flat and bitter. "The fact is, we've no resources for that. I don't like to say it, sir, but these times are bad for the Legion. Perhaps our human worlds have been at peace too long. Perhaps too many listen to the Antiacs—"

He saw that Jil was puzzled.

"The Antiacs are peace kooks," he told her. "They laugh at the Legion. Deny we ever saved mankind. Claim instead that we ourselves caused the old space wars. Say we should have gone out unarmed to meet the Medusae and the Cometeers and let them be our friends. They want to disband the Legion and get rid of AKKA—"

"AKKA?" Her grandfather gasped. "Leave ourselves naked?"

"AKKA is our great weapon." He spoke again to Jil. "A

secret weapon, entrusted to the Keeper of the Peace to be used only as our desperate last defense. The present Keeper is a woman—in fact, a second cousin of mine. Named Vivi Star.''

He smiled very solemnly at Jil when he thought of Vivi Star.

"A lovely girl when I knew her, but that was long ago. Chosen to be Keeper, she had to give up the sort of life we both had known. A sad time for me. Almost as if she had died. I suppose she's in some fortress, under Legion guard, but everything about her has to be a supreme secret now."

Wondering what the Keeper's life would really be, Jil thought the great secret of AKKA must surely be exciting enough to make up for whatever she had to leave behind. She wanted to ask if she might ever be chosen for one of the Keeper's guardians when she had grown up and trained in the Legion, but Kynan Star had already turned to her grandfather.

"Insanity, sir!" he was muttering. "Contagious insanity! The Antiacs are playing politics in the Hall of Stars. Diverting funds to their pet special interests. Already starving the Legion here in the nebula. Threatening to pull us out altogether, leaving the colonists to defend themselves—if they can."

He stood up, with a grave little bow for Jil, and asked them to excuse him. He said he was sorry he couldn't bring her father back, but perhaps Captain Macharn would get well enough to tell what had happened to the *Iron Argo*.

He walked away slowly, looking burdened with trouble and older than he was. Jil felt sorry for him and sad about her missing father. She had begun to worry, too, about the Antiacs. She didn't understand why any human being could want to be rid of AKKA and the Keeper of the Peace, and she felt afraid that when she grew up there might be no Legion left for her to join.

3

Kynan Star took off the next day for the Legion base on Alpha IV. Jil stood out in the dusty yard behind her grandfather's house, watching the vanishing speck of the *Sunmark* and the white jet trail that spread and faded behind it, trying to shake off her troubled wonder about the cliffdrillers and the Antiacs. It would take creatures worse than they were, she decided, to keep her out of the nebula.

When she asked her grandfather for more about the Antiacs, he was still too badly upset to talk about anything, but he did take her downtown with him the next day. They listened to a singer in the Quasar Club. A ratty little man with a high nasal voice and a scraggly yellow beard, the singer was named Rem Brendish.

Picking a battered astrolin, he whined "The Ballad of Giles Habibula." It was a crude satire that made her grandfather fume. The Legion of Space was an ugly racket, run by cunning thugs. AKKA was no superweapon, but just a toy popgun, too weak to hurt a fly. The stellar invaders in the old space wars, the Medusae and the Cometeers, had existed only in the boastful lies of the Legion's phony heroes. Jay Kalan and John Star, Hal Samdu and Ben Gyrel, they had all been cowardly braggarts, claiming greatness for deeds never done.

"And old Habibula was the best of them." That was his mocking refrain. "Too fat to fight, too old to run, too drunk to die, the best he did was dine and lie. He stuffed his gut and swilled his gin and told his tales to terrify."

The listeners were a little knot of worn-out prospectors, most of them bitter because the nebula had been too much for them. They tittered, and a few of them tossed coins. Her grandfather threw his wine glass. It grazed the singer's ear and stopped the song. The little man dived behind the bar, yelling for help.

"A hateful little rat." The barman ushered them hastily out, apologizing to her grandfather. "But he does pull the dust-busters in."

"Vicious slander!" Her grandfather was still brooding about it as they walked back home. "My father knew men who had known old Habibula. Maybe he did join the Legion to escape the law. But he had a way with locks, and he served the Legion well."

For a long time they stayed away from the Quasar Club. Her grandfather wouldn't talk about the Antiacs. He wouldn't talk about Captain Shon Macharn, even when her mother kept asking. One day her mother went out to the base hospital and came back seething with indignation.

"The poor dear man! He's getting better fast, though the silly medics won't believe it. They're all in a swivet, just because he had a sort of sickness they've never seen. They wanted to ship him back to the big Legion clinic on Alpha IV. When he wouldn't go, they called their specialists here to examine him.

"The dear brave man! They're all discombobulated, but he won't let them touch him. He's no guinea pig, and he wants his rights. He says he's getting out of the hospital—out of the Legion, too—before they ever stick a needle in him."

A few days later, he did get out. Her mother brought him home, saying he was his old self again. He had in fact changed amazingly, gaining flesh and vigor. His yellowed skin was pinker, the way he moved more natural. He had begun to remember.

Yet, except to her mother, he was not himself. He never laughed. His voice was still strange, too flat and too loud. He seemed absent-minded and abrupt, angry all the time. Worst of all, he still had that evil bog-rot odor. Every time Jil breathed it, she felt her stomach heave.

"He frightens me!" her grandfather muttered, more to himself than to her, once when they got away from the house. "Because he simply isn't Shon! I know the Legion did identify him. Voiceprints and fingerprints. Total biomatch. Even scraps of Shon's memory now. But still he's—something else!"

She had clutched his arm, and he saw her terror.

"But don't you fret about him," he went on quickly. "Because your mother thinks he is getting over whatever he had. If he really does, perhaps he can help us find your father. Anyhow, for her sake, we must treat him well."

Her mother, Jil thought, was treating him too well. He ate at the table with them and slept in her father's room. When he got strong enough, her mother went out with him. One night at the Quasar Club they heard Rem Brendish singing "The Ballad of Giles Habibula" and brought him home to talk to them about the Antiacs.

Though it made her grandfather furious, they said they were joining the cause. Her mother wanted money to help dear little Rem, and she began learning Antiac songs. Macharn's new voice wasn't musical at all, but he asked Brendish all about the movement and began making expensive tachyophone calls to people in the Cosmic Harmony Party, out on the older planets.

One day she found her precious laser-diamond missing from the bottom of the old space locker where she had kept it along with her last holo of her father and those odd fused beads out of the nebula. Nearly crying when she went to tell about it, she found Macharn with her mother in the musty living room.

"We meant to tell you, baby doll." Her mother tried to pat her head. "We had to sell your stone. After all, it was just a trinket. Not beautiful at all, though Rem says there's a new fad for them, and we did get quite a good price. Almost enough to pay your fare out to Alpha."

"I'm not going to Alpha—"

"But you are," Macharn said, sounding very stern and cold. "With us. On the next starship."

"Baby doll, we've a fine surprise for you." Her mother stopped to hug Macharn. "Shon and I are in love. We're getting married. Tomorrow! Our flight reservations are already made. After all these ugly years, we're getting out of this miserable mudhole, back to civilization. Isn't it wonderful!"

"I won't—won't go!" Her throat hurt. "I'll stay here with Grandfather."

"Young lady, you'll obey!" She thought Macharn was going to strike her. "If you're ill-humored about your missing pebble, you might recall that I gave it to you."

Tembling, staring at him, she whispered, "That—that wasn't you!"

"Baby doll!" Her mother was shocked. "You can't think such things. Shon's all right again, and we both want to make you happy. I know you used to love him. You ought to be delighted that he'll be your new father now."

"No!" He was a cold-faced stranger, with something terrible still in his eyes. She shrank away from him. "I won't—I can't be happy. Not with him."

"You'll learn, young lady." His voice was loud and harsh and strange. "You've a lot to learn. You ought to be grateful that we'll be putting you in school on Alpha III."

She watched for her grandfather all that endless afternoon and ran to meet him when she saw him walking home. Sobbing in his arms, she begged him to keep her with him.

"If I could—" His own voice caught, and she saw tears in his pale old eyes. "But your mother has rights. Besides—" He held her closer, and it seemed a long time before he went on. "I didn't want to tell you yet, but I'm not well."

"Oh, Grandfather—"

"Don't cry." He tried to smile. "After all, it had to happen. I've already lived a good while longer than most men do, and the medics keep down the pain."

She waited, afraid to ask about his illness.

"Don't blame the nebula," he whispered at last. "I love it, Jil, the way you do. But I took too many risks when I was young. Went too deep. Stayed too long. Caught too much radiation. It killed my own pilot sense a long time ago, back while your father was still away at the Academy. And now—"

That was all he said. She caught his hand, feeling the thin old bones, and they walked very slowly back to the house, where her mother was dithering about what to pack and Macharn was angrily demanding a scrambled tachyophone channel to the Cosmic Harmony office on Alpha III.

The wedding was in the Church of the Oversoul. That was what her mother wanted, because it had been the church of the old empire, and Macharn said he didn't care. Jil sat through the ceremony with her grandfather on a hard metal pew at the back of the gloomy old building. Macharn stalked out impatiently when it was over, her mother fluttering behind. Jil wondered how she could love him.

On that sad last day, her grandfather took her with him to Kere Nyaga's law office. It was a long dusty room above the Cluster Suns Trust. Kere Nyaga was a withered little black man, her grandfather's oldest friend. Very seldom busy, he always set a square amber bottle on his desk when they came in and rummaged through his cluttered desk to find her a sweet.

"Sit down, Miss Jil." He limped around the desk to bring her the bonbon from a package he had bought just for her. That was long ago, and he was cheerily unaware of how dry and hard and stale they had become. "Good news for you today."

For one delighted instant, she thought he had found some legal way for her to stay with her grandfather. She was darting to hug him when she heard something about the estate.

"That's right, Jil." Her grandfather put his bone-thin arm around her. "You'll be my heir. Most of what I used to have is gone, but you'll inherit the old house. And funds enough, besides, to let you choose your own career. Kere will manage the estate till you're eighteen."

She kissed him gratefully, trying not to think of the time when he would die. He came down to the starport with them that night. Knowing she would never see him again, she clung to him at he departure gate until Macharn dragged her roughly away.

4

The planets of Beacon Alpha liked to call themselves the window worlds. Safe outside, they had grown fat with wealth from the nebular trade. Alpha III was a teeming human hive, all its land and half its seas buried under city level piled on mass-packed city level. On her first morning there, Jil woke bewildered and ill.

She didn't know which way was north.

Feeling lost, she begged her mother to let her see out. The elevators took them up 200 levels, at last to a rooftop park. Still she couldn't see the sky, but at last she found Alpha, a dim yellow patch in the smog. The planet seemed to tip, and things were suddenly right again.

As right as they could be, so far outside. Even though the nebula was hidden beyond the bitter-scented smog, she knew where it was. When the time came, she would know her way back.

To please her mother, she tried to like Alpha III. It was different and sometimes exciting. She had a tiny room of her own in the robotized apartment Macharn found for them on a residence level in a sector called Hawkshead Heights—she never knew why. They all bought new clothing in what her mother said was the Alpha fashion, and she went to school.

In spite of all her trying, life there was hard to like. The apartment seemed too small. Macharn was abrupt and cold with her, often angry for very little reason, and she never got used to his odor.

Nobody had much time for her, and she longed for the nebula. Longed for her grandfather, and her walks with him down the cinder hill to visit his friends in the Pass. Longed for the thunder crash of the meteor storms on frosty winter nights, longed even for the bitter dust and sticky mud her mother hated.

She felt hemmed in, smothered under steel and plastic and roaring machines and too many people.

She never saw the sky.

Yet school was fun, and she hoped it might help her get back to the nebula. The exams for the Academy would be grueling, she knew, when she qualified to take them. If she failed, even if she never made the Legion, life in the nebula would still demand every skill she could master.

Math and physics. "The laws of space," her grandfather had told her. "You'll need them first." Interstellar navigation as soon as she was old enough. Geodesic theory, terraforming engineering, tachyonic signal systems. The military sciences: weapons technology, space strategy and tactics, personal combat.

"Baby doll!" Her mother refused to understand. "A lovely young girl, we can't let you train to become a murderous monster. I've spoken to Shon, and he agrees we simply can't let you toss your sweet young life away. You'll drop the space combat and sign up for music.

"Or else we'll stop your allowance."

She didn't like to quarrel, but she had to be ready for the Legion. It was going to be her life. Anyhow, the allowance had been too little to matter that much. When Macharn cut it off, she got a part-time job for spending money and registered for free-fall yawara. The instructor was a withered little wisp of a man who had been a black master in the Legion long ago. His name was Kita Kano.

"Our art is very ancient," he told his students. "It began with my own honored ancestors back on Earth two thousand years ago. Using it in space, under all gravities and none at all, the people of the Legion have made it a finer art, more graceful and more deadly."

His papery voice was hard to hear, his limbs twisted and stiff from some old injury the medics couldn't repair.

"An exacting art," he told them. "It demands a special aptitude. A gift more of mind than muscle, to be used with more love than fury. A sense of force and mass and rhythmic motion, never used to maim or kill. Those who follow that false path can kill only themselves. To the true master, the encounter becomes a dance of life and death, in which the blind opponent seeks the harm that then falls back upon himself.

"If you would grasp the art you must meet it boldly and wisely, yet forever humbly. You must learn to leave evil feeling behind, because fear of pride or hatred can become weapons against you. The ancient saying 'Love your foe' means that you must forget yourself to share all he feels and thinks and does, withdrawing only at the instant of his fall."

He asked her to walk across the mat, to kneel upon it, to stand again. He frowned and shook his age-faded head.

"You stumble," he told her. "You tie your body into knots and trip yourself on your own feet. You have never been taught how to move." He must have seen her welling tears, because his frown became a deep-wrinkled smile. "Yet I will accept you, Jil Gyrel, if you willingly accept yawara discipline, because I see a future master within the uninstructed child."

"Please!" she whispered. "I do accept."

Accepting, she came to love both the teacher and his art. The ancient feints and shifts and spins really did become flowing dances that she learned in the null-G gym and mastered on the high-G centrifuge. Before the first term ended, Kita Kano was calling her to the training mat to let her show the class the strangely named classic forms and modes he had grown too old for.

"Bow your head," he warned her once. "The power of yawara dwells not in the artist with his instant of apparent victory, because there never is a victory. When harm is done, your feeling should be sorrow for the fool undone by his own folly. If ever you must feel pride, let it be not in your own small skill, but in the enduring wonder of the art itself."

She toiled to master that precious art and all the others she would need in the nebula. She tried to keep the peace with her mother and avoid Macharn. As time went by, she felt glad the

Antiac movement left them so little time for her.

Her mother had begun to sing with a musical group called the Wings of Peace. Her favorite number was "The Ballad of Giles Habibula," and Jil rejoiced that her grandfather didn't have to listen. The group became famous, though she couldn't see why. Money came from somewhere. A little of it went to designers for the Alpha styles Jil never learned to like, but Macharn took most of it.

What he spent it on, she didn't even try to guess. He was traveling, sometimes off the planet, but he never talked about his work, not even to her mother. The change in him was still a dreadful mystery. Though he seemed strong again, he was never even a little bit like the great, laughing, loving man who had been her father's friend. He turned white and furious when anybody mentioned that he had ever been sick.

The day Jil turned sixteen, her mother pressed her to leave school and begin training for the Wings of Peace.

"You're growing up nicely, baby doll." Jil was still elated from a call from her grandfather that morning from Hawkshead Pass, but her mother's calculating smile killed everything. "You're getting quite a foxy figure, and good instructors in voice and dance can help you find enough of my own talent to win people for the movement if you'll just forget your silly notions—"

Jil walked out.

She was in her bedroom at home a few nights later, trying on a new school uniform, when she caught a sickening wave of Macharn's bog-rot scent. Whirling, she found him in the doorway. His bulging eyes were fixed on her, and white froth was oozing down his chin. He sprang without a word when she moved, arms spread to grab her.

Feeling his lust, she found her body moving to his motion, flowing into the mode of the flying bird, which let his savage plunge carry him above her. Almost before she knew it, he lay gasping behind her on the floor. Staring at him, swaying and faint from what she had felt in him, she heard the whispery voice of old Kita Kano.

"Act and actor, nothing at all. Only the art is eternal."

Sprawled there on the floor, Macharn had a strange seizure. His gasping changed to a pitiable moan. Agony convulsed him. Bleeding now, his lips worked as if to speak, though no words came. A pang of helpless pity wrenched her, but she left him twitching in his own reeking puddles and walked out to look for a place where she could stay.

Kita Kano helped her find it and gave her a part-time job cleaning the gym to pay the rent. A few days later, when she knew Macharn would be gone to an Antiac rally, she went back for her things. Her mother let her in, puffy-eyed from crying, begging her to forgive poor Shon and come back home.

"Baby doll, you must try to understand him. He feels so terrible about what happened. He really loves us both, and he means no harm at all. It's just those dreadful nightmares his sickness left. They keep coming back, but he would die before he'd hurt you. Do forgive him, baby doll. You must come back, because the movement needs you so."

"Mother, I'm sorry—awfully sorry for you." Her own voice was shaking. "But I'll never join the Antiacs, and I'm not coming back. All I want is the things out of my room."

"Kere Nyaga called," her mother told her then. "The same night you ran away. He talked to Shon and left a message for you. About your grandfather. He'd just died—"

"Oh, no—"

The fact stabbed through her. She remembered his birthday call, his loving voice so bright and brave it had made her hope to find him still alive when she got home to the nebula. A hard lump of pain closed her throat.

"Nyaga knew you couldn't get back for the funeral," her mother was saying. "But he left word with Shon that you were the only heir. Your legacy will be waiting for you, the day you turn eighteen."

She nodded blankly, blinking at her tears.

"By then, baby doll, you'll surely come to see what our movement is." Her mother was talking on too sweetly. "The only way to universal peace. With all our expenses so terrible, noble cause—"

She turned away to gather up her teacher tapes and uniforms.

At the gym, Kita Kano made her his assistant. She kept records and drilled new students in the basic swings and bends. He gave her private lessons in the black master modes. When she started to remind him that she had no money, his rusty quaver stopped her.

"The art itself repays me, when it allows me to instruct another master."

Throat aching, she could hardly speak to thank him.

Marking a Legion calendar, she counted the months and then the weeks until she would come of age.

Walking out of the uptown elevator one day on her way to class, she heard a voice she knew and turned to see her mother passing on the slidewalk. She stood with her back toward the elevator, talking to a man.

Rem Brendish!

It took Jil an instant to recognize him, though his nasal whine hadn't changed, or his sharp-nosed fox face. Wearing Alpha fashions, he seemed a strutting stranger. His naked, narrow-chested torso aglow with gaudy body paint, he was floating in a null-G harness, his jeweled boots just touching the walk.

" . . . too deep, Rara." She caught a few urgent words. "I love you too much to let you destroy yourself, but you know the movement can't allow you—"

That was all. She had stepped back inside the elevator. Intent on their talk, they hadn't seen her. She thought her mother looked worried and pale. Brendish was gripping her arm to anchor himself, as if he owned her. In a moment the walk had carried them out of her view.

Back that night in her own lonely little room, she wanted to call her mother. Her heart felt sick whenever she thought about those old times when her father and his great friend came home from the nebula with flashing laser-diamonds and tales of high adventure, times when nothing was bad and they could all love one another.

But she never called.

She couldn't ask about Brendish or about what she had overheard. Whatever it meant, she wanted no more of the movement. Though she felt haunted by pity and bewilderment, she still could not imagine what had changed Macharn or how her mother could love or even endure him now, but she gave up trying to understand.

It dismayed her to see the Antiacs gaining power all around her. When a Legion noncom came to screen nominees for the Academy, student rioters heckled him out of the campus with their changed slogan: "AKKA's a bomb—a bomb—abomination!"

Trying to speak at a Legion rally, she endured Antiac jeers and got a black eye. She could have used the mode of the spinning top to let her heckler break his arm, but she remembered in time that she didn't really want to cause him that much harm.

When her last term began, she asked about the Academy exams. The military-science instructor told her none would be given. The Hall of Stars had cut Academy funds, he said, and there would be no admissions from Alpha III. That hurt, but she stayed on to finish the term with honors in interstellar navigation and something else she valued more. That was the little patch, pinned on her tunic by the twisted fingers of old Kita Kano, that said she was now a black master.

At last the great day came. She quit her jobs and sold her teacher tapes and cried a little when Kita Kano warned her one last time not to be betrayed by her own pride or passion. With barely enough funds, she booked passage to Beacon Beta I.

A few hours were left. She decided to risk a farewell call on her mother.

When she reached their old apartment sector, the sector management program wouldn't let her off the elevator. Her entry code had been canceled, its synthetic singsong informed her. The citizen Macharns had vacated their proper premises, leaving no new address. Their current location was unknown, and no message could be delivered.

Returning to the starport, she felt crushed beneath an unexpected sadness. In spite of many things, she had loved her mother. Captain Shon had once been just as dear. She would probably never know what dreadful thing had caught and transformed them both.

Her spirits began to rise as the starship climbed. It would be docking on her birthday, back at Hawkshead Pass!

5

Hawkshead Pass!

Riding down the ramp, Jil was jubilant. Her school days were over, her troubles left behind. Here was the sky again, and the limitless freedom of space. Beta stood huge and red above a dusty yellow horizon, but what her mind saw was the black-beaked shadow-head printed against the flame-winged nebula. Its old spell held her, its mystery and its promise and even its peril still alluring.

Reality jolted her, if only for a moment, when she looked out and down at the old starport. In the years since she left, time had hit it hard. Docks and pads and cradles were empty, hangars closed and paintless. Everything was smaller, shabbier, crumbling into gray defeat.

Outside the fence, the leatherweed looked triumphant. Rank, thick-leafed stuff, it had survived the shockwave. The first settlers had tried to clear it from the town site, but now it was coming back, its red-black jungles overwhelming Terran grass and trees. Hating what she called its bitter stink, her mother had been forever chopping and spraying to keep it off the barren yard, but Jil breathed a little deeper now, because its penetrating pungency was the scent of liberty.

The bottom of the ramp woke her to the moment. Counting the small coins left in her purse, she decided to check her bag at the terminal and hike downtown. She asked the traffic manager about passage up the channel and on into the nebula.

"Better stay aboard," he told her. "Your liner is the only one still landing here. Inbound now for Gamma and Nebulon. Nothing else expected till she comes in again from Alpha on her next round trip."

But of course she had to see Kere Nyaga, and the mirrored arrow of another starcraft caught her eye when she looked across the leatherweed jungle to the Legion base. It was the *Sunmark,* the manager told her, standing at the repair dock. When she asked if Kynan Star was still its commander, he didn't know.

Walking into town along the road where she had come so many times with her grandfather, at first she was whistling the Legion marching tune he had taught her the year she was four, but she soon fell silent. The road was potholed and empty, walled with the dusty weeds. The town looked almost abandoned when she neared it. Paint was peeling from rusting sheet metal, and red rain streaks ran down leaning concrete walls. Suddenly she saw it as it must have been to her mother: a forlorn little outpost against killing desolation.

The Cluster Suns Trust was gone, the empty windows splashed now with spray-painted Antiac slogans. Wind-blown litter was piled on the cracking conrete steps outside, but she picked her way up them to Kere Nyaga's office. Breathless with anticipation, she pushed inside. It looked and smelled just the same, cluttered and dusty, but fragrant with the Terran roses he somehow coaxed into bloom in a tiny window box. He blinked up at her across the overloaded desk with the same worried frown she recalled.

"Mr. Nyaga—"

"Miss Jil!" He had recognized her voice, but she saw his first delight fading into shocked dismay. He sagged slowly back into his creaky chair, open-mouthed and staring. "They said you were dead!"

"I did leave home," she said. "I guess I'm dead to them."

She shrugged. "But here I am. Eighteen, by the Legion calendar. I've come about the estate—"

"But—Mr. Brendish brought documents—" He shook his time-dried head, squinting at her in dazed disbelief. "If you're alive, they've done a terrible thing!"

She waited for him to tell her. Begging her to sit, he shuffled back to his own chair and collapsed into it. Still she waited while he pulled his mind together.

"Not long after your grandfather died," he began at last, "your mother called from Alpha. Said you'd run away from home. Macharn called back a few days later to say you were dead—killed by infection from a strange, slow-acting virus the medics thought you must have caught from a laser-diamond your father brought out of the nebula.

"How was I to know?"

He spread his lean old hands, his shrunken face a black mask of sadness.

"A Mr. Rem Brendish came as your mother's legal agent. He brought legal records. Forged—that has to be what happened—but the court here accepted them. Your trust was terminated. As next of kin, your mother inherited. The estate was settled. Mr. Brendish collected the residue for your mother. A very considerable sum. You could have bought your own starcraft—"

His whispery voice faded dismally away. She sat staring past him at the yellow roses.

"But now—" She tried to pull herself together. "What can I do about it?"

"Nothing, I'm afraid." He studied her gloomily. "Nothing here. Criminal charges should be filed, but that can be done only on the planet of residence—"

"Which I don't even know. The locater program on Alpha III has nothing current on them."

"If that's true, you can hardly hope for restitution." He sat blinking at her for a time, then limped abruptly to the window box and cut a yellow rose. "Miss Jil, I wish I could do—something." Frail hand shaking, he gave her the rose. "My own circumstances—" His voice faltered. "Difficult."

"Don't blame yourself, Mr. Nyaga."

Seeing the folded blankets on the sofa beneath the window

box, she guessed that the narrow office was also his dwelling. Her grandfather had always called him too honest for his profession. She caught his arm to stop his stumbling apology.

"We've both been hurt. But I'll be fine. Here I am, already halfway into the nebula. I'll get there!"

Groping for any reasonable hope, she found herself trudging up the rutted road she used to climb with her grandfather, toward their old home on the hill. It was weed-clotted now, the ruts washed deep. The old house was gone when she reached the site, perhaps sold for scrap metal. Only the stone foundation walls remained, jutting from red thickets of sharp-reaking leatherweed.

She stood there a long time, looking sadly back to those wonderful times when she was young. What had gone wrong to spoil all their lives? That cruel question nagged her.

In her heart, she couldn't blame her mother. Selfish, perhaps. Sometimes silly. But she hadn't hated the Legion when her father was home, or been more than just a friend to his best friend. Certainly she had never been either evil or crafty enough for such a crime as this. Somehow, the changed Macharn had changed her. But what had made that dreadful change in him?

She remembered that brief glimpse of Brendish hovering over her mother on the slidewalk, clutching her like some greedy insect about to feed while he warned her not to try to leave the movement.

What was Brendish . . . ?

A sharp explosion startled her. A seed pod had burst in the leatherweed behind her. The mobile seeds rose and scattered, flying like a swarm of golden moths. One dropped in her hair and clung there, bright wings beating, as if trying to bore into her brain.

Brushing at it, she shivered. The wind had shifted as she stood on the broken foundation, blowing colder off the ice plateau beyond the mountain and edged with the taint of the bogs around Black Lake. Macharn's odor. It chilled her with a dread she didn't entirely understand.

Suddenly she knew she would never press any charges against Brendish or her mother or Macharn. They were somewhere far behind her now, and she wasn't going back. All that mattered now was the nebula ahead. She tossed Kere Nyaga's yellow rose across the broken stones and turned toward the future.

The town and the twin starports made tiny gray islets on the waves of red-black weed. She found the bright glint of the starcraft standing on the Legion field. She hiked back down the hill and on out to the base to ask for any sort of berth on the *Sunmark.*

6

The private at the gate was a young man and lonely, glad to talk and anxious to please her. He looked distressed when he had to tell her that the Legion wasn't signing anybody on, not anywhere he knew about, for sure not here at Hawkshead Base. The nearest enlistment office was out on Alpha IV.

The *Sunmark* had been at the service dock for weeks, he said, getting something done to her particle-weapons system. No, he didn't know who was her commander.

"If it's Kynan Star, I want to see him," she persisted. "Pilot-Major Star when I met him a long time ago. He has probably been promoted."

Doubtfully he called the starcraft.

"It's Star." The doubt was gone. "I guess he hasn't been promoted, but he'll send for you."

A yeoman in a service truck took her to the repair dock. Kynan Star came off the craft to meet her. Time had thinned his hair and creased his lean ray-burnt face, and he wasn't quite so straight as she recalled him.

"Jil Gyrel!" Like the private at the gate, he seemed delighted with her, but the warm smile went out when she spoke about her father. If she had come to ask for news about him, there was none.

He invited her aboard.

"You've changed since I saw you." She liked his quick boyish grin. "You must have been about seven."

They sat in his private cabin, and he opened a bottle of the Nebulon wine her father had loved.

"We were friends," he told her. "Ever since my first year at the Academy. He was teaching then, and I took his course in nebular dynamics. We flew together later. After he was lost, I begged for permission to search. Never got it granted, because the Legion was always stretched too thin. I do keep alert for clues, but you know the nebula." His lean features tightened. "It plays a hard game, by rules we've never quite been able to learn."

He sipped his wine, frowning soberly, and asked what she knew about Shon Macharn.

"Nothing good!" she said. "He never got over that sickness, whatever it was. My mother married him—I've never known why. Because he's still—still so—"

She could only shake her head.

Kynan Star sat waiting for her to go on. Feeling he would understand, she caught her breath and tried to tell him how Macharn had changed, how they had tried to make her join the Antiacs, how he had attacked her, how they had taken her inheritance.

"Once he was so wonderful! To me. To everybody." She leaned to search Star's troubled face. "What happened to him?"

"I still lie awake over that." He shrugged uneasily. "Something I hope we don't confront again. I wish he had let the medics examine him—and I still wonder why he wouldn't."

"Anyhow, that's all behind." Eagerly, she lifted her glass. "I always dreamed of a life in the Legion. Getting into the Academy looks unlikely, but at least I can enlist—"

She had seen his frown.

"I'm afraid you can't."

"Because I'm a woman?"

"Not entirely." A bleak regret seamed his face. "These have been bad times for the Legion. The Antiacs are gaining power. Cutting our forces and starving us for funds. Now their friends in the Hall of Stars are trying to pull us out of the nebula."

His tone turned sardonic.

"They claim to be afraid our armed presence would antagonize undiscovered sister cultures in the nebula that might overwise become our friends. A noble theory, maybe—till you begin meeting creatures like the cliffdrillers."

"Could you—" Her voice caught. "Could you take me on the *Sunmark*?"

"Jil, I'm sorry." As if to cover his own discomfort, he paused to refill their glasses. "But I have a full crew. Anyhow, the *Sunmark* wouldn't be the opportunity you want. We're tied up here, waiting for a replacement core for the main particle gun. Shipment has been delayed. Twice, by sabotage at the arsenal." His frown lines bit deeper. "We could be lying here for months, with nothing at all to do."

"I was hoping—hoping so much—"

"I hate to hurt you." He tried to smile. "Because I can see how much alike we are. Both of us born to old Legion families and taught to live by old traditions. I came into the Legion with ideals as fine as yours."

Sighing, he sipped his bitter wine.

"That was nearly twenty years ago. I'm still a Star—and proud to be, at least till lately. I've done my duty. Often more. I've marked starlanes and surveyed new planets. I've played my share of games with danger.

"And nobody cares."

With a tired shrug, he set down his empty glass.

"Believe me, Jil, the heroic ages have ended. If we're really ordered out of the nebula—I expect we will be—I'm going to retire. I'll look for something more rewarding. I don't know what—"

He fell silent, staring moodily at nothing, until she was rising uneasily to leave.

"Forgive me, please!" He stood up quickly. "Sometimes I think too much. Please stay; let's at least finish the wine." He looked at her again, that quick grin lighting his face. "Will you have dinner with me?"

He saw her about to refuse.

"Nothing beyond that implied." He smiled disarmingly. "Not yet, anyhow. I've been at loose ends here, and you're a welcome break." He turned graver. "I wish it had been a happier meeting for you."

"I'm going on into the nebula. Though I don't quite know how—"

He saw her falter, and his gaze grew sharper.

"What's the trouble?"

"Money." She felt herself flush, but his concern seemed real. "I was counting on that legacy. Without it, I don't even know where I'll stay tonight."

"Let me call the Hawkshead House," he urged her quickly, "to guarantee your bill." He added quizzically, "Nothing more implied."

"I couldn't ask—"

"You didn't." He beckoned her back to the table. "Let's talk about the nebula and you."

"It's all I ever really wanted." She sat again, grateful for his concern. "I used to dream that I might inherit my father's pilot sense."

"That's sex-linked, I think."

"Not in those old dreams." His quiet smile encouraged her. "I wanted to be another space hero, like your own great ancestors and all the others Captain Shon used to tell me about. Serving in the Legion and defending the people of the nebula from new space enemies. I even used to dream that I might grow up to be the Keeper."

"I had dreams." Sober again, he poured the rest of the pungent wine. "In fact, I brought them with me to the nebula —and watched them crash into cruel reality."

"The nebula isn't always cruel."

"It used to be kinder," he conceded. "Back in your grandfather's youth, it did offer room and wealth and freedom to a few of the luckiest and boldest. But the richest lodes were worked out before you were born, and there was never much but mining. Farming has nearly always failed, because the native biocosms aren't compatible with ours. Terran plants won't grow, and we can't eat most of the native stuff. Food's synthetic or imported, expensive either way. The drive for more new strikes has always taken us too far in, through deadlier dust and hotter radiation, to planets where a man's working life was too short for anything he could hope to find. We've pushed our limits too far.

"Now the nebula is pushing back."

She waited to see what he meant.

"Not with anything you can zap with a particle gun. Or even erase with AKKA. Nothing, in fact, that looks convincing in official reports to the Hall of Stars. But too many starships have disappeared the way your father's did, often now on routes we used to think were safe. Cliffdrillers attack too often, sometimes now on long-settled worlds where they had never been a problem. The medics have begun reporting other cases as baffling as Macharn's."

He shrugged unhappily.

"If the Legion is pulled out, the reason will be that we're already beaten. Partly by the peace kooks. Partly by—I don't know what. But all of it's reason enough for you to stay out."

He bent intently toward her, brown eyes oddly grave.

"You haven't asked for my advice, but I beg you to consider it. Forget the nebula. You'll find a hundred better careers back in civilization."

"I've seen Alpha III—"

"You're attractive—more than just attractive." Admiration swept the trouble from his face. "Young and evidently gifted. Splendid, if you'll let me say it. Far too fine for any future you can hope for out here."

His voice lifted when she shook her head.

"Listen, Jil! My sister lives back in Kalam III. A tachyonics professor at Kalem Tech. Let me call her. She saw too much of the nebula when she was a girl, and she has always wanted me to get out. She can steer you into something more rewarding."

"You're very generous." She felt touched. "But the nebula's all I want—"

"Sir!" A younger officer shouted hoarsely from the doorway. "Dreadful news!"

"Let's have it."

He was breathing heavily, and they had to wait for him to find his voice.

"A scrambled signal, sir. From Alpha V. About the Keeper —the Keeper of the Peace. I couldn't believe it, sir. Called back for confirmation on the secret frequency. The Special Command does confirm it, sir—"

"Confirm what, Greb?"

"The Keeper, sir. Murdered!"

"I see." Kynan Star was on his feet, his face grimly grave. "Has the killer been caught?"

"I think not, sir. Her body was just discovered. Details will follow. But, sir, that's not the worst. AKKA—AKKA—"

They waited while he gasped again for his uncertain voice. "They're afraid, sir—afraid it's lost!"

7

Gravely courteous, Kynan Star asked her to excuse him.

"I'll be going—" She was rising.

"Please." He beckoned her back. "Please wait till we know more."

She waited, shaken with a sense that the whole universe had tilted. If the Keeper was really dead, AKKA really lost, all the human worlds were suddenly defenseless. She wondered bleakly how the Antiacs would feel if they found their home planets naked to invading creatures as powerful and ruthless as the Cometeers had been.

Thinking of Kynan Star, she tried to decide what she felt about him. Respect for his quiet competence, for his long loyalty to the Legion. Appreciation for his kind concern. A deep, instinctive liking—which touched her with a vague alarm.

She hadn't come to fall in love, certainly not with an embittered veteran so many years her elder. The Legion must have filled his life, leaving him too little time or feeling for anything outside it. She recalled too well her own childhood and all that anxious waiting for her father in the nebula.

Anyhow, she wasn't ready. Macharn's attempted assault had brought her childhood nightmare back, that dreadful dream where she was sinking into the frozen bog, stifled with its evil stench. Since, avoiding her more amorous school companions without quite knowing why, she had spent most of her own energies on yawara.

What she loved was the nebula itself.

"Miss Gyrel?" The younger officer spoke from the doorway, deferentially. "The crisis is detaining Pilot Star. He asked me to explain. He is anxious to talk to you again. If you can stay, I'll bring you a meal."

She said she would stay. The meal was a Legion space ration, served in its self-heating sealer. Finding an unexpected appetite, she scraped the sealer bare and kept on waiting.

Kynan Star came striding in at last, absently whistling the Legion march. She had imagined him shattered by the impact of disaster, but somehow it had been good for him. He looked younger, more erect, alive with fresh purpose.

"Thanks, Jil." His smile seemed boyish, oddly untroubled. "I had to see you again." He glanced at the empty ration sealer, his brown eyes quizzical. "I'd meant to offer you something tastier."

"It was good enough."

He set the sealer and their empty glasses off the table and sat across from her.

"Since you heard what you did, I owe you more." His tone turned graver. "If you'll promise not to talk."

"You don't owe me anything," she told him. "But, of course, I promise."

"It's all true." He nodded, jaw set hard. "The Keeper's dead."

"AKKA—" She couldn't help that breathless question. "Is it lost?"

"That was not confirmed." He frowned at the bulkhead, with a slow headshake. "But, of course, it couldn't be confirmed. We'd be fools to proclaim that the Legion is weaponless.

"But I'm afraid—"

He sat scowling at the bulkhead until she spoke.

"You don't need to tell me anything—"

"Sorry, Jil." He smiled again, wryly. "Glad you waited. I need to talk. I'm still staggered. Groping for a fresh perspective. Because everything has changed."

His eyes dwelt upon her, warming with unconscious approval, until he pulled himself straighter and took a deeper breath.

"The Keeper was another Star," he said. "My cousin, Vivi Star. As beautiful as you when I knew her.

"That was nearly twenty years ago. I haven't seen her since or ever known where she was hidden. It turns out now that she was nearer than I imagined. Out on Alpha V. Stationed there to be ready for action against any threat out of the nebula.

"Yet unprepared for what did come."

His lean face twitched.

"An unbelievable betrayal. She must have felt safe enough. Isolated on a frozen planet, a billion kilometers out from Alpha, uninhabited except for the Legion garrison. Her secret fortress was carved into a mountain peak near the equator, under the scopes and missiles of a space fort in synchronous orbit, hanging always overhead. Except for a monthly supply ship, the Legion allowed no access whatever to the planet.

"But Vivi—Vivi's dead." He shook his head as if to deny it. "The Legion investigators got there just hours ago. They found no witnesses left alive, but evidence enough to tell a shocking story. Hard to believe, but I guess we must accept it.

"They've identified two of the traitors, though they can't explain the treason. Or much else. The evidence shows new weapons used. An alien technology. One investigator thinks space aliens were involved. Maybe out of the nebula. Nothing proven yet, but I don't know—"

He shook his head, staring bleakly past her.

"Sorry, Jil, if I don't make sense." With a fleeting grin, he gathered himself. "Though it makes no sense to me. Not even the identification. One suspect is a man I knew. Knew and trusted. Captain Coran Kloon. Nobody in the Legion had a better record. He'd been cadet commander back at the Academy, a year or so before I got there. A nebular explorer, decorated for opening up the Omega planets. Assigned several years ago to the special secret force safeguarding the Keeper and recently given command of the supply ship.

"That's how they reached her fortress and got away— escaped before there was any alarm. Kloon called the orbital fort for permission to land. Called again five hours later for permission to take off. With no reason to guess anything was wrong, the orbital command signaled permission. The ship landed as usual on a ledge below the peak, and—"

He flinched from what he had to say.

"Vivi never had a chance. Under cover of Kloon's lies, the raiders struck and got away. Struck with something the investigators are calling a cold bomb. Nothing like it known before. Silent. Most of the fortress was not alarmed. A weapon that froze its victims instantly. One squad caught sitting at mess. Stopped with forks in the air, the investigators say, like a holo image.

"And they reached Vivi—Vivi's quarters."

For a moment, his level voice had broken.

"Her body mangled. Burned. Tortured brutally. An effort, evidently, to get information about AKKA. Knowing Vivi, I know she didn't talk. But they kept trying till she died. Then got away. Still with no alarm. The crime was not discovered until time to change the guard.

"Kloon's supply ship has now been found. Adrift in space around on the other side of Alpha. All her people still frozen solid in their bunks or at their duty stations. Only one man missing from the crew. Kloon himself. Another craft must have been waiting there to pick up the raiders. No hint of where it went.

"Yet now the team has developed a lead. They've found a tunnel the raiders opened to reach the quarters of another apparent traitor, inside the fortress. Using something that drilled through a hundred meters of solid granite in those few hours without alerting anybody.

"The waste rock had been crumbled to a very queer powder. Molecular particles, the Legion team reports, carrying electrostatic charges that made them flow like liquid, draining out of the tunnel. It was drilled to Vivi's apartments from the quarters of one of the guards.

"That guard's the second suspect. A Legion corporal named Hannibal Xenophon Gul. Missing now and assumed to be gone with the raiders. His treason as hard to explain as Kloon's. An odd little fellow as people recall him, really too short and too fat and too old for the Legion. Drank too much. A sloppy soldier, with no respect for discipline. His officers tried several times to pack him off to the retirement barracks, but Vivi wanted him around her.

"Nobody knows why."

Star pushed to scowl beyond her, drumming his knuckles on the table.

"Riddles!" He shrugged and went on. "The fellow's Legion records make no sense. Anyhow, not to me. Like Kloon, he'd served in the nebula. A fully rated geodesic engineer. The file is full of commendations—otherwise he wouldn't have been among the Keeper's guards. But they've found also that he doesn't exist.

"Even his name is nonsense. Hannibal Xenophon Gul. It doesn't fit the standard census system on any planet. On examination, the investigators have found all his records forged —by whom, or why, they have yet to discover. But he has no discoverable origins. He certainly should never have been trusted there.

"With only such crazy evidence to go on, the team now suspects that the raiders came out of the nebula—"

"Cliffdrillers, do you think?"

"That reported dust makes you wonder." He shrugged. "The Legion high command doesn't like the notion, but—who knows? The whole thing's a nightmare. Actually, we've learned too little about the inner nebula and its possible creatures even to risk a guess. But that naked chance is all we have to act on. My orders now are to intercept that presumptive enemy starcraft thought to be returning to an unknown base somewhere in the nebula."

His quick grin flashed.

"What a mission, Jil! Even if they are headed this way, we've no way at all to identify their craft. If we should have to fight, our particle guns are gone. Not much we could do in any encounter except bluff or try to ram."

She couldn't help smiling. "You don't look unhappy."

The grin grew wider. "Action is better than boredom. We're sealing the ports where the guns came out and taking on reaction mass. We'll be heading up the channel into the narrows. Cruising there, watching for—we don't know what.

"Listen, Jil." He bent closer, his voice grown sober. "Here's why I wanted you to wait. I've called my sister again. She's a director of the Star Foundation, and she can arrange a scholarship for you at Kalam Tech. In nearly any field you want to choose. If you'll accept, she says she can set it up at once. It will include travel costs from here—

"Please!" He had seen her shaking her head. "I know how

you feel about the nebula, because I once shared the same illusions. The last free frontier. Romance and mystery and high adventure. But that fabulous lure has always been a lie. A lie we told ourselves, because we loved the dream behind it. When the facts wake you up, you soon discover the nebula never was a paradise. More and more, Jil, it looks—well, monstrous."

His voice had fallen again.

"I've felt that for years, Jil. Felt something hostile out there, gathering against us."

Though she hadn't spoken, he saw her doubt.

"Listen to me, Jil." He reached as if to grasp her arm. "We can't yet see what's rising against us, but some facts are plain. The Legion has been crippled. Even if AKKA is somehow safe—I'm afraid to hope for that—we'll be pulled back to defend what they call civilization. The nebula is going to be abandoned—"

"Sir!" The junior officer spoke behind her. "The mass tanks are filled, and the gun ports are ready for inspection."

"Thank you, Greb." Rising, Kynan Star gave Jil a wry little smile. "At least I tried to get you back to safety—to what I hope is safety—but I guess I'm not surprised. I only hope you're never sorry."

He went with her to the airlock and clung for a moment to her hand before he let her go.

8

Waiting outside the gate, she watched the *Sunmark* climb on its shining pillar of nuclear-heated system. High in the dust-yellowed sky, but still daringly near the planet, Star shifted from the jets to the geodesic drive. The ship vanished instantly. Only the towering cloud was left, dissolving into ragged fragments, and the dying thunder.

She longed to be with him. Taking off in a disarmed star-craft to hunt the killers of the Keeper, he seemed suddenly as heroic as any of his famous ancestors. If time and change had swept adventure from all the old worlds, it was still alive out in the nebula.

"Miss Gyrel?" The foreman of the service crew had pulled his van up behind her. "I have your bag. Pilot Star asked me to take you to the Hawkshead House."

She remembered the Hawkshead House from those old times when she used to sit in the lobby with her grandfather, listening to the good talk of pilots waiting their turn for a star-ship into the nebula. The drive outside it was a yellow-scummed mudhole now, and the faded sign leaned crazily. Rank red leatherweed was climbing the rust-streaked walls. Yet, though the years had claimed so much, she found Sister Lebb still sitting at the desk.

Sister Lebb and Sister Vorul were widows of starpilots and members by mortality right in the Starfarers Guild. Grown frail and hard of hearing since Jil left, beaming cheerily through identical wire-rimmed spectacles, they had never surrendered to change. Half asleep behind the cranky desk, Sister Lebb woke and called Sister Vorul out of the kitchen to join in her welcome.

They had loved her grandfather, and they proudly showed her a dimming holo of him on the lobby wall. They even remembered her, a tiny girl in a muddy dress, timidly asking starmen if they had known her missing father. They were delighted to see her now, and Sister Vorul limped to show her to the Meteor Room.

Even in the crunch of crisis, Kynan Star had found time to call them and vouch for her bill. Though that moved her almost to tears, she wanted to keep her independence. Sister Lebb agreed to let her wait tables and wash dishes for her board, while she waited for a way up the channel.

"A long wait, likely," the old woman warned her. "These days the big ships bring pilots of their own all the way out from Alpha. Most go on past us, never stopping even for reaction mass. The smaller craft, they don't hardly come no more, not like they did in your dear grandfather's day. Because the little people, the settlers and miners and traders and such, they're all too scared to do much in the nebula now. Scared the Legion will pull out and leave them to all the monsters they swap their wild tales about, things crawling out of worlds where men can't go."

Sister Vorul said her father had slept in the Meteor Room. It was huge and cool, with a smell of clean decay. A dusty wall case held meteorites the sisters had picked up long ago and labeled mineral specimens that pilots had brought back out of the nebula. One yellowed label read "laser-diamond," but the diamond itself was gone.

Jil liked the room and the Hawkshead House. The sisters were tolerant bosses, her own duties not too demanding. The last of the old starpilots had given up waiting for the ships that never came. The few roomers left were aging miners and traders, most of them defeated and broken long ago, eking out the leavings of their lives.

Keeping a careful silence about the Keeper's murder, Jil listened breathlessly for news. None came. The talk around the tables was all of the better, bygone times when the Gyrel Channel had been still pulsing with the flow of eager seekers into the nebula and their rich rewards returning. After a few uneasy days, she began to hope that the killers had been captured, that AKKA was somehow safe.

At last a ship did arrive. The drum of jets woke her. Sister Vorul told her in the kitchen that the *Purple Empress* had landed. A private starcraft, registered out of Samdu VI, bound for Gamma II and points beyond, she was down at the civilian service docks loading supplies and taking on reaction mass. Spacehands off the ship were soon trooping into the long dining room. Rushing in with stacked platters for the family-style breakfast, Jil heard angry profanity.

"They're riled up, Miss." A gaunt man in a steward's cap looked up at her. "The Empress ain't so pretty when you come to know her."

"A jinx ship!" a fat chef told her. "Owned by a raving maniac—I'll serve him poison if he ever gets me back aboard."

"Damned robots for officers!" a deckhand growled. "Running us to do the dirty work like we was more damn machines."

When she learned that none of them meant to go back aboard, she asked if the ship would be signing on replacements.

"Don't think of it, Miss!" The steward shook his finger at her. "The ship's a flying nightmare, not fit for anything human. For sure not for the likes of you."

"The robots ain't the worst." The fat man scowled across his plate. "Watch out for the owner."

The owner, they told her, was a financier coming out to inspect his investments on the nebula planets.

"Claims to come from somewhere back in civilization," the deckhand muttered. "But if he was ever exposed to anything civilized, it sure never took."

"Brutal bastard!" The steward pointed to a lanky starman not eating because his jaw was bandaged. "He done that. Took a swing at me. Knocked a waiter cold because he spilt a drop of soup. But his crazy temper ain't the worst. That's the way he stinks. The whole damn craft stinks like a cargo of corpses. Rank enough to make you puke."

When she heard the owner's name, she nearly dropped a platter.

"Ulnar. Mr. Edric Ulnar, but he wanted us to call him Prince Ulnar." The steward sneered. "Your Grace and Your Greatness. The bastard claims he's the rightful heir to the old emperors. Claims he's carving out a new empire for the Purple Hall out on the planets of the nebula."

Ulnar! Her mother's maiden name. Jil wondered if this despicable aristocrat could be a kinsman of her own. No close one, she decided. All the Ulnars her mother ever talked about had been as poor as they were proud.

When the dishes were done, she told Sister Lebb she was going out to ask for a berth on the Purple Empress.

"Don't do it, dearie! It's a wicked ship—I never heard the like of any other. No place for a sweet young girl."

"There aren't many ships," Jil said. "I don't mind a few risks, not if they get me into the nebula."

"I was young once. Busting with sap and sure I could do anything." Sadly wistful, the old woman sighed. "It's a cruel universe. I ache for you, dearie, but I know you can't be stopped."

She shook her head, blinking at Jil with watery eyes behind the thick-lensed glasses.

"Because I was young once, back when your grandfather was. Both of us heard the call of the nebula, the way you do. The riddles and the wonders. The challenge and the danger. It dares you to conquer it and tempts you along with what you hope to win. When you're winning, or think you are, it lets you feel you're superhuman.

"That's the cruelest trick, dearie, because it calls you on to kill you. A terrible game, the risks too hard to see and the prizes never what they seem. It's all rigged against you, with rules you never learn. My heart breaks for you, dearie, because the nebula always wins."

The thin old arms embraced her.

"I know you won't be stopped, but do take care!"

Jil thanked her, a throb of pity in her throat, and let Sister Vorul drive her out to the starport gate in their ancient battery van. Her spirits rose again when she saw the *Purple Empress*. Standing at the service dock, dwarfing the gantries around her, the ship loomed into the dusty sky, tall and proud and mirror-bright, ready for the nebula.

Robots were at work with the human crews around her.

They were functiforms, the human guard told her, all operated from the ship's computers. Crane-armed giants were tossing crates off a supply truck into the cargo hatches. A tiny mechanical spider hopped on three delicate legs to meet her on the passenger ramp.

"State your name," it sang. "State your business here."

"Jil Gyrel." She stared back into its multiple lenses. "I want to speak to the owner."

"State your business with Prince Edric Ulnar."

"I wish to ask for a place on his crew."

"The Prince prefers functiforms for all essential operations of the *Purple Empress*. He does, however, require certain human services." It hopped closer. She caught its sharp new-plastic scent. The stalked lenses extruded at her. "State your qualifications."

"I'm twenty years old." She was trying not to shrink from the merciless lenses. "Graduate of Alpha Tech 499—"

"The Prince requires no techfolk."

"I've worked at a lot of jobs."

"State recent positions you have held."

"I'm washing dishes and waiting tables now at the Hawkshead House. Before that—"

"The Prince does require such service." The lenses lifted toward her face. "You, however, are female."

"Is that bad?"

It froze.

Grateful for the chance to step back from it, she had time to look up and down the line of empty docks, wishing there could have been a starcraft with a human crew.

"Attention, Jil Gyrel!" It hopped abruptly after her. "Although previous human servitors were male, the Prince states that he will now accept female service. You will now attend to the legal conditions of your employment. Your oral responses will be recorded as a binding contract. If you wish to serve Prince Edric Ulnar as a duty-bound spacehand aboard the S.S. *Purple Empress*, you will now so affirm. Speak distinctly."

She listened to a droning interrogation. Did she agree to remain aboard the starcraft, faithfully obeying the orders of all her officers, organic or mechanical? Was she knowingly and willingly bound by interstellar law, by the planetary law of Samdu VI and by the code of the Starfarers Guild? Would she accept the Guild minimum wage, submit any disagreement to Guild arbitration and secure proper legal release from duty before attempting to leave the starcraft?

She agreed.

"Jil Gyrel," the robot hummed at last, "Prince Edric Ulnar hereby employs you for service aboard the S.S. *Purple Empress* under the legal conditions to which you have duly submitted, accepting all penalties that may be imposed by the officers thereof.

"You will report for takeoff at noon, local Legion time."

She went back to the Hawkshead House to make her farewells and pick up her bag. The refugees from the ship were sitting in the lobby, still relating alarming tales about the lunatic Prince and his demoniac robots. The sisters stared in dismay when she told them she was signing on, but nothing could break her high spirits. At last, in spite of everything, she was on her way into the nebula!

The three-legged spider met her on the ramp and hopped ahead to lead her to a narrow cabin on the service deck.

"Remain here," it whirred. "Secure for takeoff."

It closed the door. The lock clicked. She was alone. The cabin was windowless and icy cold. The motionless air had a strange, stale reek. For just a moment, shuddering to a sudden dreadful suspicion, she felt something close to panic.

What if the Ulnars had joined the cliffdrillers or other unknown creatures of the nebula in a fantastic plot to restore their long-lost imperial power? Suppose they were the Keeper's killers, escaping now into the nebula? Could the *Purple Empress* herself be the unknown craft Kynan Star had been ordered to intercept?

In another moment she had put the panic down. The notion seemed insane. Even if it should be true, she was glad to be aboard. With the murder still kept secret, she had no evidence likely to convince port authorities that anything was wrong.

Anyhow, it was already too late for any effort to carry a warning off the ship. The deck beneath her was suddenly alive with the geodesic field, and gongs in the corridors outside began booming the takeoff alert.

At last!

9

Takeoff!

She stowed her bag beneath the hard berth and lay down to wait. The gong count speeded and ceased. An instant of stillness, and then the far bellow of the jets. It grew. She felt their shudder, their fast-increasing thrust—unexpectedly cut off.

Already the geodesic drive!

With all the sounds and forces of normal space left behind, a vibrant hush filled the ship. There was only the subsonic song of the propulsion field, felt but not heard. She sat up on the edge of the berth, shivering a little from the chill but happy to be at last on her way.

Her door clicked open.

"Duty call!" The spider-robot purred. "The Prince and the Baron require human service."

She followed it into the service elevator. Two decks up, they came out into a long galley where cold light glinted on bright metal and two silent spiders were darting about in a pungent haze of cooking fumes. One brought her a heavy gold tray, enameled with a purple crown.

"The Prince requires medication." It placed a tiny crystal

cup on the tray. "You will bend one knee when you serve him. You will not speak except when he requires it."

It waved her through a doorway.

The room beyond astonished her. Semicircular, it took half the deck. The walls were hung with purple velvet, embroidered in brilliant color with battle scenes of the old empire. In the center was a massive table where two men sat.

The nearer was robed in some stiff and brilliant crimson stuff, purple-edged. His huge and deeply cushioned chair was set on a long platform, now swung around so that she couldn't see his face. Sprawled back in it, he looked lifeless.

The other blinked at her through a thin yellow beard and jumped upright, as if her own amazement had been catching. He wore a tight purple jacket, golden-fringed. Ribboned medals glittered on his narrow chest. Though his long-nosed hatchet face looked familiar, it took her a moment to recognize him.

Rem Brendish!

Her gasp of surprise filled her nostrils with that foul bog-rot stench that Shon Macharn brought back from the nebula. She heard the big chair creak and saw the man in crimson turning slowly toward her. He was Macharn, but changed again. Again, shockingly.

He had been robust and powerful when he sprang upon her in the bedroom. Sunk back now against the purple cushions, he looked puffily bloated, gravely ill. Bruiselike markings as dark as the velvet mottled his bloodless skin. His lax face sagged, white spittle glistening on the cracked and swollen lips. His dull-glazed eyes bulged wildly at her.

"Jil Gyrel!" Brendish was yelping. "How did you get here?"

She couldn't turn away from Macharn. His frothy lips had begun to quiver. Clinging to her face, the glassy eyes had dilated as if with unspeakable terror. He shuddered, moaning brokenly, swollen hands batting clumsily at the air. She couldn't move or speak until he swung the chair abruptly away.

"Jil!" Brendish turned suddenly accusing. "What do you think you're doing here?"

"I'm on your crew." She faced him unsteadily. "Working my way into the nebula."

"I see." His fox face smiling behind the scraggly beard, he

looked relieved. "We'll find enough for you to do."

"I didn't expect—" Her breath was gone, and she had to inhale that evil reek again. "Where is my mother?"

"I am Baron Brendish." His tone grew colder. "You will address me as sir."

She looked at Macharn, but he had slumped back in his chair, breathing heavily, his dreadful eyes blankly fixed.

"Sir—" Her voice shook. "Where is my mother?"

"The Princess is in her cabin."

"May I, sir . . . May I see my mother?"

"Not unless she wishes." He inspected her disdainfully. "She was deeply offended when you attacked the Prince and ran away from home. I doubt that either will ever forgive your disgraceful lack of gratitude."

"Forgive me?" Her anger flashed. "What about the plot to steal my grandfather's estate? And your own share in it? Must I forgive—"

"Quiet!" Brendish rapped. "You're a servant on the *Purple Empress*. Nothing else. The Prince requires his medication now. You will kneel when you offer it. You will not speak to him or to me without permission."

Trembling, she knelt to offer the golden tray.

With a stifled groan, like some animal in pain, Macharn reached for the crystal cup. It held something thick and black that had its own acrid pungency. His dark-mottled hand waved and shook, but at last he got it to his lips and sucked at it greedily.

A convulsion seized him then. The cup fell and shattered on the deck. A broken cry escaped him—she thought it seemed a sob of pain. He writhed in the crimson robe, gasping as if with suffocation. When his cadaverous head lolled back, she reached uneasily to help him.

"Don't!" Brendish rapped. "You will not touch him."

Just as suddenly, he seemed to be recovering. Breathing heavily but evenly, he swung toward Brendish, mouthing hoarse and broken syllables that made no sense to her.

"At once, sire." Brendish bowed low. "I'll send for it." Voice sharper, he yelped at her, "Report to the robots."

A silent spider beckoned her through the steamy galley and past the elevator, into a long room where electronic charts of the shockwave and the nebular stars glowed above banked computers. These, she guessed, were the craft's robotic brain.

One high black cabinet was marked with a silver spider-shape. She guessed that it ruled the robots themselves.

Beneath it, a massive steel door clicked and swung open. Reaching inside, the spider's quick whips brought out an odd little object. A ball of silver-colored fibers that looked like tightly curled hair, hardly larger than her own head. It felt nearly weightless when the robot dropped it on her golden tray.

"Take it to the Baron."

Back in the purple stateroom, Brendish beckoned her to set the tray in front of Macharn.

"Sire." He bowed. "The thing in question. Found in her quarters. Believed to have been alive at the time, because it uttered words and attempted to escape. The chillers knocked it down. Possibly killed it. Our tests have failed to detect any sort of life since we brought it aboard."

Chillers! Jil's heart thudded. Could they be the "cold bombs" used to disable the Keeper's defenders? She stepped back, grateful that their attention was on that singular object. Carefully motionless, she watched Macharn bending clumsily to peer at the thing and listened again to those grotesque mouthings she couldn't decode.

"Not yet, sire." Brendish darted around the table to his side. "Our agents did record its words. Identified as primitive English. Mostly nonsense. I can quote from memory: 'O, the pity of it! The churchyards yawn and hell itself breathes out contagion. O God! that men should let enemies into their bodies to steal away their brains! Rise! Rise betime against infection and the hand of grim-visaged war.' "

A hoarse groan rumbled from Macharn.

"It's still under study, sire. No clear translation has been established. On the surface, it looks like a clumsy effort to alert the garrison against us, but the peculiar idiom does perplex us. We still suspect a cryptographic code—"

A raucous squawk.

"Sire!" Brendish jumped and squealed in evident alarm. "We've done our utmost. But, sire, please consider our dilemma. We believe the object was alive. We must assume that it is still alive. Yet we lack hard data on its vital processes. I must warn you, sire, that anything more drastic might be fatal to it."

Macharn nodded clumsily, with an uncouth grunt.

"My own conclusions, sire?" Medals clinking on the purple jacket, Brendish bent to prod the fiber ball with a dirty fingernail. "I suggest that the object is native to the nebula. Perhaps in fact the same creature found and brought back by the early explorer Commander Gyrel."

He darted Jil an enigmatic glance.

"The journal of his initial expedition reports finding something he called a laser-maker. He believed that it was or had been a living being. He was hoping to get responses that would establish communication—"

Macharn interrupted with a hollow croak.

"We have searched, sire. After that initial report, Gyrel never mentioned the object again. Later students questioned his early evidence. The object was placed in the Legion Museum and apparently forgotten. Its presence in the fortress astonished our agents."

Macharn bent to blink vacantly at the silvery coils, gnarling like some restless beast.

"Sire, we've no way to know." The nasal whine turned uneasily placatory. "Please recall our limits. Whatever it is, the object does appear immensely old. Uniquely enduring. If it really has survived the passage of the shockwave and all the ages since, it could hardly have been harmed by what we have done—"

Brendish cringed from another angry bark.

"Sire, we have been cautious." He bowed in abject apology. "Please, sire! Recall your own orders. Recall our difficulties—"

His shrill appeal trailed away.

Macharn had leaned clumsily to pick the object up. He stared at it emptily, tossed it back to the tray and swung to growl at Jil. Shivering inwardly, she tried not to shrink from his pain-glazed eyes. They showed no sign that he had ever known her.

"Wine!" Brendish rapped. "The Prince is ready for his wine."

The robots set a flagon of dark-red wine and two crystal goblets on her tray. When she knelt to set them on the table, Macharn lunged to snatch the flagon, tipped it high to drain it and grunted hoarsely at her.

"Dinner!" Brendish waved her toward the galley. "Now!"

The robots sent her back with a roast fowl on a silver platter. Before she reached the table, Macharn grabbed it in both mottled hands. White foam dripping from his lips, he tore it apart with quivering fingers, crammed whole joints into his mouth, choked on bones he couldn't swallow, and spat them on the table and snatched avidly for more.

Sliding the hairball out of his way, Brendish stood watching with a wary-seeming intentness. Jil watched them both, terrified, stunned by more hints and hazards than she could even try to understand. With the platter swept bare, Macharn gobbled again.

"Wine!" Brendish yelped.

When she came back, however, to kneel with another red flagon, they both ignored her. Macharn's unnerving stare was fixed again on the laser-maker. Brushing the bones aside, Brendish slid it toward him.

"Everything, sire. Electric shocks. Red-hot needles. Acid sprays. Concussion. Ultrasonics. Baths in blazing hydrocarbons and liquid helium. The outcome was invariably the same. No observable response. No observable damage."

Macharn picked it up with a savage-seeming bray.

"Sire, we've done that," Brendish shrilled. "Testing for metabolic processes, we find none at all. It consumes no oxygen—nor, so far as we can tell, anything else. It secretes nothing that we can detect. Emits no heat or any other energy. In fact, the lab reports no actual evidence that it is or ever was alive."

Macharn snarled.

"We recognize that danger, sire." Brendish bent again, almost pleading. "Its presence at the fortress demands explanation. Any connection between our ancient enemies in the nebula and these fools outside might seem to threaten what we plan. But you can surely make allowances—"

Macharn cut him off with a bestial bellow.

"We'll do that, sire!" Brendish gasped. "We're taking extraordinary measures to keep it secure."

Macharn tossed it back to the golden tray.

"Take it!" Brendish rasped at Jil. "Back to the safe."

Walking out with it, she felt lost in whirling wonderment. A shapeless fluff of wiry hair, it looked utterly nondescript. Could it really be a living nebular creature? Brought out of the nebula by Ben Gyrel? A companion of the Keeper in that secret fortress on Alpha V? A tortured captive of the plotters now?

All that seemed too fantastic for belief. . . .

She had seen it moving! With a slow, ciliary motion, the silvery hairs were uncoiling. Their slight motion lifted it a little, rolled it toward her on the tray. Sound came out of it, almost too faint for her to hear.

". . . Gyrel?" The words were fainter than the thudding of her heart. ". . .still human?"

She swung to hide the tray from the men behind her and made herself walk slowly on. When she could breathe, she whispered, "I am human."

". . . 'scape whipping—" To hear that tiny sighing, she had to raise the tray. ". . . secure from worldly chances and mishaps to warn the Legion." She couldn't stop walking. ". . . killers of celestial peace—" Something in the galley began whirring. ". . . armed rhinoceros—" The whine was louder, but she bent to catch one last phrase. ". . . word to Hannibal Gul—"

The sighing died. The gray filaments relaxed. The creature sank back into the tray, once more only fluff. She had to carry it on into the galley, where the silver spider waited. A bright whip swept the fluff ball from her, tossed it into the open safe.

The heavy door clunged shut.

10

Brendish yelled for wine.

Holding her tray for the spiders to load, Jil tried to slow her thumping heart and get some sense of what she had to do. Kynan Star would be cruising somewhere ahead, hoping to intercept the killers. She must reach him with the little she had learned and all the riddles she hardly dared guess at.

The laser-maker?

Had it been a witness to the Keeper's murder? Clearly, it had begged her to warn the Legion. But what had it meant, whispering of an "armed rhinoceros"?

Hannibal Gul?

Why should any word go to him? The second traitor Star had named, the trusted guardsman whose quarters had been the base for the raiders? Had the laser-maker, like the Keeper, simply trusted him too far?

"Service!" Brendish gave her no time to grope for answers. "Jump to it, Jil!"

Deftly swift, the spider-robots were clinking filled glasses into her tray.

"Kneel!" Brendish rasped when she carried it back into that

purple-hung throne room. "Kneel to the Princess Ulnar!"

She saw her mother then, following a silent spider through an inner door. She, too, had been strangely changed. Very thin and very pale, she was sheathed in a low-cut gown of some brilliant, clinging, golden stuff. A single huge gem blazed at her throat. Her steps were hesitant and slow, her eyes on the robot as if she needed its direction.

"Mother!" Jil darted to meet her, glasses spilling. "Mother —it's Jil!"

Her mother paused and slowly turned. Lifting from the robot, her eyes were wide and babylike, blankly inquiring.

"Don't you even know me?"

A shadow of effort crossed her mother's bloodless face, fading back into that mindless smile. The robot's whip had caught her hand, and she turned without a word to follow it. Numbed and swaying, Jil tried to steady the clattering tray.

"You will address her as Princess." Brendish was on his feet, angrily yapping. "But never unless she requires it. She has nothing to say to you. Now serve the wine."

She served the wine.

Her mother scarcely sipped it. Sitting across the big table from Macharn, silent and inert, she seemed dreamily unaware of anything. Her empty eyes drifted to Brendish when he spoke and back to Macharn when he grunted some grating syllable, never returning to Jil. Nothing changed that lifeless smile.

When Brendish ordered food, Jil knelt again to offer it. Macharn wolfed another whole fowl. Brendish plied knife and fork with a deliberate precision, finally wiping his mouth almost daintily on a purple napkin.

Her mother touched nothing.

At last they let her go. One bright spider took the tray, and another escorted her down to the service deck. Left alone in her small bare cell, haunted by her mother's white and silent smile, she ransacked her imagination for anything to do.

Clearly enough, Brendish and Machard did not intend to let her leave the craft. Otherwise, they would never have let her see and hear so much. She had to get away, get what she knew to Kynan Star.

How?

Though she had been on starcraft before, had learned the rudiments of geodesic propulsion and interstellar navigation back at school, the *Purple Empress* was alien territory, the robots in control. Racing up the Gyrel Channel, the ship was already uncountable billions of kilometers from Hawkshead Pass, still far more from any world ahead.

No aid was possible—unless it came from Kynan Star himself. He should be waiting somewhere up the channel. Yet she could hardly hope that he would intercept the ship. For the "narrows," where he would be cruising, were only relatively narrow.

Even wider once, when the Beta burst through the shock-wave to leave the channel in its wake. Through all the centuries since, the nebular clouds had been creeping back to seal it again, their swirling turbulence so great that most of the tachyonic markers old Ben Gyrel had placed were no longer safe to follow. In the narrows they had begun to clog the channel with dusty mascons that split it into a maze of passes far too dangerous for any pilot without the latest charts and the most sophisticated astrogation gear.

Unless, of course, he had the Gyrel gift.

Star would be cruising, she thought, somewhere outside those branching passes. He might be able to watch the entrances to three or four or half a dozen, but surely not to all. If she simply waited for him to try to stop and search the *Purple Empress,* the odds were all against her.

She had to act. How? Try to get past the spiders and inside the signal center with time enough to send some warning before they overwhelmed her? Or try to get back into the room where she had glimpsed their master computer and somehow disable it? Or into the engine room to sabotage the drive?

Such notions fell to shreds in her mind. Though Brendish and Macharn seemed worse than insane, their monstrous plot had moved with an inhuman efficiency. Brendish, with his sadistic delight in humbling her, might let her continue to serve them, but he would leave her no freedom for anything else. The spiders were able jailors. She saw no way to turn the tables. Every plan she thought of seemed sure to fail, certain to invite penalties she didn't want to contemplate.

Exploring the cell, she found only the bare gray metal of walls and ceiling and deck. Nothing movable, nothing that could become a weapon or tool, nothing revealing anything about the starcraft or its masters.

She opened the door.

"You are not required." A silver spider met her. "We have no duty for you now."

"I'm going to the bathroom," she said. "I want water to drink and something to eat."

Gracefully, it hopped to block her way.

"You will not leave your quarters," it sang, "except when called to duty. Your meals will be brought to you on schedule, but no such service is scheduled for you now. If you wish lavatory or toilet facilities, they may be extended from the rear bulkhead."

"I see." She stood a moment, trying to take its measure as a yawara opponent. It was even shorter and slighter than old Kita Kano, but she had no way to guess its weight or strength or skill. Hopping suddenly closer, it swept her with its own cold lenses as if it were measuring her.

"You will remain inside," it hummed. "Your door will remain closed."

She retreated.

Inside, she found pressure switches that dropped a tiny basin and a cold-rimmed toilet out of the wall. There was no way to drink. Lying on the hard berth, she waited for her scheduled service. Her thirst and hunger grew, but no food or water came.

The berth—had it swayed beneath her? She wasn't certain, not until it rocked again. Her body felt abruptly lighter, almost floating for an instant. She sensed a change in the nearly soundless power of the geodesic drive.

Already, the narrows!

Here was her slender chance that Kynan Star might intercept the ship, though there was a far greater likelihood that it could evade him. Or maybe neither, unless the pilot was more cautious or more skillful than he seemed.

The pause and plunge of the ship had alarmed her. She had learned the theory of the geodesic drive, which in effect annihilated space ahead of the ship and generated new space behind, yielding impossible-seeming speeds many times the Newtonian velocity of light. But that effect required open space. Gravitic and magnetic fields interfered. Planetary take-offs and landings had to be made on the auxiliary nuclear jets.

All she could do was keep on waiting. The ship quivered and tossed. Her dinner never came. Aching from fatigue and strain, she thought she should try to relax. If any chance for action opened, she would need all her wits and skills.

She thought the ship had crashed into Black Lake, down beyond Hawksbeak Mountain. She had somehow got out of the wreckage, which had gone down through the broken ice behind her. She was caught in the half-frozen bog, helpless to move and suffocating in its evil reek.

People she had loved stood above her on the high ground. Her mother, lost in some sweet far-off dreamland, smiling at her emptily, not really seeing her. Shon Macharn throwing her the end of a rope but pulling it away with a strange, hoarse laugh when she reached for it. Kynan Star, wading out to help her but changing into a silver spider when the foul mud splashed him.

But she heard Rem Brendish yelping and found him hovering like a hungry insect in the air above her head, his angular frame glowing purple with luminescent body paint. Suddenly he changed into a puff of silver-colored smoke.

"Human?" His animal yelp became the laser-maker's whisper, mocking her with a riddle she had no answer for. "Who is human?"

Suddenly, it was gone. The others ran. She was all alone. The icy mud was pulling her down. It came to her waist. It rose around her shoulder. Its foul taste spilled into her mouth. It closed around her, and she couldn't breathe. But nobody cared. Nobody was human. She was dying all alone.

The bog quaked then, and she saw the mountain shattering into great black boulders that came roaring down around her. Still the cold bog held her fast. She couldn't move and she couldn't breathe, and nobody came to help.

The falling boulders battered her.

"Emergency!" A human voice, harsh with tension. "Prepare for in-flight emergency."

That woke her. She had fallen on the metal deck beside her berth. It lurched and quivered under her. Wet with sweat, yet trembling and cold, she staggered to her feet.

In the corridor outside, she heard the rapid clatter of running human feet, then the quick triple click of the spider's hop. That diminished into stillness. Except for the nearly soundless vibration of the drive, which now seemed to sink and surge unevenly, she could hear nothing. She opened the door.

The corridor was empty.

11

She darted out of her cabin, out across the rocking deck. Wary of the elevator, she slipped into the dimly lit ladder shaft beside it.

"Disaster alert!" The same grim voice blasted from speakers in the corridor. "Pilot Arkel at control command. Disaster alarm! All hands to emergency stations."

Gongs began to jangle. A red light blinked on and off above the elevator door. It opened, and a silver spider hopped across the corridor to freeze just outside her cell.

"Hear this, Jil Gyrel!" it bugled at the door. "You will remain inside."

Wondering if it would wait there for an answer, she hauled herself up the ladder toward the command deck. Pilot Arkel had sounded human and bleakly desperate. He might become an ally. A narrow chance, perhaps, but she saw no other.

The shaft was shielded from most of the ship's internal G-field; climbing was easy there. The narrow gates on each deck stood open. When her head came level, she peered cautiously out into the clang and flash of the warning system. Every corridor was empty.

Even on the salon deck, where she had served Brendish and Macharn, she saw no motion. She shivered to an eerie chill, a sense that she was alone on a ghost ship run by robots and monsters somehow dehumanized, with no help anywhere.

"All hands stand by!" The speaker system boomed again. "Ship in gravest danger now!"

That hoarse warning cheered her. Pilot Arkel sounded frantic. She climbed again, to the blink and din of another deck. Opposite the elevator, crimson symbols blazed:

ESCAPE DECK

If the ship had to be abandoned, the life pods would be here. Dropping back to hide her body in the shaft and peering out across the curving corridor, she found a winking orange sign:

ESCAPE STATION C
20 PERSONS

A way off the ship!

If she could open it. Reach and work the hatch beneath that flashing sign. Get aboard the pod. Launch it before the robots found and stopped her. Breathless and trembling, she pulled herself toward the doorway. Caution dragged her back.

Could she make it?

Likely not.

The pod's minimal geodesic equipment would not have been designed for the hazards of the narrows. Even if she could keep the tiny craft alive, neither the drive nor the signal system would have interstellar range. Unless the *Sunmark* or another friendly vessel came within hailing distance, she might wander alone through these shifting rifts till her support systems failed.

The triple click of a robot's hop made up her mind. Sinking out of sight, she listened to it approaching, passing, receding. Two minutes later, it passed again, patrolling the deck. In only two minutes, she couldn't hope to launch the pod.

When the click had gone on once more, she climbed higher. Two decks up, she came to the railing at the top of the well. Peering through, she searched the deck beyond it. The command deck. The pilot hung above her, his seat tipped back to let him see the conning screen.

A big, rawboned man with wild red hair. His face was turned toward the screen, but she could see the shine of sweat on his unshaven jaw. He spun the chair, watching the varicolored wink and flicker of the screen. Alarms hooted and clanged around him, and red warnings blazed across the console.

"All hands!" he rasped into his mike. "Propulsion fields unstable. Secure against Newtonian accelerations."

Something interrupted the soundless power of the drive. The ship fell, lurched, bounced. On the decks beneath, something crashed. Stressed metal creaked and groaned. Clinging hard to the ladder, she watched the conning screen.

Green streamers of nebular gas exploded across it, shot through with sudden scarlet arrows—particles of drift probably smaller than pinheads, but deadly if they got through the geodesic field. Shifting nets of sharp black lines mapped the interfering fields of magnetic and gravitic force spread like cosmic spider webs to snare them.

"Stellar devils!" she heard the pilot gasp. "If we live through this—"

Another klaxon blared, and he spun to confront a fresh burst of blazing peril. In his desperation, she saw a spark of hope. If she could make him listen without alerting Brendish or the robots, convince him that the Keeper was dead and the killers aboard, perhaps they could escape together.

Climbing one rung higher, she caught her breath to call—

"Arkel, I won't allow all this commotion!" The brittle voice snapped from close beside her head. "It upsets the Prince."

Brendish!

She dropped back into the well, afraid to look out. His voice came from close behind her, perhaps from the elevator door.

"So what?" the pilot muttered. "It upsets me."

"Call me sir!"

"If you think a word can save you, sir."

"What's your problem?"

"Our problem, sir." The gritty voice grew more ironic. "Magnetic forces and drifting dust are getting a bit too thick for the drive—"

"The Prince paid for competence," Brendish yapped. "Can't you read your own charts well enough to keep us in the chan—"

"Sir, you looked at my license. You looked at the charts. You ignored my advice to take the North Pass. I informed you that these others are far more difficult. As you see, they really are. You yourself picked this route through what we call Devil's Creep."

"If it's marked and charted, I see no difficulty."

"The channels change—sir! Because the Gyrel Channel is no open door through the shockwave. More a maze of narrow tunnels left in Beta's wake. Maybe clear enough once, but choked now with gas and debris pulled in behind the star. All the passes are closing now, and half the branches blind. Gyrel's old charts and markers going out of date—"

"Which we knew," Brendish sneered. "That's why the Prince paid for the pilot sense you claim on your license—"

The din of a new alarm drowned him out. Again the deck quivered and pitched, and again the pilot battled for a moment of relative calm.

"I had it once." Exhaling heavily, he sank back in his high seat. "Believe me, sir. The Gyrel gene. You won't find it often in men my age, because the radiation kills it while we're young. Mine died years ago."

"You—bastard!"

"An apt word, sir." His chuckle was sardonic. "We're most of us bastards, we who have or ever had the gift, because wives won't risk the nebula. The great Gyrels left bastards of their own to sire the rest of us—"

He cursed and flung himself at the console. The ship seemed to lift and spin and drop. Jil felt the drive falter, heard it go audible: a tiny, brain-stabbing whine.

"Damn you!" Tossed out across the deck, Brendish staggered for his balance and scrambled back out of her view. "If you wreck us—"

"In that case, sir, we'll all be dead." Grinning wanly, Arkel wiped a sleeve across his sweaty chin. "Because our luck's run out. I was lucky once, because I had the gift.

"It's magic, sir. Makes you a master of the nebula. You can see magnetic fields glowing in the dust. Feel a pinch of dust a billion kilometers ahead. Smell gamma radiation—sweet as a woman's perfume, till it begins burning the gift out of your brain. You can go anywhere, do anything—or you think you can. That's why you risk so much. You can kill the gift with exposures you hardly even feel. At first you don't know you've lost it. Even when you do, you doctor your license and keep on flying. Because the nebula's your life—"

"You—infamous—criminal!"

Shrill with fury, Brendish stumbled back into view, fox face red, tiny fists knotted. Jil dropped two rungs down.

"Perhaps I am." She heard the pilot's tired ironic chuckle. "Most of us are, here in the outlaw passes. The men with newer licenses draw berths on honest craft and steer safer courses. The rest of us have to settle for whatever stinking wrecks we happen to stumble on."

"You'll regret—"

The howl of the console cut him off.

"Sir!" Shouting against the din, Arkel sounded oddly calm. "Heavier hazards ahead. I'm activating escape station—"

"To abandon—" Brendish squeaked. "To abandon ship?"

"Not yet, sir. But I advice you to inform your Purple Prince. If we must, you'll find escape gear ready. In any case, I'm staying with the craft. Perhaps I am a bastard, but you can count on that."

Jil was dropping down the shaft.

"All hands!" His gravel voice ground out the speaker system. "Secure for safety drill."

At the escape deck, she caught the ladder to check her fall and listened for the spider's triple click. All she heard was the jangle of alarms. The winking orange symbols still identified the escape station across the curve of the narrow deck, and now a green sensor disk beneath it was marked with a red blinking signal:

ACTIVATED

She scrambled for it.

"Halt, Jil Gyrel!" the spider shrilled behind her. "You are not allowed—"

In all her drills with old Kita Kano, she had never fought a robot. Now her mind went numb with dread, because she didn't know how. The essence of yawara was the emotionless mesh of opposing minds, and the spider had no mind. Its ruling computer was no doubt emotionless enough, but far beyond the reach of any mode or move.

Yet, with no thought needed, she felt her trained body moving, flowing into the mode of the rolling boulder, one perfected by black masters 1,000 years ago to counter the unthinking rush of a dazed or insane opponent. With a fleeting thrill of wonder, she felt the spider's metal mass flying over her twisting hips, heard it crash into the deck.

She touched the sensor. The hatch clanged open. Inside, she slid into the pod. Escape drills had taught her how to do that, and the winking symbols now showed her which wheel to spin, which button to punch. The hatch clanged again. The pod lock thunked. Air hissed. A canned command crashed: "All clear for pod launch. When ready, break delay display."

She found the little hammer, shattered the luminous panel flashing DELAY.

Thunder drummed.

Only half aware of anything else, she knew the pod had been ejected.

She was off the lunatic ship!

12

Free!

The drumming thunder and the crushing thrust had been abruptly stopped. In free fall now, the pod flew on through ringing stillness. Jil floated over the controls, inhaling clean air, drunk with elation.

With the *Purple Empress* already far astern, she was well into the nebula, here on her own. For a few magic moments, with her oldest dream come true, nothing else could matter. But then her head struck the conning hood. Suddenly aware of minor aches and bruises from the launch, she twisted in the air to scan the pod.

It was a bare and narrow tube, almost too small to let her stand. Though its rated capacity may have been twenty persons, she counted only nine seats. Its equipment was minimal and mostly automatic. It had no rockets. The effective space displacement of the geodesic drive gave it a cruising range of perhaps four or five billion kilometers, a vast distance on any command human scale but far too little to reach any star. The drive was dead now, shut down by safety circuits till they were clear of the ship.

"Jil Gyrel!"

Pilot Arkel's raucous burr startled her, blasting out of a speaker in the console.

"Message to you from the S.S. *Purple Empress*. Prince Ulnar regrets that we cannot turn back to attempt to search for you or attempt any aid. Baron Brendish has informed your unfortunate mother. She wishes to express her forgiving and undying love as she and the Prince bid you this last sad farewell.

"End of message."

Silence rang again, but her first wild delight was dead. Wherever the pod happened to take her, she knew that all the puzzles of the *Purple Empress*—the cruel enigmas of her father's fate and the change in Shon Macharn, the haunting riddles of the Keeper's killing and the laser-maker's cryptic whispers—all those agonizing problems would haunt her till she solved them.

"Well, Jil!"

The pilot startled her again, his voice relaxed and not so loud.

"The Baron's gone below—you want to call him Baron. A chance now for a word of my own. Jil Gyrel! Wish I'd known you were aboard. We're kin, you know. Related through your name and the gene I was born with, though I wouldn't be surprised if you refused to claim me.

"However you feel about anything, don't try to reply. Your tachyonic transponder doesn't carry voice. All it does is send an automatic distress signal, indicating your identity and position. Range only a light-day or so. Designed to keep sending for a couple of months. That's about the limit of your power for the drive and life-support systems.

"All I can do is wish you luck. Afraid you'll need it. The Prince and the Baron made me steer into a pass called Devil's Creep. For reasons you can guess. Safer when old Ben Gyrel marked and charted it, but the shockwave keeps rolling back. If you care to trust my advice, set a course for Gamma.

"It's true we can't try to pick you up. Troubles enough of our own. Troubles I was asking for when I signed on. The Baron and the Prince admitted they were running from the Legion, but they've turned out to be an odder pair than I expected. If, by chance, you do get out alive, I hope you'll tell the Legion anything you know.

"As for me, I'm stuck—"

His voice had grown fainter as she fell behind the ship. Now it was cut off. Perhaps Brendish had come back. Feeling a rueful sympathy for Pilot Arkel, she thought he might have been an interesting man to know.

The pod was drifting on. She hauled herself into the control seat. The robotic pilot wanted her name. She punched it in and looked at the nebula in the conning hood. A dazing jolt. Here inside the shockwave, that hawk-headed shadow had vanished. Except for a few glowing rifts, dark dust-clouds hid everything around her. Even the *Purple Empress* was gone. She felt utterly alone, trapped in an infinite and directionless cosmic desolation.

She looked for the shape of Devil's Creep, but nothing had a shape. With the pickup pushed to the limit, she searched for the dusty mascons around her and the tachyonic strobes old Ben had placed to mark them, but the hood showed nothing. If the *Purple Empress* had run into trouble, despite Arkel's skill and all his instruments, what chance had she? What use was her silent gene . . .

A gong clanged.

The safety circuits had let the geodesic generator come on. The pod was suddenly alive, the console lighted, the internal G-field tugging her down to the seat. The sense of that soundless power changed her mood. All the hazards ahead had suddenly shrunk to her own size. The pod was her own starship.

Her first command!

She explored it. The service locker offered odd-tasting water and stale space rations, but not much else. The pod lacked most of the flight instruments she had learned to use. The conning hood had telescopic power enough to pick up a nearby planet or a close-passing starcraft, but its blank flicker showed nothing at all nearby.

Even the shockwave around her was only mocking emptiness. However deadly to starcraft at tachyonic velocities, its grains of dust were mostly microscopic, its expanding gas high vacuum. Again she looked for those ominous mascons rushing back to close the pass again, but they were too thin for the crude equipment to show them.

On the space-time scale of the nebula, the pod was only one more dust grain, lost in the astronomical ages and the long light-years. She might stay alive aboard it for a few months, move it a few billion kilometers and change nothing at all. Yet she still felt more elated than disheartened. At least for these brief months, she would be living out her dearest dream, flying on into the nebula.

On toward Gamma!

Even though her unlucky kinsman had confessed the loss of his pilot gift, she had no better guidance. Gamma itself was hidden in the dust ahead, but the robotic pilot projected its coordinates on the conning hood and she punched it in as her destination. Winking symbols gave her bearing and distance, relative velocity and projected time in flight.

The gong clanged again, and crimson legends flashed:

WARNING! COMPUTED FLIGHT TIME: 89 LEGION YEARS.
WARNING! INDICATED FLIGHT PLAN EXCEEDS CRUISING RANGE.
WARNING! SELECT ANOTHER DESTINATION.

She killed the warnings. With nothing else to do, because the winking data on the conning hood showed her neither the hazards in the channel nor anything outside it, she wandered back to the service locker. Recalling her recent hunger, she tried to eat an outdated ration. It refused to warm itself, and she found no appetite. Reclining the command seat, she tried to sleep. A dim sense of gathering wrongness kept her half awake.

The trouble she felt was something closer than the Keeper's murder or the loss of AKKA or the sinister riddles around Rem Brendish. Nothing she could do would delay the traitors now. The trouble wasn't even the stark likelihood that the pod would be her coffin.

What she felt was a nagging awareness of nearing danger, as bewildering as her first morning so long ago in the city-hive on Alpha III, when she woke up not knowing where she was. The feeling was hard to understand, because the pilot's shining needle did show true galactic north. Yet she couldn't shake it off. Weary of the struggle, she was more than half asleep when the console began to jangle and new symbols flickered:

WARNING! HEAVY MASCON DETECTED AHEAD
WARNING! REDUCE EFFECTIVE SPEED

She peered up into the conning hood, which had begun to wink and crawl with changing mazes of instrumental data. Though that hazardous mass of energy and dust was too diffuse for her vision to detect, the hood made it a misshapen red bull's-eye, ringed with black isodynes. Long orange arrows showed magnetic gradients. Flashing graphics indicated gamma radiation. Projected symbols flickered with readings and geodesic field intensity, relative acceleration and relative velocity.

On impulse, she hit the "clear" key to erase that whole bewildering display. Its vision function restored, the hood let her look outside for that haunting wrongness.

It was gone!

Suddenly, she had found herself.

With something better than mere sight, she could see the nebula. The mascon ahead. A thicker swirl of dust, still too far and too thin for her eyes but suddenly sharp in her mind. The nebular clouds beyond it swimming clearly into focus. She could feel their motion and sense the webwork of forces they obeyed.

Though Beta was still veiled in the dust behind, she knew its place and mass and motion as surely as she had almost always known galactic north. In her mind, she saw how it had swept out the channel, gathering meteor clouds to make those rains of fire that had delighted her childhood, leaving its wake for Ben Gyrel to map.

She felt the turbulent gas and dust rushing in again, to clog and finally seal that accidental tunnel. The mascon was only a minor eddy in those vast cosmic winds, but it whirled between her and Gamma. Arkel's advice to head for it had been a deadly blunder. Following the *Purple Empress*, though only at a tiny fraction of its speed, the pod was already trapped. Yet, in that giddy instant, danger didn't matter.

For she had the Gyrel gift!

Half her mind tried to doubt, tried to say that all she saw and felt and knew was mere illusion, a mental escape from cruel dilemmas. She could see the shape of every rushing cloud, feel the weight and flight of every deadly grain in the mascon ahead, hear the silent magnetic forces of the shock-wave like the roar of a hurricane around her.

It was real! The mutant gene was working in her. The Gyrel legacy, it was worth infinitely more than the inheritance

Macharn and Brendish had stolen. Perhaps it could even save her life.

When that first trembling elation had begun to subside, she bent to resent the robotic pilot on a new course, turning away from Gamma toward a still-open section of the narrowed pass —and hoping Pilot Arkel had found it in time.

She couldn't help that hope, even though the destruction of the *Purple Empress* would also kill the enemies aboard. She wanted answers to the riddles around Brendish and Macharn before they were erased. She didn't want her mother to die, or the laser-maker, or her unlucky kinsman.

PILOT ERROR!

That yellow warning had flared across the hood.

WARNING! NO TACHYONIC MARKER AHEAD.
WARNING! NO CHARTED DESTINATION WITHIN CRUISING RANGE.
WARNING! RESET DESTINATION HEADING TO AVOID INDICATED HAZARDS.

Sure of herself, she let it blink.

13

Eight days later, the speakers thumped.

"S.S. *Hedonian*." A woman's voice, musical and low. "Calling Escape Craft C from S.S. *Purple Empress*. We hear your signal and we're homing on it."

Within a few hours, the same warm voice was telling Jil to kill the drive and stand by for rescue. At last her conning hood picked up the starship, a faint silver fleck that swelled until she heard the clatter of the magnetic line fired to haul the pod aboard.

When crashing air had filled the lock, she opened her exit hatch and found three women waiting. They astonished her. Tall and slender, golden-haired and golden-eyed, they were nearly nude. Their beauty took her breath. All three looked precisely alike; even their voices were identical.

Trying not to stare too hard, she thanked them for picking her up.

"Captain Larron commanded your rescue when he heard your name." Devotion hushed their voices when they spoke of him. "He welcomes you aboard the *Hedonian* as his special guest."

She told them she had urgent messages to send.

"You must ask Captain Larron." The nearest frowned doubtfully. "We are flying under tachyonic silence, which cannot be broken except by his express command."

They took her to a stateroom, larger and more inviting than her cell on the *Purple Empress*. The captain would be pleased to receive her in the main salon before dinner. Suitable clothing could be provided, if she chose to wear clothing. When she said she did, the gowns they brought looked more costly than any she had ever owned and only slightly long. Beginning to feel at ease with the women, she confessed that she couldn't tell them apart.

"Nobody can, except the captain himself." They seemed amused. "We're android clones, you see, genetically identical. Distinctions between us are seldom required."

When she was ready, they took her two decks up to meet Captain Larron. The main salon was even more elegant than Macharn's purple sanctum, though not so showy. Polished gemstones and hardwoods shone. Rare metals gleamed discreetly. The captain rose to receive her, smiling genially through a heavy red-brown beard.

A huge man, and powerful. Hard muscles swelled and rippled beneath a casual tan pullover that carried no insignia of rank or status. Red-brown hair flowed down around his shoulders, as thick and lustrous as the beard.

"Welcome to the *Hedonian*!" Regarding her, his greenish eyes lit with pleasure. "We left our course to pick you up because I respect the Gyrel name, but I'd never expected any such superb reward."

He offered drinks from a well-stocked bar. Straw-colored Nebulon wine, liqueurs from Alpha and beyond, a rare Terran brandy. She asked for cold water and kept a wary distance, groping to know him and his enigmatic crew.

His rugged, dark-bronzed face looked open. He seemed at ease, his vibrant voice warmly cordial. She wanted to like him, but this *Hedonian* was another riddle, not yet so disturbing as those that came to haunt her on the *Purple Empress* but equally perplexing.

A tall, nude beauty brought iced water for her in a silver cup and the Nebulon wine for him, kneeling to them both as humbly as the spider-robots had made her kneel to Brendish and Macharn, smiling up into his face with a total devotion.

Jil sipped the water, feeling troubled by her own instinctive response to his hearty masculine vitality. His male appeal was almost an aura. Half captured by it, she could understand the girl's adoration. Alarmed, she didn't intend to let it overwhelm her.

"Captain, I've a favor to ask. A very urgent call I have to make."

In absent affection, his powerful hand had fallen on the girl's golden head. She shivered as if in ecstasy. Smiling fondly, he nodded for her to rise.

"Any other favor." He turned more gravely to Jil. "But circumstances force us to fly silent. You'll approve when you know why."

"You'll let me call when you know the situation."

"You're my guest." He smiled again. "I'm listening."

"A matter of interstellar security." She hesitated, uncertain how to convince him. "Did you know the Keeper has been killed?"

With his admiring eyes sweeping her again, he shook his head as if he hadn't really heard.

"Murdered," she told him. "Her great weapon likely lost. Maybe to conspirators plotting to restore the Ulnar Empire. They're on the *Purple Empress.* Escaping into the nebula. I think they have alien allies there. There's a Legion ship cruising in the channel. The *Sunmark*, under Pilot-Major Star. I must get what I know to him."

She saw the doubt clouding his cragged features.

"Captain, please!" she whispered. "You've got to believe. You will, when I tell you more—"

His regretful shrug stopped her.

"I don't like to doubt such a lovely witness." He was gently tolerant. "But we've just come from a stop on Alpha." He shook his head. "Not a word about any attack on the Keeper."

"Because it's a security secret," she insisted. "It has to be kept secret. The Legion can't tell our enemies that we've lost AKKA—"

She had seen his fleeting smile.

"Captain, I'm not crazy!"

"I didn't say that. But your flight in the pod must have been a pretty grim ordeal. We'll try to help you recover."

She studied his features, the iron behind the genial charm.

"Where can you drop me off?" she demanded. "When?"

"A difficult problem." He shrugged, with a momentary frown of apology. "I don't know the answer."

"Am I a prisoner?"

"Our guest," he said. "But we must keep you—"

"Why?" She was on her feet, breathing hard. "I won't submit—"

"Please sit down." He gestured persuasively. "Listen for an instant. Perhaps the Legion is really in trouble, but so are we. With the most compelling possible reason to risk no contact with them. You see, we're fugitives ourselves. If the *Sunmark* is actually cruising above us in the channel, perhaps we are the prey it's waiting for."

Unwillingly she sat.

"Another strange tale." His brown smile tried to disarm her. "Nearly as odd as your own, but I hope you'll try to believe me. We'll both be happier when we come to trust each other." He signaled the waiting girl. "Won't you have some wine?"

She shook her head, but he let the girl refill his own glass.

"I was born in the nebula." His tone was patiently appealing. "I've always known about the Gyrels, and you may have heard of my Dad. Raben Larron. Sometimes known as Robber Raben. For cause enough, I imagine."

She couldn't help liking his casual grin.

"Came out from Terra. On borrowed money, he used to say —I imagine it was stolen. Got here with nothing at all. That never mattered, because he was made for the nebula. He loved the daring. Even the danger. Shrugged off his losses and revealed when he won. Your Gyrel men were born with your pilot gene. He used to say his was the dealer gene. A gift for falling on his feet. Made his billions, yet never had enough.

"Mother was an acrobat from Derron IV. Came out on a tour he'd promoted. Fascinated at first with him and the nebula, but I guess his financial acrobatics got too giddy for her. Went home to civilization the year after I was born. Wanted me, but Dad laughed at her lawyers and took me out beyond the law.

"So I grew up with his love for the nebula. Grew up wanting to be just like him, till I found he wasn't really happy with himself. In spite of all he used to win and lose, he'd always felt himself beneath the touring bloods, with all their class and manners and social arts he didn't know.

"Sent me out the year I was twelve, to get the polish he wished he'd had. With funds enough to buy the best. I had a dozen years of high-class culture, with top-flight science to match, most of it on Terra. Learned a lot, including things he'd never expected. Lived a year with my mother again, before she saw she didn't want me. All of which made me what I am.

"Like me or not."

Smiling at her, he shrugged as if certain she must.

"Yet I'm no clone of either one. Never cared for Dad's hard games to win another billion. Never learned to care for the Terran culture and old-style class my mother worshiped. Or the universe she called civilized. Guess I never will."

Solemn again, he sipped the amber wine.

"No room back there for me." He fixed his greenish eyes on her, as if anxious to make her see how he felt. "Too many people. Too many 'isms.' My college profs used to preach cultural evolution. All their theories meant to glorify social setups invented to enslave the individual human being.

"Look at Cosmocracy—"

The emphatic sweep of his great arm spilled wine across the deck. A silent clone darted to mop it up, while his voice boomed on.

"Cosmocracy! The 'ism' of the New Empire. Claims the cosmos loves us. Hates the Legion and the Keeper as sinner against universal harmony. Schemes to crown the Ulnar pretender in a new Purple Hall. A weak-chinned idiot, when I met him once."

"The Ulnars—"

He caught himself with a self-conscious grin.

"Forgive me, Jil, but I'm afraid I hold a special animus against them and the Cosmocrats behind them, because their crazy gospel of cosmic harmony seduced the girl I loved."

Jil nodded, wondering if that animus might help him believe her story of the imperial plotters escaping aboard the *Purple Empress*. She decided not to interrupt him now.

"A thousand 'isms'!" He swung his arms, booming again. "Games men play. The winners get the glory. The others—a trillion little rats caught in a trillion tiny traps. I prefer a cleaner kind of freedom and a wider field of action. The nebula can give you anything if you've got guts or skill or luck enough."

Jil couldn't help a sympathetic smile.

"I know," she told him. "I grew up out on Alpha III, but I never learned to like it. I'm happy to be back. No matter—" Remembering, she checked herself. "No matter what happens now."

"That's entirely up to you."

He gestured genially, offering the wine.

"Go on." She erased her smile. "About your father."

"Dead. Ten years ago. Killed by an old associate who claimed he'd been misused. The news brought me home. Dad had died rich. I found I owned a planet, if you can imagine."

He grinned, savoring the phrase.

"Ultima I—I never learned who first claimed it, but he must have been Dad's own breed. Somewhat too deep inside the nebula, but rich in every heavy metal. The dusters claim it's haunted with cliffdrillers or worse, but I've always found a few tough enough to dig more wealth than I could squander.

"We're bound there now—"

"When we land—"

"Sorry, Jil." His face grew firmer. "I don't want the Legion there. That's why I had to tell you what I am. And how I have to live. My story's not quite over. As I said, there was a woman."

He leaned toward her urgently, as if anxious for her to share everything he felt.

"A woman I loved." His tone seemed wistful. "More goddess than human, at least in my own imagination. As stunning as you are, even in fact—you see her images all around me."

He nodded fondly at the meekly waiting clone.

"She loved me, or said she did. But never loved the nebula. When I wouldn't give it up, she got herself engaged to a civilized aristocrat—an arrogant fool with nothing but the Ulnar name. A hard blow, but Dad taught me ways to win."

Proudly, he smiled at the girl kneeling now to pour his wine.

"Thank you, lovelight." He gave her his strong hand to help her rise, and she clung to it with a trembling sigh of rapture. When she released it, he returned to Jil. "I still have her, after all, refined and multiplied!"

His self-delight seemed wholly innocent, almost naive.

"You see, I'd studied genetic engineering. Learned enough to hire the best in the business. Secured a few tissue cells when that reluctant goddess had a minor blemish fixed. I had them cultured, expertly modified, cloned illegally. Every blemish lifted. Every misdirected emotion transformed into absolute admiration. Replicated enough times to staff my ship and my place on Ultima—"

He checked himself with a sharp look at Jil.

"You don't approve?"

"Does that matter?"

"Other women have astonished me." He scanned her soberly. "One had worked in genetics with me. A friend, I thought—a colleague in research—till she saw the clones. I never understood why she condemned me so savagely, or why she got so rabid when I offered to donate cells of my own for the manufacture of whatever sort of superman she wanted."

"It was she who betrayed us to the Legion."

His green eyes narrowed.

"As for yourself—" He nodded at the tall clone, whose golden smile remained expressionlessly intent. "How do you feel about her?"

"If it matters, you seem terribly unfair."

"To the clones?" He shook his head as if honestly bewildered. "Without me, they would not exist. I love them. They love me—totally, with an engineered and absolute devotion. We share our happiness and harm nobody. How is that unfair?"

"If you love freedom, where is theirs?"

"If I love freedom, or think I do, that's an accident." He gestured expansively. "Due to the nebula and Dad." He surveyed her again, deliberately. "You'd deny that you were engineered. But you were, as I was. Not artificially, of course, but by all the random natural chances of genes and environment. If you love freedom, it's nothing you were ever free to choose, nothing my clones would ever choose. Forced on them, it would destroy their happiness."

Oddly anxious, he leaned to look into her eyes.

"I'm trying to explain, because I hope you won't condemn me."

"Why should you care?"

"Because we're going to be a long time together, Jil. And because so many others hate me." His bronze jaw set. "I'm a felon, convicted under the so-called gene guard law, which was enacted to keep genetic engineers from attempting to reshape the human race. I was convicted in spite of an expensive legal defense. A sound defense, based on the fact that my creations can bear no children.''

Emotion broke through his genial composure.

''My own conviction—that was no surprise. What I didn't expect was the sentence against my clones. As the judges read the law, no human clone can be allowed to exist. We're all under sentence—the legal term for killing clones is not 'execution' but 'cessation.' To the law they aren't alive, therefore they cannot die.''

His craggy features quivered.

''That's it, Jil. The reason we can't call the Legion.''

Watching him, the waiting clone had whimpered in anguish, reaching as if she longed, yet feared, to give him some caress. He paused to comfort her with a gesture and an uncertain grin before he spoke again to Jil.

''With the Legion behind us, we're in flight for our lives.''

14

She begged Larron to drop her off.

"In the pod. Somewhere up the channel, where some other craft might pick me up."

"Sorry, Jil." His regret seemed real. "That's impossible. We're keeping to the outlaw passes, which friends of the Legion avoid. Odds are you'd drift here till you died. Or do worse if you were picked up—"

"The odds don't matter," she broke in. "Not with the traitors escaping—"

"Listen, Jil." He was genially inflexible, half apologetic, half exasperated, altogether stern. "We aren't calling anybody. The nebula's full of rumors as fantastic as yours, most of them false. It's my craft and my clones, with no doubt that we'll be killed if the Legion ever overtakes us. All you can do is relax and make the best of us—"

"Relax?" She groped for words to break his craggy certainty. "I'm not crazy, Captain. The Keeper's dead—I know that. AKKA is lost. I have information that must reach the Legion—"

"If I thought that was true—" he paused to study her, shaking his head—"I might risk my own life to pass your warning on. But not my clones."

"Captain—" She tried to smooth her trembling voice. "I want no harm to you or them, but I can't just forget—"

Greenish eyes amused, he grinned behind the flowing beard.

"It all depends on where you stand. From your standpoint, one convicted criminal and a few illegal clones can't count for much against the Legion and the safety of mankind. But from mine—"

"True, I guess." She had to nod. "But can't you find some safe way to get my message out?"

"I won't throw our lives away." His grin was gone and his voice rang harder. "We can't risk any contact." He was rising. "You're my guest. I'll try to treat you well, but you'll stay my guest."

"You mean prisoner?"

He shrugged, genially unyielding.

"See you at dinner."

The clones escorted her back to her stateroom and waited with her there till time to dine. When she tried to send them away, they said their duty was now with her. They wanted to bathe her, to comb her hair, to help her dress, and they went back with her to the main salon.

At dinner she met the pilot.

"Jil Gyrel." Larron seated her across from him.

"Pilot—Master Julian Diamondwall."

A short, stout little man, he had shrewd little mud-colored eyes and an air of bitter wisdom. Yet his smooth, yellow moon face held no hint of age, and he bowed to her with a certain gloomy jauntiness. His nod to Larron was merely casual. He was clearly no subject clone, and Jil wondered if he might become a friend.

Her spirits had begun to lift. She couldn't escape a certain sympathy for Larron in his battle to create and defend the private world he wanted, or even ignore her own emotional response to his appealing male charisma.

After her musty rations on the pod, the food seemed superb. When Larron called for music, a trio of the clones chanted an ode he had composed to celebrate the nebula as the last arena of freedom. Their voices had purity and power, and she found herself sharing his love for the nebula.

The little pilot enjoyed himself. He cheered the song, ate

with gusto and drank his full share of the wine. In no apparent awe of Larron, he ogled the busy clones. Jil saw one of them start and stare as if she had been pinched. He bowed to her when the meal was over, beaming so warmly that she decided to try an appeal.

"Thank you, Pilot, for picking me up." She offered him her hand. "Are we still in Gyrel Passage?"

"Aye, lass. In the pass called Devil's Creep." He looked obliquely at Larron. "Because it's swarming with mortal mascons. It's only precious luck, Miss Gyrel, that you got to us alive." His quick little eyes came back to her. "Or do you have the pilot gift?"

"I think I do," she said. "May I see the conning screen?"

"You are mortal fortunate if you've got that power." He blinked in astonishment. "I never saw it in a woman. Nor in many men. Myself, I'm glad enough to trust a blessed robot. Come along to the bridge and meet Lord Archy—"

"Remember, Julian." Larron had been leaving, escorted by his troop of alluring nudes, but he turned abruptly back. "We're flying silent. Jil says there's a Legion battlecraft somewhere behind. You will permit no attempt of hers to reach it with any sort of signal."

"The mortal Legion?" A wheeze of dismay. "After us?"

"It's Kynan Star," Jil told him. "On the *Sunmark.* Hunting the traitors. The killers of the Keeper—"

"Jil hasn't got over her ordeal in the pod." Larron gave her a condolatory headshake. "She believes the Keeper has been murdered, but she brings no evidence. Our own destination is still Ultima I, and the Legion would never let us get there."

"Aye, sir. Miss Gyrel's a welcome guest, but we need no trouble with the mortal Legion."

Larron swung regally away, an ecstatic clone on either massive arm. The little pilot turned to Jil with a wink and a grin that made her want to trust him.

"Come along, lass. You must meet Lord Archy."

She followed him into the elevator.

"Pilot, I want to tell you who I am and how I know the Keeper has been killed—"

"If you're Jil Gyrel, I know who you are. I'm mortal glad to meet you." His bow was oddly formal. "In better times, your famous family was kind to me. It was old Lyn Gyrel who hauled me out of a gutter and took me into the blessed nebula.'' He gave her a quick yellow smile. ''He used to talk about his son back at the Academy. A bright kid named Jef. Your father, I guess.''

''Then you will believe me?''

''Ah, Miss Jil!'' He blinked at her sadly. ''I'm mortal glad to welcome you aboard—Larron's clones may be as mortal lovely as you are, but they weren't made for me. In those old days, the Gyrels were heroes of the blessed Legion and I was proud to serve with them. But those days are gone.''

He shook his head with a wheezy sigh.

''Lass, things are mortal wicked now. Larron says you want to send some message, but Lord Archy and I have reasons to keep quiet. You don't find friends of the Legion slinking up these suicide passes like worms in the gut of a mortal monster. We're miserable convicts, lass, in flight for our precious lives.''

He bowed her out onto the command deck.

''Lord Archy! Meet a friend.''

She couldn't find Lord Archy. The seat beneath the conning screen looked empty until a bright silver ball the size of her head rolled out of it and bounded toward her across the deck. Bouncing before her like a dribbled ball, it spoke in musical bell tones.

''Mr. Two, can you specify a number for our friend?''

''Her name is Jil Gyrel.'' His wrinkled grin held a hearty admiration. ''She's our special guest aboard the craft and a mortal special friend. Her number will be three.''

''We greet you, Miss Three!'' The ball bounced closer. ''If you trace descent from Command Ben Gyrel, you are indeed a highly special human. We ourselves were designed for service to him.''

''He was my grandfather's father.''

''Welcome!'' it pealed. ''Welcome aboard the *S. S. Hedonian*. We were shaped to serve Ben Gyrel. If requested, we will gladly serve Miss Three.''

''Thank you!'' she whispered. ''You may be requested.''

She had found the signal center. Consoles darkened now, it filled an alcove beyond the conning screen. Back at school on Alpha III, she had passed her tests in tachyonic communication. Given a few minutes alone with the signal gear, she would have a reasonable chance to reach the *Sunmark*. Looking away before it could betray her, she turned again to the pudgy pilot.

"My father was lost on the *Iron Argo*—"

"A mortal tragedy!" Bald as a melon, his head was cocked shrewdly at her, the squinting eyes so keen she was afraid he might read what was shaping in her mind. "We might have been aboard with him, but for the freaks of mortal fate. I'd lost my license as a nebula pilot—the result of misfortunes I don't care to recall. I didn't get the berth I asked for."

"You were lucky."

"The *Argo* was under Shon Macharn. I've heard he got back too sick to talk."

"A dreadful sickness!" Jil whispered. "He used to be wonderful, back in the days when he and my father came home together. Strong and brave and kind to me, laughing at the nebula. I don't—don't know—"

She shivered.

"He got well enough to marry my mother. But the sickness left him changed. Horribly, in ways I never understood. He's on the *Purple Empress* now, flying into the nebula ahead of us, calling himself Prince Ulnar. Involved in a crazy-seeming scheme to restore the old empire. Captain Larron won't believe me. But the conspiracy—it's real!"

His face was an ageless yellow mask, revealing no response.

"Please!" she begged him. "I know how it sounds, but I'm not insane. The plotters have been diabolic. Fooling everybody. Somehow corrupting Legion commanders. They've crippled the Legion terribly. That's why I've just got to call—"

She stopped.

The quicksilver robot was back in the pilot's position, dancing over the consoles. Diamondwall stood staring at it and off toward the signal alcove, his raspy breath heavier, his round face expressionless. She wasn't sure he was listening to her until he swung abruptly back.

"It's no mortal wonder Larron won't believe you!"

"Please, you must!" she begged him. "It's so terribly important. I don't know what they're planning, but I'm afraid. Don't laugh, please! If you had seen Macharn on the *Purple Empress*, and a evil little rat named Brendish—"

She stopped when she saw his slow headshake.

"I'm mortal sorry to hear about Shon. A brave and able starman, back when I knew him." Heavily, he sighed. "But the nebula changes all of us. Look at me!" His dull-colored eyes darted back to her. "The precious wreck of the man I might have been. Alone and broke and afoul of the law when Larron picked me up. Crawling now through fire and fury in this fearful gut, with the Legion on my tail."

"Please—" she began again, but he didn't seem to hear.

"I came out to the mortal nebula as young as you are, lass. As full of noble dreams." Those wheezy words began a tale of cruel misfortune. Miner and trader, pilot and geodesic engineer, gambler and evangelist for the Church of the Oversoul, he had never struck anything rich. His only lucky break had been stumbling on Lord Archy. He gave no detail about the rescue, but the little robot had been his loyal companion since.

"Forgive me, lass, if I talk too long. The reason is I've lived too mortal long."

He *had* talked too long. His tale had been too dramatic to seem entirely true. Now and then his sharp little eyes had narrowed too keenly at her, as if to see whether she believed him. She tried not to let her reservations show. All that really mattered was her chance to call the Legion.

"Please," she said. "Go on."

"Thank you, lass." In spite of all her doubts, she couldn't help liking his time-battered grin. "I'm mortal glad to have another human on the blessed ship, and I hope you'll come to trust me. Flying with Larron, we'll have a long time together."

"How did you meet him?"

Only half listening, she tried to measure him, to watch Lord Archy's dance beneath the conning screen, to plan what she must do. Unless he happened to know yawara, the thing should be possible. If the little robot really respected the Gyrel name . . .

"Ah, lass," he was wheezing, "Larron came along at a fearful time. I was rotting in a stinking prison. Convicted of forging my pilot's license. Condemned to radical regeneration —which means they meant to kill my blessed brain and revive it with the mind of some mortal duster dying of radiation sickness.

"An evil day, lass, when any honest starman finds himself too mortal old and ill to get a legal berth. All my friends dead and gone long ago. All but Lord Archy, and they had him, too. Condemned by the Robot Control Board and sentenced to penal disassembly, because his capacities exceed their legal limits for a self-directed functiform unit.

"Their mortal error!" A broad yellow grin. "His self-directed capacities surprised them. He got out of their penal lab and set up the rescue. For me, and Larron, too. He'd found Larron lying in the same lockup, under penalty of death with all his lovely clones. We were mortal fortunate to find the *Hedonian* still standing at the penal dock—"

Lights had come on in the signal alcove, and a buzzer purred there.

" . . . got away together." She heard his creaky voice again. "That's why we all fear the mortal Legion. . . ."

This was her chance! The robot had bounded toward the signal station and he was puffing hastily after it, his back turned to her. The mode of the swinging scythe would bring him to the deck disabled or dead.

"Mr. Two, we request attention," the robot's bell tones rang. "A proclamation from the Legion Nebular Command . . ."

A stroke of luck, she thought. With a circuit already open, her own message to the Legion should get through before Larron and his clones had any chance to stop her. Breath caught, she crouched to move.

And found she couldn't.

A wave of uncertainty stopped her. Was Julian Diamondwall actually as innocently defenseless as he tried to seem? What would actually control the self-directed robot? Loyalty to the Gyrel name? Gratitude for its rescue? Or its own circuits for self-preservation?

Her breath went out.

She lurched across the deck, recovering her balance.

Suddenly, she wasn't sure she really wanted to cause the death of Larron and his clones, or betray the little pilot and his robot, no matter how great the reason.

" . . . proclamation from Pilot-General von der Veen." The gong voice changed abruptly to the hurried rasp of a tired human throat. "Reporting invasion out of the inner nebula. Numerous planets under attack by unidentified enemy battle-craft. Legion craft have been destroyed, Legion bases lost. The

Legion Nebular Command announced with regret that all remaining forces must be withdrawn to defend the Gyrel Channel. No further protection can be extended to civilian populations, and all civilians are warned to get out of the nebula while they can—"

The hoarse voice caught.

"If they can!"

15

The *Hedonian* flew on through Devil's Creep, deeper into the nebula.

Unhappy with herself, Jil followed a clone back to her stateroom. She almost envied that bare golden beauty, so completely content, so serenely unconcerned with anything except Captain Larron's sovereign will. For she felt haunted by a guilty regret. She had failed the Legion, failed the laser-maker, maybe even failed mankind.

Why?

She lay awake a long time, looking for answers that never came. The captain and his little pilot had saved her life. Somehow, for reasons she wasn't sure about, she had come to like them both. Yet both were self-confessed convicts, holding her illegally. If she owed them anything, it couldn't be the safety of the race.

Her sleep was uneasy when it came, troubled with dreadful dreams. The clone waiting at her stateroom door had become a silver spider, reproaching her in the round bell tones of Diamondwall's Lord Archy.

"Jil Gyrel, you have betrayed humanity, and now you must

suffer punishment. Your sentence is slavery to the Purple Emperor.''

When she tried to escape, it dragged her into a purple-hung throne room. The man on the high throne was Captain Larron, mighty-muscled and red-bearded, as nude as the clones kneeling around him.

"I rule the nebula, Jil Gyrel," he boomed at her. "I've defeated the Legion and taken the secret of AKKA. My faithful clones will use it to kill all men. All women are now my slaves.'' Rising, he beckoned her toward his throne. "Jil Gyrel, you will now submit to me.''

She wanted to yield, to feel and answer the thrust of his male might. She was eagerly climbing the steps of the throne, arms open to him, when she heard the laser-maker calling from somewhere far away. A tiny sighing at first, its voice changed to the crack-voiced singsong of Master Kita Kano.

"Remember us, Jil Gyrel! Remember the armed rhinoceros and your duty to the Legion.''

Sick with shame, she turned away from the naked giant and the purple throne.

"Come to us, Jil Gyrel!'' the far singsong was calling. "The Legion needs you to capture the killers of the Keeper. Pilot-Major Kynan Star needs you to help him recover the secret of AKKA. The people of the nebula need you to defend them from the Purple Emperor and his cliffdriller slaves.

"You've betrayed them once, but you can save them now.''

Ashamed of her betrayal, she ran toward the voice.

"Jil, I want you!'' Hoarse with passion, Captain Larron was shouting after her. "Come back to me.''

In spite of Kita Kano's voice and all her duty to mankind, his male spell overwhelmed her. She ran back into his open arms, quivered with rapture when they crushed her against his black-haired body. She was raising her eager mouth to his when she caught his body reek, the evil bog-rot stick of Shon Macharn.

She tore away and ran again.

"Jil Gyrel!'' The quavery chant was still Master Kano's, but it came from a fire-diamond now. They were suddenly back on Beta I. It was a frosty winter night, and the fire-winged nebula blazed across the sky. The laser was the eye of the hawk, flashing needles of red and green, and the accusing singsong was a prayer addressed to her. "You betrayed us once, but you can save us now."

Larron had come panting close behind.

"Jil!" She felt his hot breath and heard his pounding feet. "Jil Gyrel, you know you want to be—have to be—mine."

She ran on toward the diamond laser. It was flashing now from the barren crags of Hawksbeak Mountain. Black Lake was suddenly in her way, the lifeless flats of dark caked mud spread far around it. Frantic to escape the hard-breathing giant, desperate to reach the laser and make atonement for her crime against mankind, she ran out across the brittle crust.

It splintered under her naked feet. Freezing mud swallowed her. Its foul reek took her breath. Sinking, she tried to scream for help. There was no help. Larron stood safe on the bank, his great arms around two naked clones, laughing at her shame.

"Jil Gyrel!" one of the clones sang to her, its lilting voice strangely calm. "Captain Larron expects you at breakfast."

Awake in her own stateroom, she felt stiff and sticky-eyed, still ridden by her own guilty indecision. Yet somehow she soon felt better. The waiting clones were lovely as ever, quickly attentive to her comfort. At the table, Larron seemed too gentle and too genial to have been the libidinous giant of her nightmare. His smile was a flash of hearty admiration, but he turned back at once to the long-limbed nude about to serve him. Suddenly, she was hungry. The dishes were often unfamiliar, all delightful. She ate with appetite.

"Fearful news, Captain." Diamondwall came waddling late to the table, dolefully shaking his head. "Lord Archy has been recording tachyonic bulletins. From the Legion craft as they scuttle out and the civilians left to face they don't know what. A mortal evil time for people in the nebula."

For all his gloom, however, he had a yellow smile for Jil and a wheezy greeting for the clone who glided to fill his plate.

"Attackers striking everywhere." He spoke almost casually, as if he didn't really care. "Hitting mining camps and Legion installations all across the nebula."

"Who's attacking?" Larron frowned, more concerned. "From where?"

"Nobody knows." He shrugged. "Cliffdrillers suspected but not identified."

"Can't it be the Ulnar conspiracy?" Jil peered anxiously at

Larron and back at Diamondwall. "To restore the Purple Empire?"

She was shivering to the shame of her dream and the stink and the chill of that frozen bog, but she felt better about herself when Diamondwall shrugged again and Larron shook his tawny mane.

"Nothing in the nebula works out so mortal simple." Diamondwall looked up briefly from his plate. "Any human rebels would be broadcasting ultimatums. Lord Archy says the attackers never signal anything at all."

He held out his plate for another portion of little crimson hydroponic berries that Jil could not identify, tangily sweet, smothered in a rich, golden cream.

"They've beaten the Legion." He spoke with difficulty between huge bites. "It's pulling out. Blowing up or burning yards and installations. Ordering dusters out of the nebula. Mortal nonsense! They've got no way to get out. No craft to carry them. Nowhere to go."

He fell back to his breakfast.

"Should we—" She looked uneasily at Larron. "Are we turning back?"

Larron seemed absorbed in the gold-skinned clone leaning over him, fondly watching the fleeting play of her facial expression and the fluid flow of her body motion, responding to her with his own slight and subtle gestures as if they spoke a silent private language. Clearly they were not discussing retreat from the nebula.

"Turn back?" The little pilot blinked at her sadly. "Into mortal death? The Legion may be scuttling out of the nebula, but they'll be waiting to meet the invaders in the channel. We'd be caught in between."

He paused to polish his plate.

"Ah, lass, don't forget what's outside. Radical regeneration for me. Penal disassembly for Lord Archy. Death for the captain and his clones." He raised his plate for yet another serving of the crimson berries. "Live or die, we'll do it in the nebula."

He grinned his thanks to the golden clone.

"There's a precious blessing for us, lass, in a mortal wicked wind." His yellow moon face beamed. "The Legion looks to have bigger problems now than chasing after the miserable victims of some lunatic law."

When the meal was over, he let her go with him back to the command deck. Lord Archy came flying from the conning screen to meet her.

"Greetings, Miss Three!" He bounced on the deck in front of her. "Can you supply data on deceased Terran scientist Archy Mides?"

"Who?"

"He means Archimedes," Diamondwall told her.

"Pronunciation illogical," the gong voice protested. "We request data on the primitive Terran mathematician and philosopher who originated the art of terraforming worlds." He bounded eagerly higher. "Can you supply such data?"

"Sorry," Jil said. "I think he was an early Greek, but I didn't know he was a terraforming engineer."

"He could move a planet," the bell tones pealed. "Using a powerful invention of his own, now no longer identifiable, which he called a fulcrum. We deplore the lack of further data—"

An alarm rang, and the consoles flickered red.

"Miss Three, we beg your forgiveness. The instruments require attention."

He bounded back to the conning screen.

"He named himself," Diamondwall said. "Archimedes is his hero. He has always hoped to visit Terra to look for the facts beneath the legend, but our fearful misfortunes have kept him condemned to the mortal nebula."

He lit the map tank to show her the starship's course.

"We're still caught in Devil's Creep," he told her. "Forced far below light speed and picking a way through mascons and magnetic storms that could burn us to atoms. But don't let it fret you, lass. The refugees will be running for North Pass, the mortal invaders maybe hard behind. Our way to Ultima should be clear."

"The invaders?" She peered at him uneasily. "Won't they be waiting for us there?"

"Could be." He shut off the map tank. "But we hope not. The drillers are mortal metal eaters. Larron says he's beaten them to all the richest lodes. He still has a few miners down on the planet and a duty crew on the tach statellite, but most of the pay metal's gone. Too little left, he hopes, to draw any drillers. If he's wrong . . ."

He shrugged, squinting very sharply at her.

"Mortal few live forever."

16

She slept better the next night, till a clone's song woke her.

"Miss Jil! The pilot wants you."

On the command deck she found emergency. Lord Archy was skittering about the consoles in the flash and clangor of alarms. Diamondwall waddled to meet her, puffing and perspiring.

"Ah, lass!" he gasped. "You said you had the Gyrel gift?"

"I think I do."

"If that's a fact, we need it now." He dragged her toward the conning screen. "To save our mortal lives!"

He beckoned the robot out of her way.

"Lord Archy says we're trapped. A mascon cloud has blocked the mortal pass ahead and another starcraft is sneaking up behind—"

"A Legion ship?" she whispered. "Kynan Star, on the *Sunmark*?"

"No way to know." He shrugged. "But you find no friends in Devil's Creep."

He tugged her on.

"We're in a mortal wicked fix. Larron says he'll die among

the mascons before he gives up to anybody. To the Legion or another outlaw or any fearful alien out of the nebula."

Lord Archy had skipped aside, and she slid into the pilot's seat. The alarms confused her for a moment, till she killed them. The conning screen clear again, she looked out into the nebula and felt dazed by its impact.

With far more precision and power than the simple hood she had used in the pod, the screen revealed the swarming suns of the nebular cluster, burning blue giants and mightier red ones, dark protosuns and a far-off, slow-flashing pulsar, all wrapped in turbulent gas and clotted dust that reached out to the swelling shell of the shockwave itself.

Its vastness was shattering.till, suddenly, her mental focus changed to let her perceive it with a sharper sense than all the ship's instruments. Still dazzling to her, that mutant gift let her reach across the light-years to weigh suns like pebbles in her hand, let her feel gravitic and magnetic forces like winds against her face, let her grasp all the changes of the nebula like the motions of some simple toy.

She found a tiny point of mass behind, darting after them through a narrow-seeming gap between those frowning walls. Something swifter than the clouds, denser than the dust, too small to show a shape.

Kynan—

"Can't you help us, lass?" She heard the pilot's plaintive moan. "Can Lord Archy teach you how to work the blessed hood? Our need is mortal dire—"

He fell abruptly silent.

She had already grasped the force and motion of the mascon rolling in ahead, almost in the way she had learned to feel the moods and modes of a crouched yawara master. In only a moment, she had found a route not yet blocked by its roiling blot.

"Careful, lass!" He had seen her bending to reset the flight director. "Don't you need the star maps? One mortal blunder could kill the blessed ship—"

"No blunder, Mr. Two." Lord Archy's gong tones cut him off again. "We observed Commander Ben Gyrel while he still possessed the pilot sense. Like Miss Three, he had little need for instrumental aids."

Squinting warily, Diamondwall watched until she let Lord Archy dance across the consoles to check the changes she had set up.

"Any mortal trouble now?"

"Negative, Mr. Two. We detect no difficulty rated mortal."

"Forgive me, lass!" He grinned at her gratefully. "You've pulled us out of a fearful fix. Let me leave you with Lord Archy now, while I go below to beg the clones for the stuff of precious life. Nothing starves me faster than the wolves of wicked peril."

He waddled into the elevator.

The whole pattern of the channel was visible now in her mind, as sharply seen as the starship itself. She set up a course that would carry them clear of the mascon, safely out of Devil's Creep, on to the end of the channel.

"Well done, Miss Three!" Lord Archy pealed. "We observe that you do indeed display the rare talent of Commander Ben Gyrel, who is still Dr. One. Created to serve him, we now owe service to you. You may request whatever you wish."

Sliding off the seat, she started toward the signal center. Again a stab of uncertainty stopped her. If the ship behind was in fact Kynan Star's, she could now no doubt get her message to him. Lord Archy surely wouldn't interfere. Yet, her pulse pounding and her breath rushing fast, she turned back.

Again, she didn't quite know why. Larron and his pilot were still criminals in flight from justice. Terrible invaders were still sweeping men from the nebula. What she knew could be useful to the Legion. Her duty should have been starkly clear.

Yet the nebula had already changed her. She had somehow come to feel more at home in this hazardous outlaw world than she had ever been in the teeming city levels of Alpha III. Astonished at herself, she felt a solemn sort of joy that the haunting shame of her nightmare was gone.

Back in the seat beneath the conning screen, she caught herself whistling the Legion march and paused to grin at its irony. Though Lord Archy volunteered to take a watch, she stayed there until they had come safely past the mascon and on into clearer space beyond Devil's Creep. The drive pushed up to a full, effective light speed, she went groggily back to her cabin and happily back to sleep.

A richer music rang in the voice of the clone who woke her for dinner, and a warmer welcome was waiting for her there. Larron rose to greet her, bowing with a new respect, his craggy grin more than merely cordial.

"The pilot says you saved the ship. We won't forget."

"Aye, lass." Diamondwall looked up from his high-piled plate. "Your blessed talent found the way Lord Archy could never discover—and shook off that wicked ship behind us. We left them still blundering for their lives among the mortal mascons. They're long since lost from our conning screen, and Lord Archy says they'll never overtake us now."

"Does he think—" She flinched from a probing needle of regret. "Was it a Legion starcraft?"

"The mortal Legion?" A golden clone was kneeling to offer a platter of cultured meat, and Diamondwall leaned to spear a generous slap of cultured steak. "Or another mortal outlaw? No mortal matter to us now."

He bent to his steak.

"With your aid, we're on our own." Aglow with a new approval, Larron's eyes came from the clone back to her. "The Legion and the law left behind. Ahead of us, the life I always longed for."

"But—" She looked into hard bronze grin, searching again to grasp the mind behind it. "What about the invaders?"

"No more news." He waved the platter away. "The signal spectrum has gone silent."

"I wonder why—"

"No way for us to know." His voice was oddly casual. "The attackers aren't talking. I suppose the defenders have stopped sending because they don't want anything homing on their signals."

He shrugged.

"Perhaps we'll never need to know. If the invaders really are cliffdrillers, Ultima I has little to draw them. I believe we can reach it now, and I doubt that the Legion will ever trouble us there. A barren ice world, but home to me. Now our whole universe."

His greenish gaze grew quizzical.

"Miss Gyrel, I see the questions in your face. You want to ask how long we'll be there. A day, a year, a century?" His great hands spread wide. "Life was never certain anywhere. Whatever comes, I mean to make the best of our refuge, and we'll do our utmost to keep you happy there."

She nodded, not protesting, yet deeply troubled. Life on Larron's prison planet wasn't what she had come to look for. Yet she had twice refused the chance to call Kynan Star. Whatever happened now, the choice had been her own.

They flew on into the nebula.

She spent long hours on the command deck. Lord Archy made her welcome, and she kept finding new delights in her unfolding pilot sense. With each increase in power, the geodesic field cut off more light and other Newtonian radiation, yet her new perceptions did not fade. She decided they must be tachyonic.

When Lord Archy identified Ultima, far toward the clots of spinning mass and burning energy at the nebula's core, she found that she felt it more clearly than the map tank showed it. A great blue sun, its single planet in an orbit far out. The data bank described the planet:

Huge, arid, frigid, exposed to hazardous radiation.

Her home forever?

She was back in the pilot seat, groping for any sign at all, when she felt something moving ahead. A vague blur at first, a dull-red glow as she perceived it, more distant than the planet but darting toward it faster than anything material would move. In a moment she knew that what she felt was the space-time distortion around a geodesic ship. She called Lord Archy. He called Diamondwall. Searching the position she gave them, they found nothing at all on the conning screen.

"Too mortal far for us to pick it up." Diamondwall peered sharply at her. "If your precious gift has not deceived—"

"A signal, Miss Three!" Lord Archy skimmed closer. "A tachyonic beam emanating from the point in question."

Jil started toward the signal center.

"Lass, let it be," Diamondwall called. "Tachyonics is Lord Archy's natural language. If there is a signal, he can—"

"There is a signal, Mr. Two. A human voice, but often interrupted. Using insufficient power and inadequate equipment, the sender is attempting to reach outside the nebula."

"A mortal voice? What's it saying?"

"Request your pardon, Mr. Two, but the signal is not sufficiently complete to permit accurate interpretation."

"Let us hear what you've got."

The quicksilver sphere slowly sank and slowly rose again, its motion soundless. Listening, Jil heard nothing for a time, then a sudden scratchy blast.

" . . . Legion. Calling the Legion of Space, to warn mankind—"

A human voice, but faint and strained and fast. And somehow familiar. Though it came from somewhere deep in the nebula, she knew she had known it before. Desperate, gasping out that frantic appeal, it faded before she could place it.

"Please!" she breathed. "Pick it up again!"

"If we can, Miss Three. If the signal—"

Lord Archy bounded higher, and his own round gong tones gave way again to another blare of that tortured and distorted voice.

" . . . horrible slavery. The shadowflashers rule the drillers and hordes of human puppets. Human leaders, turned to spies—"

Again it faded. Lord Archy danced faster, higher, silently. Jil could hear Diamondwall's wheezy breathing and the swift thudding of her own heart.

It swelled out again, a crashing blast.

" . . . all the nebula. I know, because of how they use me. With AKKA—"

Again it was gone.

" . . . my master about to recover control." Hoarser, faster, it came back. "Moments left. For God's sake get my warning to the Legion and mankind. I was Master-Pilot Jef—"

It became a gasping shriek, choked with unendurable agony, suddenly silenced. Lord Archy made one final bound, back to the pilot seat.

"End of transmission," his bell voice pealed. "Signal cut off."

"Mortal strange!" Diamondwall muttered. "The miserable devil must be insane—"

"My father!" Jil's own whisper seemed as hoarse and gritty as that dying scream. "Legion Pilot Jef Gyrel."

She stared at Diamondwall.

"What are shadowflashers?"

17

Diamondwall shivered.

"Don't, lass! Don't speak of mortal shadowflashers!"

"Why?" Jil gripped his pudgy arm. "What are shadowflashers?"

"Nothing real!" She felt his shudder. "They're a fearful legend, lass. Too wicked to be real."

"They seem to trouble you."

"A nightmare, lass. Far better forgotten. I heard the tale in a duster camp long ago. A tale of monstrous evil I never wanted to believe. Aye, it must have been invented by miners who'd struck it rich to scare intruders off their claims."

He tried to turn away.

"You heard my father's voice." She pulled him back to face her. "What are shadowflashers?"

"Nobody knows." He blinked at her dolefully. "That's the wicked thing. The dusters say no living man—or woman either —has ever seen a shadowflasher. The legend comes from mortal unfortunates no longer alive. From hasty records found on the bodies of the dead. From craft caught too deep in the nebula. All telling of the shadow things coming in to kill them."

"Telling what?"

"Mortal little." His mud-colored eyes shifted evasively. "Even the dying don't see their killers. They babble of flying shadow shapes, blacker than blackness. Stabbing black light that kills whatever it strikes. Freezes men in one mortal instant, so cold they shatter like glass when they fall.

"But if you ask what's inside the shadows, that's a mystery of the nebula. Aye, a fearful mystery, lass. One I hope to know no more about. Sweet life knows we all have mortal ills enough around us, without recalling such evil inventions as the shadowflashers."

"If they've got my father, we must tell the Legion."

"Lass!" Chidingly, he shook his head. "You forget the miserable refugees we are. I'll report this sad thing to Larron, but he's no mortal idiot."

He waddled away. She waited with Lord Archy, hoping for another signal. None came. The red-seeming blur of that far-off starship drifted slowly toward Ultima, until she lost it in the redder, vaster glow of the star's gravitic disk. She gave up then and went below to ask for Larron.

"He's playing the sensorion," a clone told her. "You may go in, but you must not interrupt."

The sensor screen inside the door was a wall of blackness. Sound crashed around her when she stepped in. Sound somehow more intense than merely loud, more felt than merely heard. Throbbing through her body, its force overwhelmed her. Its rhythm seized and ruled the rhythm of her heart, the rhythm of her breath. It compelled her farther into the dark, drew her out into light—or seeming light—beyond.

Looking for Larron, she found herself standing—the illusion was total—on a long slope of loose red sand. The sound had become a hot wind howling around her, whipping dust into her eyes. Stubbornly, she climbed the dune. The sand caved beneath her feet, and the scorching wind tore at her. But still she climbed until at last, triumphant, she topped the crest.

Suddenly, then, the dune became a great wave breaking. The sound was a hurricane roaring. Crouching on a sliver of wreckage, she rode the wave toward a perilous shore. White water geysered off cragged rocks. Icy spray whipped and blinded her.

When she could see again, she had beaten the thundering surf. Stumbling up the shelving beach, she found a towering mountain ahead, bare crags lifting, lifting forever, toward the high, snowy cone. She climbed it, and the sound became an avalanche thundering down upon her.

She clung to a jutting point and let the sliding ice roar around her. Again she climbed, against shrieking winds and raking hail. She jumped bottomless blue crevasses and inched her way up straight ice cliffs. At last, victorious, she stood on the summit.

Beneath her the snow slopes quaked. The mountain grumbled, rived with sudden crimson fissures. Blazing lavas flowed below, and the sound was the volcano's crater-throated roar. Searing fire and choking sulphur smoke exploded, blowing her into the sky.

But she found wings. Shining films of fairy opalescence, they lifted her out of thundering eruption, up through blue-stabbing lightning and choking fumes and rains of incandescent stone, out at last from the angry planet into the silent peace of space.

"Well, Jil?"

The spinning world and all the space around it were abruptly gone. She stood on a scrap of bare deck beneath an arched projection dome. It took her a moment to find Larron, sitting at the center of it in his circles of keyboards and controls. Breathing as if from heavy exertion, he was naked to the waist, his black-haired torso filmed with sweat.

"You wanted to see me?"

She had been possessed. The music—something more than music had filled all her being with sensation and emotion. Ebbing slowly, it left her totally drained, as if she had in fact been battling savage elements, yet still aglow with a triumphant sense of her own invincible self.

Breathless and trembling, she didn't try to speak. For Larron had been transformed in her mind. All that unconquerable might had in fact been his own, shared with her through his creative art. An awed admiration swept her, a humbling wave of something close to the absolute devotion of the clones.

For a moment she couldn't recall why she had come.

"My father—" she whispered then. "Calling from a starship moving toward the planet. Just a few words. Broken words. But he told us a lot about the enemy. They're things called shadowflashers. They rule the cliffdrillers, and they somehow capture and control human beings—that must be what happened to Shon Macharn. They've killed the Keeper. They've disabled AKKA. They're sweeping people out of the nebula.

"And they don't intend to stop—"

"Jil! Please!" His great brown hand beckoned her toward him. "Part of that is probably true. The news disturbs me— that was why I needed to play. But we can't do anything about it."

"We must! We can! At least we can relay my father's warning."

"Listen, Jil." He shook his head. "If Legion starcraft are still operating in the nebula, they picked that signal up. If they aren't, we couldn't reach them. In any case, we can't betray our own refuge."

"Refuge?" She stared at him. "How can there be any refuge?"

He bent back to the keyboard. Those mighty chords drummed again, lifted her on shimmering wings, left her joyously sure of her own vital power. They shuddered back into stillness. The glow died out of the holo dome.

"We aren't caught yet." Larron swung to grin at her. "We're still flying silent. Risking no more than we must, Ultima I is still the only chance I see. If luck breaks for us, we'll have a long time together there."

"If it doesn't—"

He shrugged as if tossing off all adversity. Still trapped in the spell of his music, she felt overcome. He was near and magnificent. Suddenly, illogically, she didn't care what came against them. He was strong enough to defend his private universe against nearly anything. Even if his world ended, he would never yield defeat.

"Captain Larron!" A clone's adoring song broke the moment. "Your dinner is waiting."

After dinner she went back to the command deck. That far-off starcraft was still lost somewhere behind the planet, and Lord Archy had received no further signal. Captain Larron had ordered the drive field cut farther back to keep their tachyonic wake harder to detect.

The next day she picked up a second starcraft, still too far for the conning screen to show it, followed from the direction of Devil's Camp. Diamondwall looked alarmed when she reported it to him, but Larron seemed almost unconcerned.

"I doubt they've seen us. Their conning gear can't be that much better than ours." He frowned thoughtfully at Jil. "Could be your Legion friends, if they got out in time to see what course we took. But we'll be landing well ahead, with time enough to hide."

When she woke next morning, the soundless song of the geodesic drive had ceased. The jets were drumming before she reached the command deck, and she found Lord Archy taking them into orbit around Ultima I. Larron rose from the signal center.

"I was trying to call my people on the tach satellite." He shook his head. "All I get is a recorded signal. Left when they pulled out. Reporting what happened down on the planet. Raiders believed to be cliffdrillers. Ate every scrap of metal, to quote the report. Mining and milling machinery, building and docks and whatever shipping failed to get off.

"Message ends with a warning left for us. Don't contact survivors. They'd be animals by now. Freezing and starving and desperate."

He shrugged, dismissing them.

"What's left is all ours, Jil!" A bleak elation lit his face. "A world of our own!"

"In spite of all that—" she stared—"you mean to land?"

"At Freeholm." His green eyes narrowed, studying her. "Still reported safe when my people left. Safer now for us, certainly, than any craft in open space. The raiders seem to have swept the planet clean. If the Larron luck holds, they won't be back. Whatever comes—"

His hard arm swept her against him, the pressure almost painful. He grinned down at her, his eyes unafraid. Captured, overwhelmed again, she let her body yield against him.

"A stern world, Jil. But you'll learn to love it."

"Captain!" Two tall nude clones were waiting for him at the elevator doorway. "The biolab reporting."

"Take a look!" Nodding at the clones, he squee::ed Jil again, murmuring in her ear. "Our new home. There in the conning screen."

He turned to go with the golden clones. Jil stood where she was, still feeling the crush of his great arm, held again by his lingering scent and the reckless ring of his voice as she had been in the sensorion. Looking after the serenely beaming clones, she wondered if their synthetic perfection had erased all rivalry.

"Miss Three." Lord Archy broke her spell. "Do you wish a view of Ultima I?"

Magnified in the screen, the planet was a dazzle of white, its polar regions featureless. Only a few reddish spots and slashes, nearer the equator and nearly too faint to see, suggested anything but ice. Its empty desolation chilled her until she found the cheering thought that it showed very little to interest more invaders.

A sudden new perception drew her mind aside. A crimson-seeming blur, exploding into space behind them. It flared brighter, flashing at her so fast her arm came up to shield her head, but fading just as quickly. Where it had been she found a tiny point of density, crawling on an orbit above their own.

"Another starcraft," she told Lord Archy. "Dropping out of geodesic drive behind us."

He found it in the screen, a bright point without dimension. Moments later, the signal center flashed and chimed to an incoming call. She had moved to answer, but the robot checked her.

"Miss Three, we have the signal also." The gong tones changed. She heard the voice of Kynan Star, hard with tension, hurried, harshly formal. "Legion Nebular Command, calling S.S. *Hedonian*. Acting under emergency decrees to defend the peace of the Hall of Stars, we demand that you allow us to close and board for—"

An incandescent needle flashed across the conning screen to stab the image of the starcraft.

Star's voice was cut off.

18

Larron strode out of the elevator, Diamondwall panting behind him.

"The mortal Legion? Here already?"

"Affirmative, Mr. Two."

"Dogging us into the guts of the mortal nebula?" The pilot squinted unbelievingly at Larron. "Haven't they heard about the fearful shadowflashers? And their own orders to pull out in time to save their blessed hides?"

"Ask it—" As if in awe of the robot, Larron swung to Diamondwall. "Ask it for detail."

"Data, sir." Lord Archy skipped to Larron's feet. "Nine point five minutes ago we observed a starcraft emerging from geodesic drive. Computation of flight trajectory indicates origin in or near Devil's Creep. Craft dropped into circumpolar orbit around Ultima I, mean radius 37,661 kilometers."

Larron looked back at Diamondwall.

"Was the craft identified?"

"Affirmative, sir." The silver bubble still quivered at his feet. "Tachyphone signal identified it as Legion warcraft *Sunmark*, Pilot-Major Star in command. Addressing S.S. *Hedo-*

nian, he demanded permission to board. His signal was interrupted by a missile moving at trans-Newtonian velocity."

"Do you know where?"

"Affirmative, sir. Trajectory computed. Point of indicated origin coincides with position of another starcraft, arriving from direction of nebular core."

"Was the Legion craft destroyed?"

"Uncertain, sir. No signal received since instant of impact."

"One point for us." Larron nodded, with a sharp look at Jil. "I doubt that your Legion friends will be troubling us again."

"But—the other mortal craft?" Diamondwall blinked at him. "Drillers or flashers or whatever frightful things? If they're still cruising ahead of us, armed with such a fearful weapon—"

"Up to now they're fighting for us." Larron grinned. "We'll proceed to land at Freeholm."

"To be slaughtered there? Like bugs beneath a blessed boot?"

"Better there than here." Larron shrugged. "Down at Freeholm, we'll be better hidden. We'll keep signal silence. Hope they don't detect us."

They came down to Freeholm.

Jil walked down the ramp into a dense ice fog. Chilled steam from the jets, it boiled down around her, hiding everything. The bite of it took her breath, and she had to wait for it to rise and clear before she could see their landing place, or even the soaring mirror tower of the hull.

What the lifting fog uncovered was a long sandstone shelf, naked except for scattered clumps of rust-colored leatherweed. Bare yellow cliffs climbed behind it toward the high glare of the ice plateau and the sun's frigid dazzle. Stony slopes below them tumbled down into a yawning canyon that looked hundreds of kilometers across and dozens deep, its hazy floor patched with dull-red weed.

Searching for a building, she found nothing at all until Larron blew piercing notes from a sonic key to open a doorway into the sandstone. It was dark at first, the air inside stale and cold, but lights came on and ventilators began to hum. Larron led them on into a high-arched rock-hewn hall.

"A cunning hideout." Puffing as he waddled, Diamondwall

swung to squint about him. "But the starcraft's still outside, a mortal lightning rod to draw the fire of that fearful gun."

"No hazard," Larron said. "We'll be moving the craft as soon as she's unloaded. To a concealed silo above us on the icecap. Two hundred kilometers away. If the cliffdrillers come back, they can eat the craft and welcome. We won't be needing it again. Freeholm itself was built with minimal use of metal, and that buried deep."

He turned and strode to Jil.

"Like it?" His great arm crushed her to him, and the ringing power of his voice recalled the spell of his sensorion. "Our own empire!"

"Yours, maybe." She turned her lips from his, trying to resist her own responsive urge. "But I'm afraid not for long. Not with the Legion and the invaders already hunting us."

"Listen, Jil." His genial boom had become a murmur of intimate caress. "There is a storm around us, on a course we can't predict. But some storms have eyes. Small islands of calm, untouched by fury raging all around them. If the invaders pass us by, Freeholm can be an isle of joy for us.

"Of love, Jil—"

"But if they find us—"

He chuckled, his craggy face oddly unconcerned.

"Truly, Jil, we needn't care. Because there'd be nothing we can do. Knowing you, I know you want to fight. We're weaponless and powerless. The storm's beyond our stopping. Yet, here in its eye, we may have the best refuge of all."

The clones around them had stopped silently to wait. Most of them still smiled at him with benign devotion, but the nearest one peered at her more sharply.

He crushed her against him.

"I know our little universe isn't quite what you came out looking for." His gentle murmur was not too low for the attentive clones to hear. "But, Jil! Please don't hate it. Or me! Every day I thank my luck for the chain of chance that brought you to me."

"I don't think your clones are quite so delighted."

"If that's all, never fret!" He chuckled again. "Here, Jil, my wish will be the law."

Letting her pull away, he strode on into the deep-dug retreat. Nearly all the clones followed, clustering closer, but two stayed with Jil. Their smiles no longer quite so warm, they escorted her down a branching tunnel to the suite they said would be hers.

She invited them inside.

"If you don't mind, there's a question I've wanted to ask." She studied their golden perfection, trying to guess how totally Larron owned them. "Don't you ever wish you were free?"

They looked bewildered.

"Liberated from your duty to the captain?" she said. "Free to find lives of your own?"

"Miss Gyrel!" Only the nearer spoke, but both nude forms had stiffened with indignation. "Certainly we do not. He created us to serve him. His total happiness is all we ever seek."

"Suppose—" Uneasy with them, she hesitated. "Suppose he loved someone else?"

"No!" They spoke together vehemently. "That could not be," the nearer added, looking hard at her. "Because we were made to fit his wishes. No other will ever be. And we must ask you not to speak of that again."

"I won't."

Uneasier than ever, she let them show her the apartment. Three long rooms, equipped with an elegance that astonished her. The heavy tapestries glowed with luminous scenes from Larron's sensorion. In image after image, a magnificent red-bearded giant battled wind and wave and volcano, climbing at last on shining wings into high and open space. There were no windows, but one wide wall was a holo tank that commanded vast vistas from the conning dome above.

Freeholm ran on local time, they told her. The planet's day was nearly thirty hours, but she would soon become accustomed to it. It was sunset now, and her dinner would be served here in her suite.

She ate alone when it came, unhappily. The food and wine may have been superb, but the trimphant giant striding through the heroic tapestries around her was too clearly Larron. She was racked with her hot revolt against his appeal, furious with herself for feeling so eager to see him again.

The clones came back to take the serving cart away and left her alone again. The planet's night dragged on forever. Unable to sleep, she watched the holo tank. Moonless night had fallen, but spotlights blazed on a gang of clones unloading the *Hedonian.*

In bright, tight-fitted cosmonalls, they were graceful as dancers. The tank brought no sound. It seemed to her that they toiled in joyous unison, controlled by their total devotion to Larron and serenely unaware that anything could ever change.

She felt a pang of envy for them.

The last bags and drums and crates came off. She watched Diamondwall waddle up the gangway, watched silent ice fog explode from the jets, watched the craft slide up into the dark. The spotlights were off. Wondering uneasily if it could have been observed from out in space, she went at last to sleep.

Day, when it came, was a white blaze that began on the high icecap, crawled down the yellow cliffs to the bare sandstone and the straggling leatherweed around the hidden dome, dropped at last to sweep the final cloths of purple darkness out of the canyon. After a hundred times, she thought, or ten thousand, its slow drama might become maddening.

Silent, more silent than they had ever been, the clones brought her breakfast and a message. Captain Larron had ordered them to ask her if she wished to tour Freeholm.

"Please!"

Gracious enough, though she felt a cool reserve, they showed her the refuge. The main hall, which was a cavernous throne room. The captain's study. The huge null-G gym. The sensorion, larger than the one on the ship. Storerooms and food facilities on the lower level. Power came from a nuclear plant, they told her, 3,000 meters down. She didn't ask if anybody thought cliffdrillers could detect it. The clones themselves clearly feared nothing at all, unless perhaps Larron's interest in her.

They found the captain himself in the genetics lab, surrounded by white-robed clones and crates off the ship. He came eagerly to seize her hand in his great fist, the force of his grip almost painful. Beaming through the beard, he took her inside to see the half-installed equipment.

"We're prepared for more than cloning," he told her. "I suppose you've heard of the old efforts to perfect a longevity serum. Originally undertaken, I believe, to extend the Keeper's life, but abandoned because of unexpected side effects and outlawed later because of a rumor that the Ulnars were supporting such experiments, hoping to turn themselves into elitist immortals.

"In my own genetics research, I stumbled across records of certain illicit studies, undertaken serveral Terran centuries ago. I contrived to copy the records, and I've brought equipment to carry on the work. If we succeed—and we will succeed—our little universe can endure forever."

He swung to seize both her arms and sweep her closer. Aware of the staring clones, she tried to pull herself away. Ignoring them, he held her.

"Please—"

Laughing softly, he bent his red-beared face to hers. She felt his hot breath, and his hard lips stopped her voice. She shuddered, yielding, her heart pounding. Faintly, far away, a clone called something she didn't try to hear.

"We'll have time enough." He let her go, turning to follow the clones. "Forever!"

Cooler than ever, her escorts took her up to the conning dome. Patterned after a starcraft's command deck, it was equipped with signal center and conning screen, as well as controls for air, heat and power throughout the refuge. She found it empty, and the clones let her stay.

Exploring the wide panoramas of ice and sky, of barren rock and dusty weed, of the chasm's hazy gape, she was glad to be out of her windowless cells, glad to be alone. She needed time to come to terms with this narrow prison and her own feelings for its warden. Rebellion seethed inside her, and a savage anger at herself. Because she knew a time would come when she would yield completely to him.

Outside the dome, Ultima I seemed strangely uneventful. The sun was a tiny, cold-blue disk against the filtered screen, crawling very slowly into the unclouded sky above the far canyon rim. Unheard breezes swirled thin yellow dust among the leatherweed clumps. Black shadows diminished. That was all, until she found an orange fleck creeping down the ice.

The fleck became a many-wheeled mechanical worm, slithering down narrow trails to the sandstone bench. Nearby, it rolled out of her view, but in a few minutes Diamondwall came puffing up the ramp into the dome, Lord Archy skipping ahead.

"Ah, lass, so here you are!" His yellow face lit. "We've hid the blessed craft. For the mortal moment, anyhow." His pleased look was gone. "But Lord Archy says it can't stay hid. Not with two mortal starcraft searching from the sky."

Silently, the robot soared past her to the conning screen. "Wicked hawks!" He squinted anxiously at her. "Hunting us like precious fresh-hatched chicks. Can't you pick them up, lass, with your blessed pilot gift?"

"Not here." She shook her head. "Any strong gravity field washes it out."

They moved to watch Lord Archy dancing over the consoles. The screen darkened. Star images flecked it. At last she saw a faint green point creeping among them.

"Information, Miss Three," he pealed. "We observe wreckage of the Legion battlecraft. Its orbital motion remains unchanged since it was attacked. We compute a high probability that all personnel were killed."

"Mortal good luck if they were," Diamondwall muttered. "But don't forget the wicked ship that hit it—"

"Reminder, Mr. Two. We do not forget. Additional information: We continue observing and computing orbital motion of alien battlecraft."

"Where is it?" Jil whispered. "Near?"

"Report, Miss Three. Alien battlecraft is now following circumpolar orbit, mean altitude three hundred kilometers—"

"Flying low enough," Diamondwall wheezed. "Searching every precious inch of the mortal planet!"

"Can they find us?"

"Aye, lass. I think they will. Unless they're blind as blessed bats. They'll see the trail we left in the snow, returning from where we hid the mortal craft—"

Shuddering, he swung away from her.

"I'm famished, lass. Nothing on the blessed icecraft but rusty water and musty space rations. If we're hiding like mortal mice from a pack of prowling cats, I need food and precious wine to nerve me for the wicked instant—"

Wheezy voice fading, he reeled into the elevator.

Jil stayed with the robot. They watched the sky. The cold sun climbed to the empty zenith and sank back toward the ice plateau. In spite of the gravity, she felt the alien battlecraft before Lord Archy found it on the screen. It was falling out of the south, already so low the screen showed its strange teardrop shape. No retrojets were burning, and she thought at first that it too had been disabled.

"Observation, Miss Three," the robot's gong voice rang. "Alien battlecraft detected on landing trajectory."

"Out of control?"

"Negative, Miss Three. We observe no rockets firing. Data lacking on mode of propulsion. But landing trajectory appears to be fully controlled."

"Coming down here?"

"Negative, Miss Three. Alien craft descending toward location of concealed S. S. *Hedonian*."

It had dropped beneath the ice horizon before they heard its passage overhead: a sudden thunder crash that shook the dome and rolled very slowly into silence. The intercoms flickered with the startled faces of Diamondwall and Larron, demanding news.

"Data lacking, Mr. Two—"

The bell notes broke abruptly off.

"Information, Miss Three." The little robot skittered toward her. "We are receiving signal from alien battlecraft. Voice transmission on reserved Legion frequency. Name of speaker stated. Master-Pilot Jef Gyrel."

"My father!" Jil whispered. "What's he saying?"

19

The robot's bell voice changed.

"Calling anybody—anybody human!"

Hoarse and strained and breathless, it was her father again, his voice remembered from those good times so long ago when he and Captain Shon Macharn used to come home out of the nebula.

"Calling—calling anybody off—S.S. *Hedonian*." Odd interruptions broke its desperate rush. "I'm Legion Pilot Jef Gyrel. Down on the ice—ice field where you hid the starcraft. Nobody here, but I must have help. For God's sake—"

A strangled pause.

"Pick me up! My last—last chance to get away. From years of hideous slavery. A helpless human—human tool used against mankind. My warning must get to the Legion. For God's sake—answer! Now! My master—master parasite—it will surely kill me when it gets control again.

"If you can still move and speak—"

A ragged, long-drawn scream.

"My father!" Jil whispered. "Call him back—"

"Don't!" Larron's command rang out of the intercom. "We'll maintain signal silence."

"But, sir—" Unbelieving, Jil spun to face his green-imaged scowl. "My own father! With the truth about the invaders. Don't you see we must—"

"I see we must save ourselves. His own signal has created danger enough from those human marauders the satellite crew warned us about. If they homed on our signal—"

"If they heard my father, that harm's done now." Trembling and desperate, she leaned toward the intercom. "Captain, that's my father!"

"Jil, I'm sorry." His voice fell, almost tenderly. "But we can't get involved. We'd only waste ourselves. All we can hope to do—with whatever luck and common sense we can command—is try to save our own little universe."

His tone grew colder.

"Please, Jil. For your own sake." He turned to the robot. "Continue to monitor all Legion frequencies. Record any further signals and report them to the pilot and to me."

"Command received," Lord Archy tolled.

"Jil, I think you need a drink." Larron's greenish image smiled again at her. "I'll expect you at dinner in an hour."

"I—I'm waiting here," she whispered. "If my father calls again—"

"You may wait." He nodded. "But you will make no effort whatever to respond."

His image vanished, but Diamondwall's remained.

"Aye, lass!" The green moon face looked stark with apprehension. "Larron says we can live forever here, so long as we stay hid. We'd be mortal fools to tell the shadowflashers where we are—or invite some crazy human cannibal to roast our blessed bones tonight."

Then he, too, was gone.

Alone with the robot, waiting forlornly, she paced the crystal dome. Outside, the arctic sun blazed on ice and rock and rusty leatherweed. The world seemed frozen, soundless, already dead.

"New data, Miss Three." The robot startled her. "Voice signal from your father."

Breathless, she spun to listen.

"Legion Pilot Jef Gyrel." A hoarse and hurried rasp. "Calling—anybody! Can't wait longer. Leaving shadow-flasher craft, down near *Hedonian*. Will try to follow your snow track. Can't—can't get far. Need emergency—emergency medical aid to kill—to kill shadowflasher parasite.

"For God's sake—pick me up!"

The frantic whisper died.

"End of transmission," Lord Archy pealed.

She caught a gasping breath.

"Listen, Lord Archy!"

"Comment, Miss Three. Command nonessential. We monitor your voice at all times."

"I want to ask some questions." She peered at her own image, trembling and tiny, in his silvery curve. "You will not report them to anybody else."

"Command accepted, Miss Three."

"You returned from the ship on the icecraft. Where is the icecraft now?"

Soaring nearer, he paused in the air.

"Data, Miss Three. The icecraft was left beneath a sandstone ledge, fifty meters to the right of the entry door, concealed behind a fabric curtain." He dropped to the deck, bounded back. "Miss Three, do you require our aid?"

"Only information now. How is the icecraft powered?"

"By electric motors, Miss Three. Driven from a small reactor."

"How is it operated?"

"Operation requires a sonic key, Miss Three. The same key unlocks both the icecraft and the entrance doors to Freeholm. The icecraft is controlled by a wheel, moved forward or back to govern acceleration, turned right or left to guide it."

Again he hung motionless.

"Warning, Miss Three. The entrance is guarded."

"Thanks—" Her voice caught. "Don't tell anybody!"

"New data, Miss Three." A tiny chime, almost too faint for her to hear. "Larron approaching."

She turned to the elevator and saw him emerging.

"Jil, dear!"

Alone, no clones along, he strode to meet her. His great black-haired hands caught her, crushed her into his odorous embrace. She felt the thudding of his heart, heard the sharp intake of his breath, saw his eager face bent to hers. Trembling, she twisted away from his seeking mouth.

Dropping to let her weight draw him forward, she glided into the mode of the goring bull, one devised long ago by the first masters on old Terra for defense against heavier foes.

Later masters had designed the mode of the standing wall to counter it, but if Larron knew yawara she had taken him by surprise.

Headfirst, his heavy body crumpled to the floor.

Lord Archy skittered toward her.

"Is he dead, Miss Three?"

"Disabled," she said. "Only temporarily, I hope." She scanned the gasping body, the quiet dome, the frozen emptiness outside. "Give me ten minutes. You may then call the clones to care for him.

"Will you obey?"

"Affirmative, Miss Three. Your name is Jil Gyrel. You possess the mutant gift of Dr. One, who created us. We rate you his just successor." Lord Archy soared higher. "We accept your commands."

Her own heart thudding, she darted into the elevator.

In the entrance alcove, she heard quick clone voices. Two clones in skintight crimson spun toward her from the intercom. One wore a projectile gun, the other a sheathed sonic key.

"Warning, Miss Gyrel. This area is restricted. Admittance requires a special order from Captain Larron.

"We have no order to let you pass." The nearer frowned at the other.

Warily they crouched.

"Call the captain," she said. "You'll find I have no duties inside—"

"Halt!" The nearer reached for the gun. "Don't move—"

Near enough, she dipped into the mode of the flying dog. Before the gun had been entirely drawn, the ancient move had swept her down to lift and fling the nearer clone, brought her up to meet the other with the even older mode of the cleaving ax.

She reached into the pile of quivering limbs to find the sonic key. It was a bright metal tube, tipped with yellow plastic and studded with colored buttons. She twisted the tip, tried the buttons. The red one did nothing she could see, but the green lifted the entrance gate.

She dashed outside into blinding light and bitter cold. The clinging gown the clones had dressed her in was too thin for it. Crouched against it, she caught her breath and ran for the sandstone ledge. Painted to look like rock, the fabric screen was hard to see. It felt rock-hard when she tried to push through it. She tried the blue stud. It made a piercing whistle, and the false rock rolled up to reveal the icecraft.

An orange-painted metal insect, three-jointed, with multiple rollers for legs. At its window-eyed head, an oval door swung open. She climbed through oil-smelling iciness into the high cab and peered uncertainly around it. Her breath began to fog the windows. Fingers already stiff, she pushed the wheel. Motors whined, and the craft lunged against unyielding sandstone.

The collision tossed her off the seat and dazed her, making her recognize a bitter irony. Alpha III had no roads, and old Kita Kano had never taught her to drive. Already chilled and trembling, she climbed back to the wheel and moved it more cautiously. The machine jolted out of the cave. Lurching back and forth till she got the feel of it, smashing leatherweed, it took her to the foot of the climbing trail.

Metal clanged behind her. In the mirror she saw crimson figures darting out of the black-yawning tunnel, crouching to fire. A second projectile banged. As fast as she dared, she steered up the narrow path. Rock fragments exploded from the cliff above her.

Grinning at their clatter against the machine, she felt drunk with elation. Larron had held her captive too long; his power had been too oppressive. Free of his disturbing fascination, she felt a lingering pity. His great body would surely soon recover, but she wondered if his sensorion would ever again express the same mythic might.

She ignored another crash. If the clones had no better weapons, they could hardly harm her. Pursuit seemed unlikely —she had seen no other vehicle. Around a bend in the trail, she felt safe enough to stop.

Searching the cab, she found yellow cosmonalls behind the seat. Torn and soiled, but better than her gown. A fan whirred, and she felt warmer air. Driving on, she began to gain a little skill by blind trial and clumsy error.

The trail was sometimes giddily narrow. On one steep gravel slope, she went into a sickening skid. On another, she slid on treacherous ice. Higher, she stalled in windblown snow. She had to back up and try again.

At last she came to level ice.

The cold sun was low ahead, blinding on the ice. Squinting

into the merciless glare, she tried to follow the winding print the craft had left earlier across a boundless waste of naked hummocks and shifting drifts. The roller marks were shallow, sometimes hard to see.

The sun went down. In the frigid dusk, the wind-swept hollows became black pits yawning, and hummocks loomed like leaping monsters. She found the lights, too feeble against the moonless dark. Again and again she lost the trail, searched blindly back and forth until she picked it up again.

Could she find her father before he wandered off the dimming track? Or before this killing cold overcame him? Even if she did, could they trace their way back to Freeholm before blowing snow had erased the trail? Would Larron let them in? Would he—could he—give medical aid against that unknown parasite?

And the shadowflasher battlecraft?

If her father had somehow disabled its alien crew to bring it down on the ice, would they stay disabled? Or would they be pursuing? Might the ship itself take off again to follow and attack?

Hunched and shivering at the wheel, she tried to shake off those haunting apprehensions. Each slick ice slope was peril enough, each veil of flying snow another enemy, each gap in the track a deadlier challenge. Numbness crept up from her tingling hands and feet, dulling every sense, until all she knew was the shifting glare of her lights on the hazards just ahead.

A gaunt scarecrow—

A faint shadow shape, looming for an instant and gone again before she really saw it. A trick of her straining eyes, she thought, a phantom of her lights on a wisp of flying snow, until it came again, limping across a long ice hollow. It stopped and stiffly turned. It stumbled toward her, beckoning.

After all the years, her father!

20

She stopped the icecraft and opened the door.

"Thank—thank God!"

He dragged himself into the cab. His fingers were dirty-nailed talons, his hair and beard jaggedly cut and matted with filth. He wore the faded tatters of a Legion space jacket. Beneath it, a crudely patched coverall of something stiff and black. His eyes were terrible: deeply sunken, wildly staring, rimmed with scabbed and swollen purple flesh.

"I am Legion Pilot—Jef Gyrel—"

A hollow rasp, louder and more violent than Lord Archy had made it seem. Sinking weakly into the seat, he leaned to blink at her with those dreadful eyes.

"You—off the *Hedonian?*"

All she could do was nod.

"Medic? I need aid—"

"I think—" Her own whisper seemed as hoarse and broken as his own. "I'll try to get help for you."

She thrust and twisted at the wheel to turn back toward Freeholm. As they slid around, his odor froze her. A foul bog-rot stench, thickening in the cab. Her stomach churned.

"First—listen!" he was grating. "Message to send. Most urgent. To inform the Legion about shadowflashers. Can you send—"

She shuddered, seeing nothing, her numb hands loose on the wheel. The machine skidded sidewise on bare ice, plunged at a long drift when the rollers got traction, stalled there.

". . . can you?" She heard his gritty voice again. "Call—"

Too sick to speak, she pulled the craft into reverse. It lurched out of the drift, spun down a naked slope. Swirls of windblown snow hid everything around them. Too dazed to think, she didn't know where to look for the trail.

"I'm a Legion pilot." The skid had thrown him half off the seat. He pulled himself painfully back and shook his cadaverous head at her. His husky whisper slowed, pleading to be understood. "Lost in the nebula. Enslaved by a monstrous parasite. Eating my body—"

He must have seen her shudder.

"Shocked?" She couldn't bear to look, but she heard his rusty rasping. "You should be shocked. I'm not the only one. They're swarming out in armies. Out of the nebular core. To take and rule every human being. Worse than nightmare!"

He gasped for breath and spoke again with savage force.

"You've got—got to help me!"

"If—" She tried to nod. "If I can."

"My time—running out. A few more hours. Unless—unless I get help." He bent to search her with those appalling eyes. "Are you a medic?"

An aching lump had closed her throat. She turned again from his dreadful face, back to the wheel. They lurched through curtains of crawling snow. The trail was lost until she saw a dim hint of it, curving up another drift. Gulping at the lump, she found a shaken voice.

"I'm Jil Gyrel." She saw his start. "Your daughter."

"Jil?" The eyes seemed to glaze. "My—my little Jil?" The swollen lips sagged open on rotting yellow teeth, and the matted head shook heavily. "A woman now? I never knew—knew how long—how long I've lived in hell. Or thought to see you ever."

"Can you tell me—" She couldn't help shrinking away from his odor, and her voice failed again. "Father—" A ragged whisper. "Father! What happened to you?"

"A woman now?"

He twisted stiffly in the seat to look at her. Puffy flesh twitched behind the filthy beard, as if he had tried to smile, but only for an instant before it relaxed again into a mask of empty and agonized despair.

"How long?" He shook his head, the dull eyes blinking at her blankly. "It seemed—seemed forever. But I had no Terran time. I never knew how long."

She slid her window halfway down. Cruel cold slashed at her face, but it let her breathe.

"Tell me, Father!" She tried to smile. "I can't help unless I know—whatever—"

She couldn't go on.

"So you must." He nodded stiffly, still staring. "Though it —it will hurt." He sat straighter, as if to gather himself. "You were seven when Shon and I left the Pass. We took the *Iron Argo* deep into the nebula—too deep—looking for—"

His labored grating came slowly, as if he had to gather memories or strength. She kept her eyes on the trail, trying not to look at him, not to let the odor make her retch.

"Probing for traces—traces of life before the shockwave. We didn't—didn't guess—"

He sagged back, gasping, as if to gather strength.

"Went too deep!" His glazed eyes still stared blankly at the dark. "Took too much radiation. Got sucked down to Fermi V. A world on the Red List—rated too hazardous for landing. Should have been nobody there."

He lurched a little toward her, wild head shaking. His voice had slowed and sunk again until she had to listen hard, yet what he said was becoming oddly deliberate. Already rehearsed in his mind, perhaps, against this precious chance to speak.

"Caught us there. Woman's voice calling. Said she was a miner's woman. Said cliffdrillers had hit an outlaw camp. Wiped it out. No time for craft to get away. Only a handful of refugees left alive, begging for help.

"I didn't want to land. No room for refugees. The laser trail seemed to be leading us on toward stars beyond the core. But Shon had a softer heart, and the voice promised us holos. Infrared holos of the drillers, made the night they ate the camp.

"Data we wanted. We came down. The spot looked safe enough. A flat, dry gravel delta, eighty kilometers out from where she said the camp had been. A dozen ragged people, women and kids, huddled around a sledge loaded with the transceiver and a few cans of water and not much else.

"We tried to be cautious. Came down a kilometer off. Warned them to keep away. Shon walked out to talk to the woman. Our bl-blunder!"

He hunched abruptly forward, scarred hands knotted, shivering so hard that she slid the window up.

"Because she wasn't a woman—not any longer!"

He sagged back against the cushions, hideous eyes blindly staring. Jil glanced into them and hastily away. Strangely dilated, ringed with purple decay, they were wells of agony she thought she couldn't endure. She listened a long time to the rasp of his labored breathing, wondering if he had fallen asleep.

"Father—" The word was hard to say. "What was she?"

Painfully he roused himself.

"My own little Jil—" He shook his dreadful head at her. "How can I tell you?"

"You must. To let me help."

"She had a shadowflasher—" His hoarse quaver faded, came back with a savage emphasis. "A shadowflasher in her!" He twisted in the seat, squinting those tormented eyes at her. "A diabolical parasite!"

He stopped again, staring into the dark.

At first, when she swung back to retrace her own trail, the fresh roller marks had been easy enough to see, but already the blowing snow had begun to cover them. Leaning over the wheel, frowning into the blinding dazzle of their lights against the flying flakes, she tried not to think of parasites.

"We'd heard of flashers." He seemed calmer when he spoke again, so drained of everything that the whine of the motors almost drowned his faint and labored voice. "Duster tales, never confirmed. Like the drillers, the flashers don't get caught.

"But they exist!

"That's what I want to tell the Legion. Maybe migrants from outside the nebula, like we are. If so they got here first. Well adapted long ago. Waiting to welcome us."

He paused to make a strange rumble that may have been a bitter laugh.

"The adult monsters thrive in radiation hot enough to kill a man. But the young need shelter—shelter and food." His breath rasped louder. "Parasites! Living inside organic creatures. Creatures they control and torture and consume.

"And take their time about it."

His dark-rimmed eyes blinked at her.

"If you are my little Jil—" His terrible head shook painfully. "Grown to be a woman!"

He slumped heavily back, silent again.

Driving on, she felt grateful for the probing cold, because it had numbed her to the horror living in him. Grateful, too, for the dimness of the track. Tracing it took nearly all her mind, with little left for shadowflashers.

"Shon was gone too long," his ragged croak went on at last. "Hands empty when he did come back. And two parasites inside him.

"One—one—"

A violent convulsion had seized him. His voice became a rattling moan. She saw glistening foam on his sagging lip, and a thin red trickle where a yellow snag had torn it. The bog-rot stench was suddenly overwhelming. Her stomach roiling, she slid the window down.

"One—for me!"

His voice had grown so faint she had to slow the motors.

"I got the odor when I met him." With a dreadful grin, he nodded at the open window. "Before I could speak, Shon stuck one finger at me. The thing jumped out of it, like a fat red spark.

"Hit me in the mouth.

"Burning like fire. I howled for help. Shon just stood there, watching. Watching my agony. I fell on the deck. Before I got up, the thing—thing had taken me. Ridden me—ridden me ever since. The pain goes on. Grows and grows.

"All the eternity—the unending hell—while you've been growing up."

His feeble voice had failed again. Feeling his terrible stare, she couldn't help glancing at him. Sick, shaking her head as if to deny the horror in him, she turned back to search for the vanishing trail.

"It stole my mind." She couldn't escape his gritty rasp. "Took my body for a tool. Used me like Shon and all the others. Spies, Jil! Diabolical spies. Teaching the monsters all they want to know about the Legion and our weapons.

"While we suffer—if you knew how we suffer—"

Again he stopped to gasp for breath and strength, and again she couldn't look.

"Shockwave—shockwave hurt them." His raspy whisper slower, he was fighting to make sense. "Left no organic hosts to hatch their eggs. Now we—we've revived them.

"Ideal meat—"

Not looking, she felt his icy grip on her arm.

"Jil, I got away." He must have leaned closer, because the stench was overwhelming. "But not for long, unless you get— get me help. Because the thing in me is grown. Changing inside me like an insect larva.

"I've seen—seen it happen. The transformation breaks control. But not for long. They know the danger. Commonly ride in pairs to watch each other. But the invasion has stretched them thin. My master—alone. Cliffdriller—"

He broke into a gasping moan, his cold claw cruelly tight and jerking at her arm.

"Cliffdriller crew—" The broken words raced faster. "When the shape change hit the thing inside me, I got—got my body back. Made the drillers land us on the ice. Smashed the navigation gear so they can't fly the craft. Got aboard *Hedonian*. Nobody there. No answer when I called. Had to take the trail.

"Thank—thank God you found me!"

She couldn't tell him she had lost the trail.

21

Wrapped in whirling snow, all she could see was the blaze of her lights against it and, sometimes, a narrow fan of white-drifted hollows and hummocks ahead. The wind had filled the shallow roller prints.

When she groped to find herself, the whole snowscape seemed to tip and spin. Bottomless hollows and looming ice hummocks leered at her, all alike. She stopped the machine to watch the driving snow, hoping for a clue in the wind direction, but the great flakes seemed to swirl from everywhere.

She made herself glance at her father. He had collapsed into the far corner of the seat, perhaps asleep. His scab-rimmed eyes were closed, but his mouth yawned wide on the broken teeth, streaks of foam and blood drying on his beard.

Sick from his reek, she felt sicker from her lost orientation. Sicker than she had been on that first bad morning on Alpha III. She groped for her pilot sense, found only giddiness. A cruel irony struck her. The mutation, adapting the Gyrels for life in space, had unfitted them for planets.

Groping for anything, she drove on to the crest of the next hummock and stopped there to search again for the trail. The dazzle of her lights against the driving snow still hid everything. She turned them out.

Darkness.

She waited to let her eyes adjust. Still there was only total blackness. The planet was moonless. If any starlight filtered through the clouds, it was too faint for her to see. She felt trapped in a suffocating dungeon.

A wave of panic paralyzed her. Her father's drama, so dreadful she could hardly bear to think about it. The monster in him, soon to wake and kill him. The stakes so great, the odds so grim. Shivering, she thrust at the wheel. Any direction was better than none. Almost at random, she drove on across the crest and down the unbroken slope beyond.

Above the motor whine, she heard her father breathing. A croaking snore, interrupted with rattling moans. His mouth was gaping wider when she looked again, his swollen tongue protruding, black-splotched and bleeding. He lurched forward suddenly, screaming.

"Out!"

His bog-rot stench filled the cab again, so thick she couldn't breathe. Chilled and shivering from a sudden sweat of illness, she saw him scrabbling at the door.

"Lock—" The thick-tongued gasping was hardly intelligible. "Whatever—don't let me in!"

The cab door came open. Thrashing, shrieking, he plunged outside. The machine rolled on for a few more meters until she could stop and spin back. The lights picked him up, a flat little huddle in the snow.

She stopped again beside him.

" . . . back!" The motors quiet, she heard his quavering yell: "Lock the cab!"

She sat motionless.

"Save yourself!" A scarecrow moving, he jerked to his feet. "Get the warning—to anybody human—"

Icy air had rushed through the open door. It was clean to breathe, and a deep gulp of it roused her. Shuddering, she leaned to lock the door, backed a few meters away.

His ragged arms spread, waving her farther. He turned and tried to run. Limping, staggering, he fell on his face. For a moment he lay unmoving. Then his thin limbs jerked and began to flail the ice. Moving like nothing human, his body pitched and twisted.

Something black came out of it.

A swelling cloud. Like a wisp of smoke at first, it became blacker and denser than smoke had ever been. It grew larger than her machine, a monstrous blot swelling against the glare of her lights on flying snow.

It was alive. Its black shape flowed, and blackness darted out of it. Arrows of blackness probing into the night, thrusting at the ice, striking at the machine, stabbing at her.

She knew she should move farther away, but her hands were frozen on the wheel. Trembling, shaking her head in a hopeless effort not to believe what she saw, she watched that black-flashing cloud swell again, draw itself back into something denser, lift at last, leaving something on the ice.

Something very small, flat and torn and scarlet.

Shock left her shuddering and powerless. She tried to pull her gaze away. She knew she had to move. Yet she sat there, chilled and stunned, till she saw the black cloud stirring. Lifting, spinning, drifting after her. An arrow of blackness flashed into the cab.

Colder than cold, it went to her bones. It stopped her breathing. It left her skin tingling strangely, as if a million sticky insect limbs were crawling on her. Left a crimson after-image blazing in her eyes. And it jolted her out of her daze.

She whirled the machine and fled.

Hoping to delay pursuit, she turned the lights off. In the heavy dark, the black thing vanished. Blind, she felt the machine pounding over frozen drifts, heard the skidding rollers screaming through ice-floored hollows. It jolted and careened, but no danger mattered.

Sheer panic swept her on and on, until she found herself sliding and pitching down a steep slope that seemed to have no end. When she reversed the rollers, it spun sidewise and finally stalled, half-buried in windblown snow. Afraid to use the lights, she waited there for day.

The icy night seemed endless.

Her father's fate had left a burning wound in her mind, the facts too hideous to think about, yet too near and dreadful to forget. Huddled under the wheel, she tried to imagine what day might bring, tried to think what she could do.

Get back to Freeholm? Even that seemed barely possible. Larron had hidden his refuge well. Though the winds might die by dawn, the last traces of the trail would surely be gone. If by chance she did get back, would Larron let her transmit the warning? Not likely. Not since he had felt the mode of the goring bull.

Yet hope refused to die. She slapped her body to fight the creeping cold. Fumbling numbly, she found a knob that turned the heater up. Trying not to think of shadowflashers or her father, she let her body sag back into the seat.

Cold sunlight woke her.

The storm had stopped. Rubbing sticky eyes, she peered out of the cab, down into a purple chasm. Her blind flight had brought her back to the edge of the ice, almost over the rim of that awesome canyon she had first seen from space.

The machine had stalled in the last deep drift of snow blown off the ice. The boulder slope below her fell sharply to the giddy brink. With her little skill, she scarcely dared touch the wheel again. Yet day had come. She was alive. She saw no shadowflasher.

She found water bags and space rations behind the seat. Her appetite surprised her. Her first effort failed to move the machine, but it crept a little forward when she tried less power. She found that she could rock it, each lunge longer. Another skid took her breath, but at last it tipped back to level ice.

The canyon yawned just below, still night-clotted. Sunlight blazed all along its icy brink. Searching the ragged bends of that, she found a far-off, rust-red streak. Leatherweed, she thought, on the ledge outside hidden Freeholm.

Many kilometers from her, but there was no wind yet and the sun had brought direction back. She steered for where the descending trail must be. The ice sloped again, toward shelving sandstone. She found roller prints still visible, then the rocky path.

At its foot, Lord Archy met her.

"Greetings, Miss Three. May we guide you to Mr. Two?"

She followed his dancing bubble toward a leatherweed thicket. Diamondwall waddled out of it to meet her.

"Waiting for you, lass." He hauled himself into the cab, blinking at her woefully. "Things have gone mortal wrong."

"I saw my father." Her voice shook. "Found him—it's hard to speak about. He has been possessed by a horrible thing inside him. He said—said they have others. Spying on us. Betraying—"

She had to gasp for breath.

"Please—please believe me!"

"I believe you, lass." He nodded bleakly. "I know the fearful truth."

"Then you've got to call the Legion—"

"Too late, lass. Too mortal late!"

"I saw—saw my father die." She shivered. "Saw the—the thing come out of him. A shadowflasher. Too dreadful to believe. If you had seen it, you'd take any risk. Even Larron would—"

"Lass, lass!" Blinking dismally, he shook his head. "You haven't heard the mortal misfortune that happened to us here. As fearful as any shadowflasher.

"Last night the wicked drillers came."

She sat listening blankly, stunned almost beyond understanding his wheezy rush of words.

"Drilled their way to us through the mortal rock. Crumbling granite into flour. Hit us with no warning. Took the reactors first, and left us dying in the mortal dark. Lord Archy and I were lucky. They caught us up in the blessed dome, and we got out alive.

"Larron, too, with a handful of his precious clones. All the rest buried alive or smothered in that mortal dust when the tunnels caved in." He shuddered, squinting at her gloomily. "In the fearful end, they may be the lucky ones. Because I see no mortal hope for any of us."

With a doleful headshake, he gestured toward a thin smoke plume rising a few hundred meters down the ledge.

"Larron and the clones he has left. Mostly mortal naked. Huddled over a smoldering blaze of dead leatherweed, trying to save themselves from freezing. Not a blessed bite to eat. Nor water either, unless they can climb for ice to melt."

"We can help," Jil said. "I found space rations and water bags in the locker back of the seat, and the craft will give them at least a little shelter. Let's drive on—"

"Wait, lass!" He clutched at the wheel. "You don't yet know the moral worst. I had Lord Archy climb to look for you. Two thousand meters up, he saw you coming back and found evil trouble brewing out across the icecap, where we left the blessed ship.

"A strange spacecraft, like he never saw before, down beside our silo."

"The shadowflasher battlecraft!" she whispered. "The one

my father came on. He said he'd managed to disable it when he broke free of the parasite. Smashed the navigation gear—"

"So that's why!" He nodded. "Lord Archy says they've pulled our precious *Hedonian* out of the silo. He saw it taking off. Wobbling in the sky till they got the hang of the controls, but turning back this way now. He thinks they're coming here. I don't know why—the drillers left mortal little for anything to take."

"I'm afraid—afraid I know!" She shivered. "There's a flasher in it. Looking for hosts."

"Hosts?" His old voice quavered high. "What are hosts?"

"Creatures—" Her own voice caught. "Creatures to breed its young."

"Not *me*, lass! It can't use me. I'm too mortal old to be trained."

"It takes no training. They plant the eggs in your body, my father said. The monsters hatch and grow inside you, feeding on your flesh and taking your brain to work you like a puppet—"

"Don't, lass! Don't!" His voice became a squall. "For sweet life's sake, conceal the blessed craft and pray they overlook us."

She drove the machine into the thicket. Panting with terror and exertion, he helped her tear off leatherweed fronds to brush away the track it left and hide it from the sky. Watching from the icecraft through the tangle of bitter-scented leaves, they waited for the flashers.

22

Larron's clones squatted around their smoldering fire. He came striding out of the thickets to join them, a bronze-beared patriarch, massive and commanding. Others followed, nude and shivering, limping under loads of long brown fronds.

When Diamondwall ran his window down for a better view, Jil caught the bitter pungence of burning leatherweed. The scent brought her girlhood back. Hawkshead Pass, and the sulphur-reek of the meteor storms, and the rank weeds her mother had tried to fight in her grandfather's yard.

Her mother?

Cruel questions rose to haunt her. What had the plotters done to her mother? Had the parasite in Shon Macharn planted a shadowflasher egg in her? To ensure her loyalty to the "movement"? And turn her, finally, into that mindless shadow thing aboard the *Purple Empress*?

Jil shivered. The notion seemed too hideous to be true, yet she couldn't shake it off. It explained too many things, and it turned her old resentments into aching pity and a haunting shame. If she had ever guessed—

Rem Brendish?

She recalled him as she had glimpsed him back on Alpha III, suspended in his null-G gear with her mother on the slidewalk, hovering over her like some monstrous insect. If her mother had been possessed, what was he? Another tortured tool, forced to compose his Antiac ballad as one more weapon in the secret war on the Legion?

She wondered. His sparrow body had not been ravished. Yet his deeds seemed hardly human. She found no answers. The parasites were far too horrible to think about, yet too near to be escaped. She pulled herself straighter in the seat, inhaling the leatherweed smoke. To her, it had always been exhilarating.

She looked at Larron, leaning to stir the fire with a long leatherweed bloom stalk. Standing back, he waved it like a wand. She heard the boom of his voice again, saw a nude and blood-streaked clone tossing her load of fronds into swirling smoke. Yellow flame flared again.

Even now, with his small world destroyed, he was still magnificent. She felt a throb of admiration, another twinge of regret for the way he had been humbled by the mode of the goring bull. . . .

Lord Archy bounded off Diamondwall's pudgy knees.

"Information, Miss Three," his bell voice rolled. "We detect the S.S. *Hedonian*. Descending to land."

The bright-walled starship came down on the exploding cushion of its jets, too near Larron and his huddled clones. The hot white cloud roared over them. Suddenly silent, it spread and cooled and slowly rose. Looking where the fire had been, she found it blown away.

The clones were gone. It took her a moment to discover them, lying sprawled against the fringe of leatherweed where that reckless blast had flung them. Only Larron remained erect, facing the tall starcraft, still gripping his blackened bloom stalk.

The lock clanged open. The gangway rattled out. Jil's flesh crawled when she saw the shadowflasher flowing out. A shapeless cloud of total darkness, it swelled as it emerged, lifting, drifting toward Larron.

He strode to meet it, boldly swinging his brittle club. Jil's eyes blurred, and she felt a sudden ache in her throat. Even now, facing hazards more dreadful than any he had created on the sensorion, he was still the mythic giant.

Unbeatable, he marched to meet the cloud.

Thin beams of total blackness arrowed out of it. At the motionless clones. At the leatherweed clumps and the tall, yellow sandstone cliffs. At Larron himself. She saw him stagger, recover his balance, march defiantly on.

"Lord of worlds!" In sudden panic, Diamondwall ran his cab window up. "The mortal demon—"

Gasping terror hushed him.

She saw blackness lashing at them. Shivering to its chill, Jil heard Diamondwall moaning a warning not to move or breathe for life's mortal sake. Frozen, they waited till the shadow blade was gone. Daring at last to move, she saw it stabbing into thickets farther on.

She looked again for Larron.

Whirling his slender club, he stalked to meet the cloud. It lifted a little, dropped back to swallow him. His voice rang out of it. A bellow of defiance that became a shriek of agony, choked abruptly off. The cloud rose slowly, floated back toward the starcraft. Larron was left where he had met it, lying face up on the bare sandstone.

But then a final flash of blackness stabbed him into a dreadful mockery of life. His body twitched, writhed. The limbs thrashed. The body rolled over. Awkwardly, it came up on all fours. It crawled back toward the clones. Clumsily, it rose. It stumbled on, gaining speed and precision as its new owner mastered it.

The shadowflasher was gone, back into the ship. At her still half-open window, Jil felt a breath of icy air, heavy with the steam of the jets and edged with that bog-rot stench. Shivering, stomach heaving, she shut the window.

The clones had begun stumbling to their feet, limping to meet Larron. One came to her knees and fell limply back. Still a slow and ungainly puppet, he bent to gather her into his arms, blundered with her toward the gangway. The others followed him into the starcraft.

She heard the clang of the closing lock. The cab trembled to the roaring of the jets. White vapor rushed across the rocky shelf, hiding everything. Thunder drummed inside the cloud, boomed against the cliff behind, slowly climbed and slowly died. When she could see, the ship was gone.

"Ah, lass!" Diamondwall sat trembling in the cab beside her, his moon face livid. "A fearful terror! I've met monstrous horrors in my time. Sights that would freeze your blessed brain. But none half so evil.

"Lass, we've lived too mortal long!"

Still feeling chilled and sick, Jil opened the window again to breathe clean air.

"Still," she whispered, "we are alive."

"If you want to call it life." He blinked at her dismally. "Marooned on a mortal ice world. Hiding like miserable vermin from black vampires seeking to breed in our bodies while we die of fearful famine."

"We do have cartons of food," she reminded him. "Here in the back of the cab."

"Food?" His plaintive quaver mocked her. "Mortal space rations, dried to bitter rocks and green with mortal mold. Without a drop of blessed wine to help them down."

"We'll search," she said. "Perhaps we'll find something better. But the first thing is to send my father's warning on. By any means we can." She looked at the instrument panel. "No tach system, but at least we have radio—"

"Radio!" A terrified squeak. "Lass, don't speak of radio. Not with the black vampires still seeking our blessed bodies to incubate their mortal eggs and feed their fearful hatch. Don't think of the mortal radio—"

"Mr. Diamondwall." She caught his soft-fleshed arm. "The Legion needs what we know. If we're going to die here, we've very little to lose."

"Lass!" His small eyes rolled. "We have our blessed bodies and our own precious brains. Can you call that little?" He caught a raspy breath. "You should be grateful for the mortal truth. There's nobody radio could reach."

"Are you sure? Larron thought there could be survivors—"

"All frozen dead by now," he muttered. "Mortal lucky for them."

"Lord Archy"—she looked at the little robot, who had perched on the control wheel—"you're tachyonic. Can't you reach—anybody?"

"Negative, Miss Three." He dropped to her knee. "Our contact range is limited. We detect no other signal system operating within that range except the one aboard the S.S. *Hedonian.*"

"You can detect the *Hedonian*?"

"Affirmative, Miss Three."

"Where is it now?"

"Observing, Miss Three." For a moment he shimmered silently. "Reporting, Miss Three. S.S. *Hedonian* is now five hundred twenty point seven kilometers from Freeholm, lifting out of polar orbit and shifting into geodesic drive."

"Can you get the heading?"

"Affirmative, Miss Three."

"Where is it heading?"

"Toward nebular core, Miss Three. Destination area not accurately charted. Destination planet impossible to establish."

"Is it sending anything?"

"Affirmative, Miss Three. Tachyonic signals are emanating from it."

"Can you read them?"

"Negative, Miss Three. Code unknown."

"Could there be anybody human—" She shuddered from the phrase. "Anybody else hiding on the planet?"

"Data incomplete, Miss Three. However, we detect no evidence of power generation or transmission from any planetary source. Computed probability of additional human survivors: point zero zero one."

"He means it's mortal unlikely we'll ever be rescued," Diamondwall moaned. "You can't deny it, lass. We're marooned to starve and freeze and die alone. Our only precious hope is never to be found, because the finders would be cursed black vampires come to breed their fearful offspring in us."

"Let's take a look." Jil turned away from his anguished yellow face. "Perhaps we'll find something useful."

"Mortal little left!" he muttered. "The blessed clones must have searched, and we saw them famished and naked to this wicked chill, waiting to feed the fearful flashers."

She backed the icecraft out of the thicket and drove around the ledge. A narrow scrap of flat sandstone, never 200 meters wide, not three kilometers long. Scattered with the rust-colored leatherweed masses and very little else.

She stopped where Freeholm had been. Now there was only a steep little delta of snow-white dust spread from the crumbled cliff. She saw tracks of bare feet across the edge of it where a clone must have stepped.

She looked for the hidden cave where she had found the vehicle, but it had vanished under the dust. Half a kilometer along the cliff, she found another overhang wide enough to conceal the machine. There they stopped.

"Our last blessed shelter." Diamondwall squinted gloomily around it. "Ah, lass! Larron's precious paradise, where he promised to keep us alive forever, fed and tended by his loving clones.

"Our mortal grave!"

His small eyes brighter, he watched her search the machine for food and supplies and kept an avid tally on what she found. Three cartons of space rations, standard Legion issue, one of them already broken. Eighteen three-liter water bags. An aid kit. A tattered operations manual for the icecraft.

"That is mortal all?" His heavy body sagged in total despair. "Nothing to save our blessed lives when those moldy morsels are gone? Nothing to give us one shining spark of hope? Not even a single drop of precious wine?"

"All," she said.

"Ah, so, lass." He squinted into the open ration carton. "If we must gnaw these mortal rocks, let's begin before we grow too weak for the fearful task."

"Go ahead," she told him. "I'm not hungry yet."

His appetite astonishing, he unsealed and heated one standard meal, consumed it, reached for another, then for a third.

"Look again, lass," he begged her. "This mortal trash is too dry for any honest spacehand. Look for a bottle of blessed wine."

She found no wine. Moaning its lack, he belched and sprawled back in his seat. Soon he was snoring. Climbing out, she left him in the cab with Lord Archy.

Aimless, haunted by the shadowflashers, she wandered through the sharp-scented leatherweed. Standing at the edge of the ledge, she looked off into the canyon. The weathered sandstone fell straight beneath her, kilometer on giddy kilometer, down to the distant bouldered slopes that dropped on and on to a far-off floor.

The eternal grandeur of the chasm was itself alluring. Its soaring ramparts written with the whole tectonic history of the planet, the far fields of leatherweed perhaps a relic of the lost culture of the laser-makers, here before the shockwave passed. Its enduring mystery caught and drew her.

Trembling, cold with a solemn sorrow, she pulled herself away, wandering nowhere. With the Legion reeling in defeat, with people everywhere destined to survive only as hosts for unthinkable parasites, with her last hope lost, she could see no rational reason for life. Yet she wasn't ready to die.

"Permission, Miss Three?" The robot's gong voice rang through dusty leatherweed. "Permission to report signal received?"

"Granted!" Shouting, she ran toward his voice. "Signal from where?"

Lord Archy came bounding high to meet her.

"From the Legion, Miss Three."

23

Lord Archy skipped closer.

"Life Pod B from Legion starship *Sunmark*," his bell notes rang. "Attempting to call S.S. *Hedonian*."

"May I hear the message?"

"Affirmative, Miss Three."

"Please."

"Recorded, Miss Three." The voice was suddenly Kynan Star's, hoarse with fatigue, hard with urgency. "Pilot-Major Star to S.S. *Hedonian*. We know where you landed. We demand your immediate surrender."

"Answer him," Jil said. "Tell him where we are."

"Advice, Miss Three." The gong tones rolled again. "We compute high probability that Pilot-Major Star cannot discover our location unless we enable him to home on our signal.

"We advise, therefore, against reply."

"He can't hurt us," Jil said. "Give him our location."

"Question, Miss Three. Are you aware that Mr. Two has instructed us to maintain signal silence?"

"True," she said. "But I left Mr. Two asleep. I think Pilot

Star will be a friend. Call him back.''

The little robot dropped back to the bare sandstone. For a moment it lay nearly motionless there, a flattened quicksilver sphere, pulsing slightly to its own internal rhythms. Her own little image shimmered in it.

"Decision, Miss Three." It rose again. "Your command required logical analysis. Upon logical analysis, we rate your instruction supersessive to Mr. Two's."

Sinking again, it lay quivering on the rock.

"Information, Miss Three. We are calling Pilot Star."

She waited. A little whirlwind rustled through the leatherweed, lifting bitter scents of smoke and dust.

"Jil Gyrel!" Star's voice spoke from the quicksilver bubble, breathless with astonishment. "How did you get here?"

Peering down at her own diminished image, shrugging off her own sense of startled doubt, she groped for all she could recall of the worn, embittered starman whom she had come to like and trust so much.

"By—by odd accident." With so much to tell, she had to search for the words. "A pretty grim story. I shipped out of Hawkshead Pass on the *Purple Empress*. Found Shon Macharn in command. Ruled by a shadowflasher parasite, though I didn't know it then. I escaped in a life pod. The *Hedonian* picked me up in the channel."

"Who's with you now?"

"Only Pilot Diamondwall—"

"Diamondwall?" His voice grew harder. "A short, fat man?"

"And his robot—"

"Keep it sending. I'm homing on its signal."

Lord Archy bounced again.

"Information, Miss Three. Transmission terminated."

"Keep sending," she said. "Guide him down."

"Command accepted, Miss Three."

They found Diamondwall still snoring in the cab. Jil shook him awake to tell him that Star's life pod was coming in.

"Ah, lass, you're a fearful fool!" He blinked at her in glassy-eyed dismay. "Didn't you think we had troubles enough? Left to perish of cold and hunger on this wicked rock, in the shadow of the monstrous shadowflashers. Isn't all that misfortune enough, without calling the mortal Legion down upon us?"

"With things that bad—" She tried to grin at him. "How can Star make them worse?"

The pod came in. A tiny cloud from the retrojets mushroomed in the blue-black sky. Delayed thunder reverberated against the tall yellow cliffs. A triple parachute bloomed. A bright dot swung under it, swelling. For a breathless moment she thought the pod would miss the ledge, but it fell into the leatherweed fifty meters from the brink.

Star was out of it before they reached him, limping through a cloud of gold-winged seeds startled by his fall. Head bare and balding, green cosmonalls soiled and torn, he looked smaller and older than she recalled him, too deeply stooped to be a soldier.

He crouched warily to meet them, projectile gun drawn.

"Kynan!" Jil jumped out of the icecraft. "It's just the pilot and me—"

"Stand back!"

Hard-voiced, he waved her aside and limped toward the machine. Diamondwall was still in the cab, the robot dancing on the seat beside him.

"Don't fire!" she heard him gasp. "Put up your wicked weapon, for life's mortal sake! Find some precious mite of pity for a poor old man and a sweet young girl, hiding here from the fearful black vampires."

"Believe me, sir, we've no quarrel with the mortal Legion—"

"Out!" He gestured with the gun. "Get out, Gul!"

"Gul?" His wheezy voice turned shrill. "I've no mortal notion who you take me for. I am Master Pilot Julian Diamondwall—"

"You are Corporal Hannibal Xenophon Gul." Star cut him off. "You are under arrest. If you question my authority, I'm acting as Legion commander in the inner nebula. If you ask why you're wanted, the charges would fill a book."

"Sir, if you take me for any evil miscreant, you've made some mortal blund—"

"Listen, Jil." He glanced warily at her. "I don't know what else he may have done, but my own list of charges runs all the way from mutiny and desertion to treason against the Hall of Stars and complicity in the murder of the Keeper of the Peace."

His gun swung toward the cab.

"Climb out!"

"A fearful error, sir—"

"Stop your robot," he rapped. "Instruct it not to move except at my command."

The quaking man moved as if to leave the cab but sank weakly back.

"A monstrous mistake!" A quavering squall. "Believe me, sir. I love the precious Hall of Stars. To save my own precious life, I wouldn't think of harm to the precious Keeper of the Peace."

His frightened eyes rolled at Jil.

"You're mortal wrong, sir, if you assume that I can command Lord Archy. They've both turned against me. Miss Gyrel, young and lovely as she looks, has enticed him to her own command."

His soft flesh quaked to a long-drawn sigh.

"Sir, I beg you to think again of whatever sad circumstance has led to your fearful accusations. In a long and tragic life, I've loved the blessed Legion and feared the mortal law. I'm old and broken now. Aye, and dying on this world of wicked ice, famished for a scrap of rotten ration or a drop of sour wine—"

"Jil?" Star glanced at her. "Is the robot yours?"

"I asked him to guide you down."

"Get him away from the prisoner."

"Lord Archy," she called. "Come to me."

The robot rolled to her feet.

"Is he armed?"

"I don't think so." Bewildered, she peered at the man in the cab. "I don't understand—"

"Ah, lass!" He blinked at her in piteous appeal. "For life's precious sake, tell him who I am. A forlorn little victim of mortal mischance, trapped by the idiot blunders of some bumbling bureaucrat, already on the brink of dreadful death—"

"Jil, do you know who he is?"

"He was pilot of the *Hedonian*—"

"Here's who he is. A total traitor. A key conspirator in the shadowflasher plot to steal the secret of AKKA."

"A fearful falsehood—"

"Quiet!" Star thrust the gun to stop him. "Gul was a corporal in the Keeper's guard. All his Legion records forged.

Missing after the murder. Traced with his robot to Alpha IV, where he took the name Diamondwall and escaped again with Larron, who had been convicted—"

"Sir! Sir!" He was shivering, but sweat ran down his pale moon face. "You have been the victim of a monstrous misapprehension. Julian Diamondwall has never been a spy—"

"Anything you say may come up against you, but we've got to have the truth. The full truth, Gul, about your whole conspiracy.

"Now!"

"Sir, you'll get no confession out of me." His wheezy whine had turned defiant. "For a mortal·solid reason. Your monstrous charge is false."

"Silence, Gul! I want to know what was done to Vivi—" His hoarse voice quivered. "Knowing her, I know your torture didn't break her. What we don't know is what the killers took and where they went."

"Lass, lass!" His mud-colored eyes squinted at Jil. "You might recall we saved your precious life—"

"Listen to me, Gul. Something else was missing. Something important to Vivi, which she called a laser-maker."

Jil's breath caught.

"Missing," Star rapped. "What became of it?"

"If I knew—" The fat man shrugged in dismal bewilderment. "What's a mortal laser-maker?"

"One thing I want to know." Star frowned. "An object Ben Gyrel brought back out of the nebula. He believed it was alive, or had been, though the xenobiologists found no confirmation. Vivi had it in her quarters on Alpha V. I want to know who took it."

"Sir, on my own precious life, I don't know—"

"Kynan!" Jil whispered. "I've seen—I think I've seen—the laser-maker."

"Stand back!" he snapped at her. "Don't interfere!"

"Was it a little ball? A gray fluff of wiry hair?"

"Lass!" A muffled yelp. "Have you met Miss William?"

"Jil!" Star's gun swept toward her. "Where?"

"On the *Purple Empress*." She shrank from the gun. "Macharn and Brendish—the monsters in them—had it aboard. Locked in a safe. Under torture for something they thought it knew."

"AKKA!" The fat man goggled at her and swung to squint

at Star. "Sir, this makes a mortal difference. If the black vampires have got Miss William, it's time for me to talk."

"Jil, stand by the cab." Star beckoned with the gun, crouching back to cover them both. "Talk!"

"Careful, sir!" The little man lifted both pudgy hands. "For life's precious sake, get your mortal weapon off us. What I have to say may startle you, and we can't risk any fearful accident."

Warily, Star lowered the gun.

"Thank you, sir! And brace yourself for shocks." He straightened in the seat and caught a sighing breath. "If you loved the blessed Keeper, so did I. The secret I carry came from her. I swore to her that I would guard it to the mortal limit of my life. But if the black vampires have taken Miss William—"

He flinched as if in pain.

"Sir, my revelation must begin with a sadly neglected hero of the Legion. Perhaps you recall some incidental mention of a noble old soldier named Giles Habibula?"

"Habibula?" Star blinked. "The man in the ballad?"

"Ah, sir!" He shook his head in sad protest. "That dirty bit of doggerel was a vicious peace-kook libel on the bravest man who ever risked his precious neck in the service of mankind. It was his undaunted daring and his rare craft with hidden things that turned the tides of mortal war against the monstrous Medusae and the evil Cometeers."

His dull-colored eyes rolled at Jil.

"Giles Habibula! Ah, lass, I want you to know the name. Because the race he saved has forgotten the mortal debt that's too long due him. Men name planets for Kalam and Samdu. They raise golden statues to the Stars. And sing wicked lies about a greater hero—"

"Gul! If you have a point, get to it."

"Sir, here's my mortal point." His fat brown chin thrust at Star in sudden belligerence. "I am not Hannibal Xenophon Gul, though it's true I used to use the name. There's no such soldier in the blessed Legion. There never was."

He squinted sharply at Jil.

"I am Giles Habibula!"

24

A snort of disbelief.

"Damned gasbag!" Star's gun came up. "You know old Habibula has been dead for generations."

Jil stared.

At Star, worn and drawn, reeling unsteadily under weariness and strain. At the man in the cab, wiping sweat from his broad yellow face and blinking scornfully at Star. The bright-winged seeds had settled again, but the sharp reek of crushed leather-weed still edged the icy air.

"Aye, sir," the fat man gasped. "I know his precious name is dead. Mortal dead and long forgotten. Except in a lying ballad, sir. The mortal song that calls him a stinking glutton and a slinking coward."

His quavery voice had sunk, and he sighed as if from black despair.

"Ah, lass!" His muddy eyes blinked at Jil. "If you must ever search for a crumb of blessed justice, don't look on any human planet. Better trust the shadowflashers. And believe Giles Habibula.

"Aye, lass, a man of craft and daring, who gave the best of

a long lifetime to the blessed Legion. He fought the monstrous Medusae and the evil Cometeers and hosts of other wicked foes on a hundred hostile planets. He crowned his magnificent career with a final desperate sacrifice. A deed so daring it could never be revealed."

He swung accusingly to Star.

"And what, sir, was his reward? Mortal medals struck in his blessed honor? Memorials erected? A festival day celebrated in praise of his name? Not so, sir! Never on any precious human planet. Instead, he was blotted out of history. His noblest deed unknown. Malicious slanders sung to mock his faded memory—"

"I've had enough!" Star thrust the gun higher. "Unless you've got some truth in you."

"Will you know it when I tell it?" His whine turned sardonic. "Wearing the blessed Legion green, you must have heard the epic legends that once set Giles Habibula high among the hallowed heroes of mankind. What you've never known is his last and noblest deed of valor, the most heroic act of all.

"He gave up his own precious name to save the Keeper of the Peace."

His shrewd little eyes challenged the gun.

"Sir, if you want the mortal facts, put your wicked toy aside."

"Bluster enough," Star grunted. "Get to your point."

"Ah, lass!" He glanced aside at Jil. "The mortal inhumanity of man!" He sighed and peered at Star. "As an officer in the Legion, sir, you must know the Keeper's mortal peril from all the men and monsters who seek to steal her blessed weapon.

"We've always fought to guard her precious life. I've offered mine for hers time and precious time again. What I reveal to you now—a fact few except the blessed Keepers have ever known or guessed—is the greatest risk I ever took.

"Aye, sir, the most noble sacrifice.

"I was called to make it when the medics had invented a longevity serum. An untested drug they hoped would save the precious Keeper from all the hazards of age and illness and mortal mischance. Mortal mice had survived it, and they wanted to test it on a human volunteer.

"Sir, I gave myself.

"Like another chittering rodent. I lay on a cold iron cot in their stinking lab and let them squirt their stuff into my own tormented flesh." His soft fat shook. "Sir, it made me fearful ill—brought me so close to hideous death they never dared risk it on the blessed Keeper.

"But I beat that ghastly illness, sir. As boldly as I beat the Medusae and the wicked Cometeers. When finally I recovered, they promised that I would never die." Dismally, he shook his head. "Immortality, sir. But nothing you might envy.

"Though they gave me what they say will be undying life, I've paid a fearful cost. They'd promised me a chance that their serum might restore my precious youth. What I found was my shaking age and all my fearful infirmities preserved forever.

"I've suffered for it, sir." Voice breaking, he appealed to Jil. "Lass, lass! You can't imagine the mortal agony I've endured. All the cruel indignities and crushing agonies of time, drawn out forever. My ancient friends and comrades gone. Condemned to eternal torment for the sake of the Keeper and the Legion and the precious peace, while generation on long generation passed me by. No man—"

He blinked at Jil, sobbing.

"I've suffered, lass. Longer than any miserable victim of wicked mischance has ever suffered in all human history—"

"Gul!"

"For life's sweet sake—aye, for the precious life of all mankind!—give me another blessed instant, sir, for a stranger tale than you ever heard. From a man of many names. In my tragic plight, I've been driven to invent them. Julian Diamondwall. Hannibal Xenophon Gul. Half a hundred others, if you care to inquire.

"But I was once Giles Habibula—I swear that, sir, on my sacred duty to the precious Keeper of the Peace. For I've been true, sir. In spite of every cruel and undeserved misfortune, I've kept my faith with the precious Legion.

"Here's the piteous story, sir. The mortal truth, if you can see your way to recognize it. Aged and wretched as I was—far older now, sir, than any other has ever been—I sacrificed my blessed freedom to build a new defense for the mortal human race against all ill mischance.

"The Keeper knew her precious life was never safe. Stored in her blessed brain alone, our great weapon had always been in mortal danger. She invented a plan to share it among three of us—"

"Share it?" Star gaped at him. "Are you trying to claim you know the secret of AKKA?"

"Only one precious item of it, sir." Scowling bitterly, he blinked at Star. "That's the mortal misfortune of all humanity in this hour of fearful doom. The secret was divided among the three of us, who might hope to hold it forever. Lord Archy, Miss William and myself. All three of us must rejoin our separate shares to put it back together."

"And who's this Miss William?"

"The blessed being we call the laser-maker, sir." With a heavy sigh, he turned to Jil. "You say you saw her, lass. A hapless prisoner in the hands of the mortal flashers now, carried back into the nebula's fearful gut, where we may never reach her."

"If all this is true—"

Star's hand had fallen with the gun. He frowned at the fat man, dazedly shaking his head.

"Sir, it's mortal truth. Let the lovely lass be my witness."

"Kynan," Jil whispered, "I think we must believe him. I saw the laser-maker. She spoke to me."

Star swung back to him.

"If you are Habibula—if you were in the Keeper's fort when the raiders struck—how did you get here?"

"By nerve and wit and mortal daring, sir."

"If you expect me to believe—" Star raised the gun and shook his head. "Tell me how you did it."

"If I must recall that frightful time—" He wheezed for breath. "A mortal horror that begs for wine to wash the fearful memory away, when there's not a blessed drop in billions of kilometers—"

"Get to the truth."

"Ah, sir! In the dear Keeper's name, all I say is mortal truth."

"Let's have it."

"An evil night! But one thing first. Believe me, sir." His wheezy voice rose almost defiantly. "A night of dreadful terror, but it left no mortal blot on my own precious conscience, sir."

"Maybe," Star muttered. "I'm listening."

"If your mortal mind is open, sir—" His mud-colored eyes

squinted skeptically at Jil, shrewdly back at Star. "There were three of us, as I told you, sir. One stayed always near the Keeper to make mortal sure that she was safe. On that dreadful night, the watch was Miss William's.

"Lord Archy and I were down in the Laser Lounge, where a mortal corporal could buy his blessed drop of ease and peace. Lord Archy felt their freezing weapon flash when they first hit the guards. He warned me of fearful trouble. We were in the ladder well, rushing to defend the precious Keeper, when another flash came mortal close.

"A near thing, sir. Mortal near! I woke frozen stiff in the bottom of the blessed well. Lord Archy had revived and radiated precious heat to bring me back to life. We climbed again, back to the Keeper's suite. In time to find her, sir—find her—"

Tears shone in his muddy eyes, and he shuddered to a heavy sob.

"A wicked thing, sir! For life's sweet sake, don't make me dwell on the fearful horror of it. The Keeper—we found the blessed Keeper dead, sir. Miss William gone. The precious weapon—"

He blew his nose.

"Mortal little left to tell us who the ugly traitors were and who was left what we could trust. Mortal little, sir, and the Legion team already landing from the orbital fort to fumble and blunder over that.

"We were sadly shaken, sir. Yet we found a mite of prudence and the precious wit to hide ourselves—"

"You hid?" Star rapped. "Hid from the investigators?"

"And mortal wise to do it." The fat man shrugged, shrill voice sharper. "Do you take me for a doddering dunderhead? I knew no more than those bungling idiots did about who had done the frightful crime. They thought they knew I had been involved. With so many trusted men gone wrong—aye, sir, loyal companions I had served with many years—I didn't know who else might turn against us.

"A wicked pickle, sir." The old man blinked back into Star's hard face. "Miss William carried off, and the blessed Legion all against us. I admit it, sir. For once I was afraid. Yet we knew our duty, sir. The mortal duty we had been trained and sworn for. Aye, when the evil hour came, we did what we had to.

"Lord Archy with me. If you don't know him, old Ben Gyrel had him designed for service in hazardous environments. With the precious Keeper killed, with the moral Legion teams howling in like hungry hounds to hunt us down and pin the mortal murder on us, that was a fearful test for him."

His fat hand waved at the little silver sphere, now lying at her feet, silently quivering.

"Aye, sir. A harder test than he was built for, but he passed it mortal well. He watched those prowling popinjays off the Legion bases, blundering through the blessed Keeper's quarters and mucking up any mortal clues the raiders might have left. He kept a tach link with Miss William. He scouted out a way for us to leave the fort and sneak aboard a blessed Legion battlecraft.

"We stowed away in a life pod till it landed on Alpha IV. Looking for a safer ship, we found Larron's *Hedonian* standing at the penal dock. Under guard, with all his precious clones locked aboard and Larron in the prison, waiting for their mortal mockery of justice.

"A blessed break for us. We seized it, sir. And made a blessed break for him. I took the name of Julian Diamondwall. Lord Archy got into a power station to black out the base. I called upon an ancient slight to ease Larron out of his death cell and back aboard with his clones.

"We took off for the blessed nebula.

"And there you have it, sir, if you've got the wit to know the mortal truth."

25

A lone golden seed fluttered over Star's strain-bitten head.

Jil saw his gun waver, saw him sway where he stood, saw the agony on his gray-stubbled face.

"Kynan, put it up," she begged him. "You've pushed yourself too hard. You need rest, and we aren't going anywhere. We can't go anywhere."

"If I knew—"

His hollowed eyes flashed at Jil and back to the man in the cab, his grim, drawn face a battleground of doubt and hope and desperate exhaustion.

"We've got too much at stake," his worn voice rasped. "And I've come too far to stop."

He steadied the gun at the man in the cab.

"If you could show me proof—"

"Proof, sir?" the fat man gasped. "If you won't take my mortal word, what proof would you expect? We've been in flight, sir. Flight from you and all the blessed Legion. From all the wicked monsters grown from dreadful eggs planted in the precious flesh of my old comrades, turning them to spies and traitors. Aye, sir, the hot core of the flaming nebula had become a safer haven for us than any mortal human habitation."

His muddy eyes blinked defiance.

"We hoped to find Miss William, sir. Hoped to unite the three of us and join our separate bits of the sacred secret to defend the mortal human race. Is that a stinking crime, sir?"

"If I could believe—" Star shook his head. "By your account, you've been living lies for human generations. With the stakes so high, I'm afraid to trust you now."

"Kynan"—Jil caught her breath—"I think we must."

"Why?" His unhappy eyes appealed to her. "Have you a reason?"

"What the laser-maker said." She frowned, trying to remember. "Just a few words. Whispered low so Brendish wouldn't hear. Strange words. About an armed rhinoceros. but it was begging me to warn the Legion. And get word to Hannibal Gul.

"It must have trusted him."

"Miss William!" the fat man muttered. "Don't call her *it*."

"If she trusted you—" Star scowled at him. "What's an armed rhinoceros?"

"Don't ask me, sir. Her talk was always mortal strange." He squinted at the robot. "You could ask Lord Archy."

Jil bent to the shimmering bubble. "Can you explain?"

"Negative, Miss Three. Referential data missing for term 'armed rhinoceros.'"

"If it talks, ask what it knows." Star's gun jabbed at the robot. "About the laser-maker and AKKA and this man who claims to be Habibula."

"It?" the fat man flared. "He's Lord Archy."

"Lord Archy—" She paused to phrase the question. "Is this man Giles Habibula?"

"Affirmative, Miss Three."

"Is it true that you and he and Miss William know the secret of AKKA?"

"Data restricted, Miss Three."

"Which could mean yes." She glanced at Star. "If this is Habibula, you heard what he said about the attack on the Keeper and his escape from Alpha V?"

"Affirmative, Miss Three."

"Is what he said true?"

"Comment, Miss Three. Our referential definitions of term 'truth' rated inadequate."

She frowned at her tiny image dancing in his silver curve.

"Did you travel with him from Alpha III to Alpha IV? And aid Captain Larron's escape from prison there?"

"Affirmative, Miss Three."

"Where is Miss William now?"

"Data lacking, Miss Three."

"You did have tach contact with her?"

"Affirmative, Miss Three."

"Where was she when you reached her last?"

"Aboard S.S. *Purple Empress*, Miss Three. In flight through Devil's Creep into the nebula."

"What stopped the contact?"

"Her captors were demanding facts she was unable to reveal. They exposed her to extreme stresses, which forced her to withdraw."

Nodding, Jil turned to Star.

"Proof enough, I think."

"Unless the robot's lying—"

"Data, sir." The bright bubble lifted off the rock. "We are programmed for factual accuracy."

"At least to say you are." With a bitter grin for Jil, he looked back at the fat man. "If you came looking for the laser-maker, what are you doing here?"

"We've come a mortal distance, sir. The best way we could." He caught a raspy breath. "Lord Archy and I are bound by a sacred obligation to guard our own precious lives. But you must recall, sir, that we also share the sacred secret. Miss William's rescue would do no mortal good—not to you or the mortal Hall of Stars—if one of us is dead."

Star's lean jaw set hard. For a long time he stood nearly motionless, narrowed eyes fixed on the fat man. At last, abruptly, he snapped the gun back to his belt.

"Okay!" He nodded at Jil with a heavy sigh. "A bigger lump than I like to swallow. Adjusting to it will take time." He tried to smile at the man in the cab. "I guess—I guess you do make sense. I only wish—wish I'd met you sooner. If we'd known in time—"

"If—" The fat man mopped at his wet face. "The saddest mortal word men ever said. If we three had known the evil truth while we were all together, we might have mounted the blessed weapon then, to sweep the black vampires out of the nebula."

Dismally he gestured at the chasm beyond the fringe of dusty weeds.

"But we're trapped and dying now like squeaking rats in this mortal pit—"

"Not since I know what our duty is." Star's tired eyes turned to Jil. "To join with you. To follow Miss William. To set her free. To recover AKKA and hit the enemy."

"A noble plan, sir." His voice ironic, the fat man nodded at the useless life pod lying in the tangled rigging of the yellow parachutes. "But if I may ask, sir, how are you getting back to your mortal starcraft?"

"To the *Sunmark?*" Star looked blank. "We can't get back. Anyhow, it's gone." His face turned grim. "Hit by—I don't know what. We'd picked up a hostile craft, but it was far out of range. I don't know what the missile was. Nothing like it in the Legion arsenal. Must have homed on my own tach signal, at trans-Newtonian velocity. Hit us aft, toward the geodynes. I was lucky to get out. The only one alive—"

His bent shoulders shrugged, as if to shake off that disaster.

"We must take your *Hedonian.*"

"*Hedonian?*" The fat man blinked at him, startled. "If you care to face the precious truth, sir, the mortal flashers have taken the *Hedonian.*"

"Not yet." Star shook his head. "I was following it out of orbit when the missile hit me. Saw where it landed. Saw it again as I came down here. Standing out on the ice."

"Wrong, sir. They've got the blessed craft. Came here in it for Larron and his precious clones. Gone now. Lord Archy traced it, taking off for the inner nebula."

"But—" Star's tired eyes appealed to Jil. "I saw—something—"

"That must have been the flasher craft," she told him. "It had found the *Hedonian*. Landed near it. My father sabotaged it while he was free from—"

She shuddered from the recollection.

"They left the wreck of their own craft and took off in ours."

"I—I see."

Star's breath went out, and his lean frame sagged. He shook his head at the pod. Red from strain and cruel fatigue, his eyes clung to hers.

"I guess—guess you were right," he whispered. "I've

pushed too hard, too long. Even when I knew no hope was left." He grinned at her groggily, as if half drunk with sheer exhaustion. "You know, Jil, I'm almost glad we have to quit."

"But we can't quit!"

Her own voice lifting, she looked at the fat man and back at him.

"Not now. Not since we know AKKA can be recovered."

"Ah, lass!" Wheezily reproving her, the fat man shook his head. "You make me wish I was a child again, with nothing worse to do than dream of toys and mortal holidays."

Reeling unsteadily, Star gripped the edge of the cab to hold himself erect.

"Jil," he whispered, "I envy you. Because I recall what I used to be when I first came out to the nebula. Young. Alive. Ready for nearly anything. But I've been here too many years. Suffered too many defeats. This time—"

He sagged again, to a heavy sigh.

"There's no more use—"

She turned to the man in the cab.

"Lass, don't look at me!" He raised a puffy hand. "I've no magic carpet to get us off the mortal planet!"

"We've got to try—something."

She turned to search the rust-red thickets along the narrow ledge and the white dust slope where Freeholm had been. Though no wind had risen yet, the air was colder in the growing shadow of the cliffs, and purple dusk had begun to thicken in the pit beyond the empty life pod in its yellow tangle.

"Can't we somehow signal?" Her eyes came back to the silver bubble quivering at her feet. "Can't Lord Archy call—anybody?"

"Think first, lass!" the fat man gasped. "Do you want to call the monsters back to plant their evil seed in us? For sweet life's sake, don't let some idle daydream lure us into mortal folly!"

She had turned to the robot.

"Can't you—"

"Negative, Miss Three." It soared off the rock. "We have tested our extreme signal range on all Legion tach channels.

No receiver operational within signal reach. No starcraft detected anywhere except abandoned shadowflasher battleship—"

Her breath catching, she looked at Star.

"Lass!" The fat man went shrill with consternation. "For the sake of all our mortal lives, don't think of such fearful insanity!"

26

Giles Habibula quaked in terror, gaping at Star.

"Don't let her say it, sir! I love the precious lass, for her nerve and blessed beauty. Aye, sir, the first lovely glimpse of her called me back to mountain springs on old Terra. But she's gone daft, sir. But if she's gone mad enough to beg for blessed death, here's a cleaner way."

He gestured toward the blue abyss.

"As sure as anything waiting on the mortal icecap, with precious less toil and pain."

Jil had turned to Star.

"If the flasher ship is still there, let's take a look." She shrugged at the dusty weeds around them, and the useless life pod. "There's nothing for us here—"

"Sir, don't listen to her babble." The old man's voice rose raggedly. "The wreck's too mortal far across the ice, worth our precious lives to reach. If the black vampires left it, they meant no blessed favors for us. It will be locked and booby-trapped and likely guarded by their wicked drillers."

"That may be." She had to nod. "But we've nothing left to lose—"

"Nothing, lass?" His yellow moon face quivered. "Nothing but our mortal lives! The blessed Keeper knows I'd walk through blazing flames to save the laser-maker and her precious secret, but I've never been the fearful fool who would waste himself on such an idiotic errand."

He swung massively to Star.

"Don't let yourself imagine, sir, that I've ever been a slinking coward. If you know your interstellar history, you know I made my mortal mark long ago, leading our noblest heroes against the Medusae and the wicked Cometeers.

"But look at what the lass is asking. She wants us to leave our precious haven here and offer our blessed bodies to breed new generations of fearful shadowflashers. If you want some monstrous worm gnawing your insides out and stealing your mortal brain—"

"She's right." Star raised a hand to check him. "I don't like the odds, but I guess it's the only game there is. We're with you, Jil."

The freezing dusk found them in the icecraft, creeping up the trail toward the icecap. They had loaded what they could salvage from the pod. Kynan Star lay asleep on the rear seat, overtaken by exhaustion. Giles Habibula grumbled over a second supper.

"Pig swill!" The meaty aroma from the self-heating kit seemed rich enough, but his high voice quivered bitterly. "Stinking slop a hog would scorn!"

The moonless dark was thick before they reached the canyon rim. At the wheel, Jil turned on the lights.

"Don't, lass!" He looked up from yet another ration with an apprehensive gasp. "Must you show every precious move we make to the cliffdrillers or the shadowflashers or something else as mortal evil?

"For sweet life's sake, turn out the wicked lights!"

"I can't see the trail—"

"Then give the blessed wheel to Lord Archy."

"It's not an easy drive—"

"Permission, Miss Three?" The little robot lifted off the seat between them. "May we assure you that operating the icecraft without lights would offer us no undue difficulty? We are familiar with the route to the spot where we left the S.S. *Hedonian*. If you request such service, we are fully competent to drive you there."

"Let him do it, lass. He was engineered for such tasks, and he does them mortal well."

A little reluctantly, she turned out the lights. Lord Archy bounded to the wheel, and the machine climbed on. On one side of that perilous trail, the greenish glow of the nebular sky revealed shadowy masses of ice or rock. On the other, empty blackness yawned. Her breath caught when they spun around a turn, but Habibula was unconcerned. Soon she heard his whistling snore.

Skidding and pitching, they came up the last frozen slope to the ice plateau. The wide sky glowed, coldly green and dully red, streaked and splotched with dead-black dust. Beneath that faint and eerie light, the snowscape lay immense and strange.

Though the frigid air was now still, she saw no trace of roller marks across the snow. She looked for stars. Those she found were few and far between, blurred in hazy halos. It seemed to her that the robot was veering back toward the canyon rim, but she wasn't sure of anything. Suddenly lost, as painfully as she had been on that first morning on Alpha III, she sat yearning for the freedom of space, where she could feel the stars again. She envied Lord Archy and slowly came to trust his silent skill.

"Miss Three, we are near the shadowflasher starship."

Jarred awake by the rolling gong tones, she sat up and rubbed her eyes. Habibula lay snoring beside her, and Lord Archy still perched on the wheel. The machine was lumbering up a long ice slope. When they lurched over the crest, she saw the battlecraft.

It stood alone amid the dunes of drifted snow, perhaps two kilometers ahead. Looming high against the cold blue dawn, it was black and enormous. Shaped like a half-filled balloon, it was round at the top, sharply tapered toward the narrow column that rested on the ice.

Her heart beat harder, as if she had been on the yawara mats testing the skills of an unknown master. The strange machine challenged them with unplumbed dangers. Conquered, it could carry them on to some slender chance for life and even triumph.

"Stop!" Giles Habibula was gasping. "For sweet life's sake!" She felt his shuddering fingers on her arm. "Lass, are you gone mad? Must you push our precious heads into some wicked shadowflasher snare before we're half awake? We're mortal idiots if we take the ship to be a blessed treasure wrapped in ribbon for us. Instead, we're more apt to find it a fearful trap set and baited, loaded down with hidden horrors and left to lure us to a dreadful death."

His voice quavered higher.

"Lord Archy, I command you! Stop."

"Information, Mr. Two," the bell tones answered him. "We remind you that Miss Three carries the name and blood of Dr. One. When your commands conflict, we rate hers supersessive."

"Lass, command the mortal idiot to stop! Order him to hide us back of a blessed ice peak and use all his energy detectors to search for booby traps and snares and fearful deadfalls. If we're to risk our precious necks any nearer, let's wait for shelter in the blessed dark."

"Night's no safer." Kynan Star sat up, stretching stiffly. "Driller raids have nearly always come under cover of darkness."

"Caution, lass!" Habibula shivered. "I've seen hopeless battles won, but never by a dead hero. We're mortal fortunate to have Lord Archy with us. He was engineered for work in spots too dangerous for men, and now's the precious moment when he can serve us best. Send him out ahead."

She looked at Star for his opinion. When he nodded, she took the wheel. Pulling down the slope ahead until the machine was almost hidden, she slid a window open and sent Lord Archy toward the battlecraft. While they waited, Giles Habibula heated a ration kit, lamented what he called its evil reek and ate it avidly.

They watched the balloon-shaped battlecraft. Nothing about it moved or changed. The small sun rose. Its arctic light glittered on the ice and cast a black and endless shadow from the ship. A long hour had gone before they saw the silver glint of the robot returning.

"Reporting, Miss Three." It dropped back to the seat and lay there quivering with its own inner dynamisms. "We detect no energy from inside the craft except radiation from damped nuclear reactors assumed to power the propulsion system. We detect no indication of organic or any other kind of life aboard."

Turning to Habibula and Star, Jil found them looking

expectantly at her.

"In that case," she said, "we can go in."

"With caution, lass!" Habibula begged her. "With mortal caution!"

They went in. She steered along a narrowing spiral, keeping when she could to cover behind hummocks and drifts. Twice Star had her stop while he climbed on the cab to study the black battlecraft. When he asked her at last to drive straight in, they were on the sunward side. Thirty meters from the narrow base, he beckoned her to stop.

"It touches down on a sliding cylinder." The window open, he leaned to point. His breathless whisper was hard for her to hear. "A landing buffer. Likely also used for takeoff lift. Elevators or ladder wells inside the cylinder. There's the door."

He turned to her.

· "Shall we take a look?"

"That's what we came for."

Moving to leave the cab, he nodded for Habibula to come with him.

"Must we, lass?" the old man moaned. "Must we tempt the black vampires with our naked flesh?" Squinting sharply at her, he shook his head. "If we risk their hideous sting, let's all go together. Kynan has our only gun, and we want no mortal risk that anyone might drive away in panic, leaving precious comrades to face a fearful fate alone."

Silently, she followed them.

"Thank you, lass!" he whispered. "There's blessed strength in numbers."

Snow crunched beneath their boots. No wind had risen, and she heard no other sound. Her breath was white mist, and the still cold stung her face. Bulging out above them, the black ship hid more than half the sky. She saw no sign of life about it. Gun drawn, Star led the way into the narrow angle between two great metal struts that had bitten deep into the ice. Mouth half open, Habibula peered up at the thick black flanges and massive beams that linked them to the central cylinder.

"Mortal strange!" Shivering, he shook his head. "Hurts your blessed brain to see it."

"Another technology!" Star seemed equally awed. "Though somehow half familiar. All this gear folds back against the hull after takeoff to make a clean aerodynamic teardrop. If we could get this craft back for Legion engineers to study—"

"If any mortal Legion engineers are left to study it!"

Silently, he pushed on between the towering struts. Jil and Habibula followed, Lord Archy bounding beside them. The massive door was closed, but she saw Star lifting a heavy metal plate hinged to the face of it. In a shallow recess beneath was a row of slots, each with a colored knob at the end.

"A lock, I suppose." He turned to Habibula. "A job for you."

"In sweet life's name, don't look at me," the old man shrilled. "Nothing I can do."

"I've read history," Star told him. "I know you're a lock-smith."

He shrank from the door, squinting uneasily at Jil.

"Forgive me, lass, but I have no mortal magic. Not for any such wicked task as this. Once, it's true, I had a way with locks. A certain slight dexterity gained in the bitter years of my tragic youth, before I ever escaped into the precious Legion. But that was long ago.

"Aye, lass, too mortal long."

"Try it, Giles."

"Lass!" He shrank from the lock, blinking reproachfully at her and then at his own yellow hands. "For life's precious sake, look at these miserable claws. Withered and quivering with my fearful burden of age. Numb to the bone with this mortal cold. The touch and the precious gift they once possessed were lost long generations ago."

"We've got to get inside."

Squinting at the lock, he sighed and shook his head.

"A fearful riddle. Twelve mortal levers linked to work or lock the tumblers. Twelve clicks on every lever. Twelve blessed colors. No hint of a clue to where you begin and what you repeat."

He let the heavy plate clang down.

"The wicked thing's impossible. Cold reason can't help us. Mortal math will tell you why, in precious powers of twelve. You could try combinations till the universe ends and never come within a million mortal miles of the secret key."

"Giles, we must—"

"Lass, I can't." He hunched himself against the cold. "When I used to have an art with locks, I sometimes used another way when cold reason failed. That was a feeling for the minds of their makers. Because any lock's a problem in psychology. Before you can seek out its secrets, you must share the mind and the heart and the mortal soul of the inventor."

"Please try again—"

"That's the craft of it, lass." His back to the door, he shrugged her plea away. "The precious secret of the master cracksman. Because any problem lock's a work of mortal art, built of emotion more than metal. That's what beats me now."

He shivered, exhaling icy fog.

"If the black vampires have any souls at all, they're too deadly evil for any sane man to reach for. I'll want no contact with them, lass. Because I already know too mortal much of how they seek to rule and drive our helpless bodies while they eat our blessed brains."

He staggered away from the door.

"Forgive me, lass. It breaks my poor old heart to fail you, but the fearful thing needs mortal skills I never knew. If you're bound to get aboard, let's seek out another entrance. Perhaps there's some hatch or port Lord Archy might open for us."

Star led the way. The ship's vast mass had rived the ice far around it, and they had to scramble through hazardous pits and peaks. Three times they got back to the great central shaft to examine puzzling projections. None of them marked any kind of door.

"Mr. Habibula, please!" Jil caught his arm. "You'll have to try the lock again, before we freeze—"

"Dear life, lass!" His wheezy scream cut her off. "Look behind you! Mortal monsters, eating up our own precious craft—"

Looking where his shaking arm had pointed, she found the icecraft. Already half buried in the snow, it was sinking fast. Beyond it, vast things were bursting out of the drifts. Great gray shapes like nothing she had ever known or imagined, shedding bits of clinging ice, jumping with a dreadful clumsy swiftness to ring them in.

27

The things closed in.

Kynan Star knelt behind a ledge of heaved-up ice to fire. His exploding projectiles flashed and crashed against gray, gigantic shapes. Metal fragments whined away into the windless chill. The great, ungainly things kept leaping closer.

"Drillers!" Giles Habibula broke into a waddling run. "Mortal drillers left to trap us!"

He vanished behind the nearest strut. Transfixed with shock, Jil watched the icecraft sink swiftly deeper. A white geyser plumed high. Shattered ice hailed back into a swirl of vanishing frost.

It was gone.

Something rumbled. The ice shook under her. Where the vehicle had sunk, the crust crumbled upward, flung by a sudden mushrooming cloud of white steam and flying ice. Beneath it, a black bulge lifted. A huge gray barrel followed, unfolding massive, awkward-looking legs. It raised itself on them, an enormous headless insect. The barrel body tipped toward her, as if the whole end of it had been a single black and lidless eye.

Star fired at it, twice. His projectiles burst against the bulge, so near the thunder cracks hurt her ears. The flashes dazzled her. A sharp, steamy reek took her breath. Untroubled, the thing dipped and rocked and jumped high, crashing down meters nearer.

She saw Lord Archy bounding into its path.

"Permission, Miss Three." Deaf from the blasts, she hardly heard him. "If we may advise Pilot-Major Star, the cliff-drillers cannot be damaged by his weapon."

"Can anything—" she gasped. "Can't we do anything to stop them?"

"Negative, Miss Three." He danced briefly back. "We compute zero probability that any human action can defeat them."

Again he skittered to meet the stalking monster. She heard no other sound, saw no weapon used, yet it froze where it stood. In the sudden stillness, she heard Star's gun click, reloading. She heard Giles Habibula panting and moaning behind her, heard a clatter from the access plate over the lock as he scrabbled at the door.

Breathless, she stared at the stopped cliffdrillers.

Machines!

They were all gray metal, their ponderous limbs enormous levers that worked on shielded hinges. As Lord Archy skipped closer, they all moved again, tipping armored barrel bodies as if to watch him.

They made no sound that she could hear. Once the ice snapped and quivered under her boots, as if weakened by their burrowing, and yielding now to the starcraft's weight. Pale fog drifted from her nostrils. Her face tingled and her fingers ached. She wanted the warmth of motion, but awe held her still.

Lord Archy soared silently higher.

Abruptly, in equally soundless unison, the cliffdrillers tipped their black ends downward. Folding those great gray levers back into their massive barrels, they dived into the ice. It roared and shook beneath her, erupting in billowing steam.

And they were gone. Their thunder became a muted rumble, dying into silence. A few snowflakes swirled out of the vanishing cloud. Pools of black water were left where the black machines had dived, still smoking with their heat.

"I thought—" Jil whispered. "Thought they had us."

"Near enough."

Star holstered his gun, and they scrambled out across broken ice to where Lord Archy shimmered in the chill sunlight.

"You stopped them?"

"Affirmative, Miss Three. We commanded them to go."

"They obeyed you?" Star goggled at him. "Why?"

"Because of what they are, sir."

"What are they?"

"Our own kind, sir. Self-directed devices, designed as we were for exploration and mining operations on planets too hazardous for the beings who made them. They informed us that the shockwave destroyed their makers. They have survived alone through all the Terran millenniums since, seeking materials with which to replicate themselves and searching for their lost masters."

"Why are they attacking us?"

"Permission, sir. For definition. Their appearance was not an attack. They were designed for peaceful uses only, with no capacity for violence—"

"Wrong!" Kynan Star exploded. "Their cowardly night assaults have killed thousands of people on scores of planets all across the nebula. Are you claiming they were here to welcome us?"

"Negative, sir. They are incapable of extending welcome."

"Then what were they up to?"

"Explanation, sir. They were acting under orders to protect the starcraft. They were moving to block our way aboard, but they meant us no harm."

"Whose orders?"

"The shadowflashers, sir."

"If they obey the flashers, they're hardly harmless!"

"Amplification, sir. The shadowflashers have been using them to destroy human shipping and mining installations, but only through unsupported promises to help them find their lost makers. They lack any capacity for interstellar fight, and it is the shadowflashers who have scattered them through the nebula, controlling them through false information that their extinct makers still exist—"

"Can't they see they've harmed humanity?"

"Negative, sir."

Perched now on a point of ice, pealing its words with the

rhythm of a tolling bell, the little robot seemed nearly as remote from human emotion as those metal moles it had sent back beneath the ice.

"Their control programs were never elaborate. In their ages of replication, certain of their original injunctions have been lost. Their orders here were simply to bar intruders from the starcraft. Within their limits, they were attempting to obey."

"Thanks for what you did." Star grinned. "I didn't understand."

"Information, sir. We exist to serve Dr. One and those we rate with him." Lord Archy skipped toward Jil. "We require no gratitude."

Star frowned again. "How did you make them obey?"

"We know their language, sir. We learned it a Terran century ago."

"You knew them?" Jil whispered. "Back then?"

"Affirmative, Miss Three." Lord Archy lay quivering at her feet. "They attempted to consume us. Our own maker, Dr. One, had landed the S.S. *Legion Argo* on an uncharted planet. He sent us out to survey it. When we returned, we found Dr. One dead from exposure to excessive radiation. The starcraft had been totally consumed.

"The cliffdrillers were attracted to us by our own energy fields and metal content. We were able to evade them, but only through frequent flight. Observing their subsonic signals, we were at last able to attempt communication."

"You talked—to them?" Jil peered at the smoking pools where they had sunk into the ice, and blankly back at the silvery spheroid. "And made them obey you?"

"Affirmative, Miss Three. At least to the limits of their narrow capacity for obedience."

"How?"

Lord Archy skittered uncertainly toward Jil and back to his perch on the ice.

"A demanding problem, Miss Three. Rated among the most difficult we have ever been required to solve. Because we were trapped between two conflicting commands in our own control program. We are forbidden to communicate inaccurate data, but also instructed to preserve our own existence. The choice we made was difficult, but Mr. Two has since approved it."

"No doubt!" Star muttered. "But go ahead."

"Please!" Jil was shivering. "If the drillers can be ruled, we need to know how."

"We informed them that we also are robotic," Lord Archy pealed. "A factual datum. For the sake of our own survival, however, we followed it with the ambiguous statement that we were created to command them."

He came skimming to Jil.

"Question, Miss Three. Addressed to you as Dr. One's rated successor. Do you wish us to revoke or modify our instructions? We do retain capacity to recall the cliff-drillers—"

"No!" She wanted to stroke his shimmering curve. "Thanks for what you did!" ·

"No gratitude required—"

He broke off abruptly, darting toward the starship.

"A call, Miss Three! An urgent call from Mr. Two."

They scrambled over blocks of broken ice to follow him around the massive, deep-sunk strut. Beyond it, they found the heavy door wide open. Giles Habibula stood peering from it, a fat hand lifted against the glare of ice and sun.

"Pilot Star?" he was shrilling. "Miss Gyrel? Ah, here you come! I thought the fearful things had taken you away."

"You opened the door?"

"Perhaps—perhaps I did." Trembling, he mopped his face. "I remember the wicked monsters swarming out of the drift. I knew Pilot Star's gun could never save us, and my thin old blood was chilled to mortal ice—"

He shuddered, blinking into the steaming pools where the cliffdrillers had dived back into the ice.

"A frightful time! More mortal tension than a sane mind can stand. I blacked out, lass. The next I knew I was here inside and those fearful things were gone. Perhaps the precious skills I had forgotten came back to work the wicked lock."

He clung to the edge of the valve, wheezing with relief.

"Aye, lass! The fearful drillers must have been a stroke of fortune for us. It was their wicked attack that woke the blazing genius of my blessed youth. If only for a single mortal moment—"

Heavily he sighed.

"That's the wicked pity of it, lass. Only one mortal moment, one I can't recall. Now I'm old again. Aye, old and ill and sick with mortal shock. Trapped aboard this ship of nightmare monsters—"

"Let's find if we can fly it."

They climbed inside. Giles Habibula hauled at a lever that closed the door. The room around them was circular and small.

"An elevator?" Jil asked him.

"Aye, and a ladder well beside it."

"Can you take us up?"

"Think first, lass." He blinked uneasily. "Think of all the fearful snares and hazards waiting. We could blunder into mortal shadowflashers left aboard. We could come upon their piteous victims, left with the horrid larva breeding in their bodies, ready now to awake and sting their dreadful eggs into our own precious flesh. We could step into booby traps left to kill us—"

"We'll see," Jil said. "Take us up."

"You mistake us, lass." Dismally he shook his head. "We're no mortal demigods, like those old heroes of the Legion who beat the Medusae and the evil Cometeers. A fearful error, lass. If you think we can fly the abandoned wreck of an alien battlecraft to rescue Miss William and recover AKKA and defeat the vampire invasion, you're mortal wrong. You ask too mortal much.

"Look at us, lass!

"Two old and broken men. A tiny, worn-out machine. And yourself, lass—lovely as the mortal dawn, but too tender in your precious girlhood to know the shape and feel of fearful evil."

"I saw a shadowflasher—" The recollection took her voice. "Saw it finish off my father—"

"Listen to me, lass!" He waved a shaking hand. "Listen to the odds. Aye, the fearful odds against us."

"The odds have always been against the Legion." Feebly she tried to grin. "When you fought the Medusae and the Cometeers—"

"We were younger then." His voice quavered higher. "Pilot Star may be unburdened by my own fearful curse—the mortal burden of immortality—but you must grant he's lost the fine edge of youth. We've both fought too mortal long for the blessed Legion—for people who forgot us or never cared to know. We've given all we had, and suffered too mortal much.

"I don't like to deny you, lass, because you are such a lovely woman. Aye, you make me long for the precious youth I'd lost before your blessed grandfather was born, or his noble grandfather. But all your mortal beauty can't compel us to risk our precious necks on a fool's mission that can only end with shadowflashers breeding in our blessed brains.

"You aren't our commander—"

"I don't claim to be." Flushing, she looked at Kynan Star. "I'm not even in the Legion."

Star stood a long time silent, frowning at her.

"Jil, I think you are." He spoke at last, his trouble-furrowed face still solemn. "There's truth in what Giles says. I've fought too long and lost too much. I've been beaten—running on nerve and nothing else—since that missile out of nowhere hit the *Sunmark*—"

His wan face twitched.

"If you want the cold truth, Jil, I don't see a chance in a trillion that we could fly a wrecked alien battlecraft to any sort of victory. If you do—"

With a wistful grin at her, he swung to Habibula.

"That's why she must take command."

"Sir, are you a mortal idiot?"

"Could be." He shrugged. "Could be her nerve is mostly ignorance. But there's nothing else for us to do, and I'm still a soldier in the Legion. As you are, Giles. Black as things may get, you know we don't give up."

He swung back to Jil.

"You wanted to join the Legion. Now you're in. Getting this far into the ship is a break I didn't expect. We must make the most of it. Giles and I and Lord Archy do have abilities and skills. But we've got to have you, Jil. Your will to keep on trying, when Giles and I know we're done for.

"You're our leader now."

Tears stung her eyes.

"I—" Something tried to choke her, but she gulped it down and turned to Giles Habibula. "If you can work the elevator, take us up."

28

Habibula took them up.

An icy stillness filled the shadowflasher battlecraft, and a stale bog-rot stink increased as they rose. On the first deck, he opened the elevator door on soundless darkness, strange machines looming through it. Strange to Jil, but Habibula blinked in amazement.

"Geodynes!" he gasped. "A geodesic drive. The same mortal sort I used to nurse on our first little Legion starcraft, flying out to fight the Medusae and the evil Cometeers. Ten times larger, but still designed alike."

"A sad bit of history." Kynan Star nodded bleakly. "Because it tells what happened to our lost space explorers. The shadowflashers have been trapping them and stealing their science as well as their bodies."

"Our turn now." Jil looked at Habibula. "Giles, can you run these machines?"

"For life's sweet sake!" He recoiled as if from a blow. "Lass, you don't know what you ask! These may be geodynes, but they're none I ever knew. Every mortal part ten times bigger. Likely different in a thousand wicked ways. Reshaped by monstrous brains it would drive me mad to know."

"You've got to run them, Giles—"

"Don't ask me, lass! In the fearful press of peril, you've forgotten what I am. The oldest man that ever was! Tottering toward my blessed grave in spite of all the mortal medics."

Dolefully he shook his head.

"Ah, lass, you must recall what mortal time can do. I was a young man once. Young and full of fire as you are. No task too hard for me then, nor hazard too fearful. Aye, mortal danger was food to me then, and blessed drink. I wagered life and blessed limb a thousand times, for no mortal more than a smile like your own.

"In those precious days I was a master geodesic engineer. It was my rare skills that took the mortal Legion out to beat the Medusae and the wicked Cometeers. But, lass, that was long generations past. This sort of drive was obsolete a Legion century ago, and I'm a mortal human wreck.

"Don't ask!"

On the next deck up, dark corridors radiated from the elevator. The foul shadowflasher stink hung heavier there, and Jil shivered in the icy gloom. Gun drawn, Star led them into one dim corridor. Along both sides, roughly welded shelves of unpainted steel were stacked nine high, empty of anything.

"A slave ship, lass!" Trembling, Giles Habibula pointed. "Look at the wicked bins. Meant to stow human prisoners stacked like logs of mortal wood on their way to fearful slavery for the black vampires. With the evil eggs already stung into their blessed flesh to turn them into suffering puppets."

"I'm afraid that's true." Kynan Star nodded bleakly. "It's what they plan for mankind."

Four more decks, dim-lit and soundless, were filled with the same bare shelves. On the next they found a long galley and a row of vacant spaces. Giles Habibula waddled into one of them, and came back whimpering over a hard brownish brick.

"Lass, what are we to eat?" He blinked at her accusingly. "The wicked drillers wasted all we brought from the ruin of Freeholm. Here's all I found." With a grimace of disgust, he sniffed at the brick. "Hard as a mortal rock and not one precious tenth as tasty, by the foul reek of it.

"Must we—" His shrill tones broke, and his quivering face shone with tears. "Must we die, lass? Perish of mortal famine in this fearful cage?"

"If it's all there is, my father must have been able to eat it. I imagine we can."

"Eat—this?" Scowling at the brick, he flung it into the shadows. "I'd sooner boil my blessed boots."

They turned back to the elevator.

"No luxury liner." Kynan Star paused to point at a ragged weld above the door. "The whole craft has the look of hasty mass production. Which could mean they've set their slaves to building fleets to transport more slaves into the nebula."

"To set them to building more mortal ships, to catch more millions of mortal slaves!"

At the top stop, they emerged on the command deck. Jil found it half familiar. The conning screen, with pilot seat and control consoles swung beneath. Map tank and flight computers.

"Stolen!" Kynan Star muttered. "Like the geodynes."

Other shapes were stranger.

"What are those?" Jil pointed at three thick metal cylinders spaced around the rim of the deck. "Life pods?"

Giles Habibula toddled to inspect them.

"No life pods, lass." He made a doleful face. "They'd never fret about saving mortal slaves."

Star spent longer on his own inspection and came back looking bleak.

"Launchers," he muttered. "For the missile that knocked out the *Sunmark*. Another sad betrayal!"

He scowled at them again.

"Geodesic missiles." He turned back to Jil. "Years ago, back on Terra, I heard rumors that Legion engineers were about to arm us with them. Missiles fast enough to intercept geodesic craft. With accuracy and range the particle gun could never match. Then we heard the project was abandoned."

His gaunt head shook.

"Called impossible. Forbidden by non-Newtonian physics. The story they gave us. The Legion never got them. Seems the flashers did. I guess from unlucky engineers and the parasites that rode them."

"But we have them now!" Jil whispered. "If we can fly the ship—"

"We don't." His deep-sunk eyes looked sick. "They've all been fired. Racks empty."

"My father's doing, I imagine." Somberly she nodded. "When he disabled the craft."

"Mortal thorough!" Habibula gestured at the consoles. "Nothing left but wicked ruin. Flight computer smashed. Circuit crystals out of the map tank ground to powder on the deck."

"Somehow—" Jil caught an uneven breath. "In spite of everything, we've got to take it up—"

"Lass! Do you want to kill us all?"

"The only chance—"

"No actual chance." Star stood frowning at the wrecked computer. "We'd never get it off the ice. Not without instruments. No jets, remember. The flashers take off and land on just the geodynes—a practice so hazardous to both the ship and the landing spot that the Legion outlaws it."

He swung to shake his head at her.

"Sorry, Jil. I like your nerve, but you've got to see the limits. Even if we got the starcraft off the planet without smashing it to vapor, we couldn't navigate it anywhere. Not without charts and a flight computer—"

"Lass—" Quivering and gasped for breath, Habibula came waddling to seize her arm. "Could you, lass?"

"I don't know." She stared uncertainly at the shattered crystals glittering on the deck. "It's all so strange."

"A fearful risk." Swaying unsteadily, he turned to Star. "Anybody else would leave us lost in space forever or kill us in collision, but the lass does carry old Ben's precious gene. She steered us out of Devil's Creep.

"With her Gyrel luck—"

"Can you?" Star blinked at her, startled. "Without instruments?"

"I can try."

"Think first, lass! Think mortal well!" Shrill with alarm, he turned to Star. "Consider the frightful risk. Even if the lass can lift us back to space alive—what then? Fearful shadowflasher fleets all around us, and our own mortal missiles gone. Even if we get through them to meet a Legion battlecraft, we'd be taken for an enemy—"

"We won't be meeting the Legion," she told him. "Because we'll fly the other way, to overtake the *Purple Empress* and rescue the laser-maker—"

"Lass, have you lost your mortal mind?" His yellow face reflected outraged scorn. "Just the precious four of us. Adrift in a wicked alien starship. Without a chart to guide us. Without a blessed weapon. Without food a mortal hog would eat."

"Giles—"

"Listen, lass!" His whine rose higher. "You speak of recovering the secret of AKKA as if it were mortal simple as picking up a pebble. Even if we could fly the wicked ship, we'd never find Miss William. Not with a thousand fearful worlds to search."

"We'll do what we can." Jil turned to Kynan Star. "She's important to the shadowflashers. They're probably taking her to some strong point. Perhaps the same planet where they're making arms and building starships. If we could locate that—"

"If we were shining supermen." Giles Habibula shrugged and shook his head forlornly. "The sort I used to fly with—"

"Lord Archy—" She turned to him. "You worked with Miss William. Did you learn facts about the nebula from her?"

"Affirmative, Miss Three."

"Do you know facts about the shadowflashers?"

"Affirmative, Miss Three."

"Do they have a master planet?"

"We request definition of master planet."

"Their home world? The planet where they build ships and weapons?"

"Data lacking, Miss Three."

"Have you any facts that might help us find Miss William?"

"Data lacking on her present location, Miss Three. Data lacking on destination of the S.S. *Purple Empress*. Data lacking on recent military operations in nebular space. No relevant data discovered."

"Keep looking, please." Jil frowned. "Do you know Miss William's history? Anything about her native planet?"

"Affirmative, Miss Three. Data available on her planet of origin."

"What is it?"

"Planet orbits single component of triple sun located beyond nebular core. Concealed from human worlds by thick nebular dust. Consequently not shown on human star charts."

"Mortal far from here," Giles Habibula muttered uneasily. "And mortal far from where old Ben Gyrel picked her up."

"Have you more data?" Jil asked. "About how she got so far from home?"

"Affirmative, Miss Three. Her race was symbiotic. Her own kind lacked mobility. Their symbionts were highly mobile. Union rated extremely beneficial to both. Miss William informed us that they flourished in association. They had developed sophisticated starcraft and spread their culture across many planets before the shadowflashers came.

"Miss William was engaged in development of tachyonic defenses against the shadowflashers. The arrival of the shockwave terminated that development.

"It also terminated the war. Though Miss William's people can endure intense radiation, their symbionts could not. They died. Lacking them, most of her people perished. The shockwave also terminated the shadowflasher expansion, because it had killed the organic hosts they require for reproduction."

"What happened to Miss William?"

"Data, Miss Three. Miss William informed us that the shockwave caught her far from home. Rated a child, she still possessed some slight mobility, which enabled her to survive. Yet she had no way to leave the planet. She was there when Dr. One landed.

"We established alternative avenues of contact, first sonic, then radio and tachyonic. She wished to return to her home world to search for other survivors there. Dr. One promised to aid her, but he died before we could reach the triple sun."

"Thank you, Lord Archy."

"No gratitude required."

"If she should escape, I imagine she'd try to go home." Jil turned to the men. "I think we should try to reach her people. If they were fighting the flashers before the shockwave hit, they might have something useful for us."

She tried to smile into Habibula's doleful gloom.

"The best chance I see—"

"If you want to toss our precious lives away."

"The only chance." Star was nodding soberly. "Let's inspect the ship."

They separated. Habibula went down to check the geodesic drive and came back to investigate the galley. When at last they gathered again on the command deck, he wambled to the pilot's scat and sank into it feebly, moaning as if with hopeless despair.

"The geodynes?" Jil whispered. "Can't you run them?"

"No problem, lass," he puffed. "Not with the mortal geodynes. They're great clumsy things, built with sledge-hammers. Power enough to smash a precious planet when you try to take us up. Unless you're mortal careful! Here's the wicked problem."

He showed her a little brown brick.

"All the mortal monsters had for their blessed slaves to eat." He made a dismal face. "Foul swill. I tried it in the galley. Soaked and boiled, baked and fried, crushed and broiled. Every way is worse. We'll famish, lass."

"You may come to like it better." She grinned at him. "When we get hungry enough."

The air system had been copied from Legion equipment. It seemed to be in working order. The water tanks were nearly empty, but the condensers would at least yield drinking water.

"Controls inspected, Miss Three," Lord Archy pealed. "Ship's intercom and signal equipment remain functional, but sabotaged map tank and flight computer cannot be repaired."

"So we're blind!" Giles Habibula croaked. "Trapped and starving in a mortal coffin."

"Not quite blind," Jil said. "The conning hood does show the sky, though the telescopic functions and computer graphics are gone. Here on the planet, I can't feel anything outside the ship. But my sense of space will come back when we get up—I hope."

She had turned to the consoles, and Giles Habibula heaved himself uneasily upright to give her the pilot's chair.

Kynan Star followed her to it.

"Jil, you understand the hazards." His tone showed doubt that she did. "The geodesic field propels a ship by non-Newtonian forces, canceling space ahead and creating new space behind. The danger comes from interference with Newtonian mass and force. Gravitic or magnetic fields. That's why the Legion has always required auxiliary rockets for takeoffs and landings."

Settling herself beneath the conning hood, she managed not to say she had learned all that long ago from her instructors back on Alpha III.

"Giles," she called, "please energize the drive."

"Lass, lass!" He blinked at her forlornly. "Must you kill us all? Trying a stunt that would send any mortal Legion pilot to criminal reconstruction?"

He shook his head when he got no answer.

"Aye, lass." She heard his reluctant wheeze. "Better to do it now than endure the mortal waiting."

He waddled into the elevator.

29

Star gave her a lean-jawed grin.

"Standing by—and I love you, Jil!"

Habibula's quaver came over the intercom.

"Power's up, lass. If you want to risk our blessed lives on these mortal geodynes."

She slid into the seat beneath the blank conning screen. The Legion-patterned consoles around it had made her feel almost at ease, but they burned red with warnings when she pulled the wheel to the lift position.

PILOT ERROR!
FLIGHT COMPUTER OUT!
MAP TANK OUT!
NO FLIGHT PLAN FILED!

Gingerly she pushed the wheel.

Something mauled her, crushed her breath out, dragged her hand off the wheel, slammed the seat down to the deck. The ship spun around her. She was falling into a well of icy blackness, where she couldn't move or see or think. Trying to breathe, she caught a nauseous bog-rot reek.

"Lord of space!" Habibula's moan came faintly over the intercom. "Let me die!"

Light came abruptly back. The seat lurched and creaked, lifting her back to the consoles. Gasping for breath, she peered into the conning screen. Though all the astrogation aids were gone, it held a visual image of the nebula.

Gas clouds glowing, cold green and smoldering red. Blobs and streaks of dense black dust. Haze-veiled mascons. All of it brighter toward the core, where the hot blue pulsar throbbed like a heart, a little slower than her own.

Sharper than sight, her returning space perceptions began to reveal the planet they had left. The canyon below Freeholm, now a sea of purple shadow. The wide white curve of the ice-cap, 300 kilometers below. A great fountain of shattered ice and broken rock lifting out of a ragged crater where the star-craft had stood, spreading with a strange deliberation, raining slowly back.

A booby trap exploding?

She wondered for a moment before she understood what it was: stuff caught and flung spaceward by leakage from the ship's poorly shielded geodesic field. Appalled by the uncontrollable power of it, she was almost afraid to touch the controls again.

But they were up!

Alive! Climbing fast! As they lifted farther out of the planet's gravity well, her space perceptions cleared. She found Gamma, a faint orange glow toward the human periphery, and the denser clouds around the nebular core. Suddenly, she felt at home in the nebula.

The shockwave walled it, darkness beyond. The core burned ahead, like a fire floating at the center of a cave. Its flames shone red and green, and the dust was its black smoke. She searched for the triple sun. In vain. It was lost somewhere beyond the fire, but she saw the long curve they must trace to bring it into view.

Nerved again, she seized the wheel, pushed it cautiously. Though she felt no motion now, the planet dropped fast. The space ahead was suddenly aglow with orbital remnants of the solar cloud, too much mass for the drive. She had to pull the wheel back and look for open lanes through the cometary drift.

"A mortal mauling, lass!" The whimper of Giles Habibula came faintly from the intercom. "Broke every bone in my blessed body. Left us wrecked to freeze and starve and perish on the wicked ice—"

"We're in space," she told him. "On our way!"

"Lass!" his plaintive wheeze reproached her. "Don't lie to a dying man. I want the fearful truth."

"Data, Mr. Two," Lord Archy's bell voice rang from the intercom. "Reporting confirmation that we are in space."

With a final moan, he fell silent. Feeling out the way with perceptions she might never understand, she searched out a flight path and kept them on it. Star dropped down the ladder well to inspect the craft again. He came back whistling the Legion march.

"Jil, I think—I hope—we really do have a chance! Lord Archy reports no damage to the hull. Giles admits the geo- dynes are running mortal well. No new hazard that I can find. And we're back in non-Newtonian flight."

His haggard head shook slowly.

"Can't quite believe it. I'd been beaten, Jil. Too far down to try anything again. I—" His tired voice caught. "Jil, you've let us live again."

Touched by his emotion, she turned to look at him. Stooped and balding, swaying as if only stark effort kept him straight. Lean and drawn from killing strain, his green Legion cosmo- nalls soiled and torn, black beads of drying blood along an un- tended scratch across his grizzled cheek. A glow of feeling for him warmed her.

"Kynan—" Her own voice quivered. She wanted to reach out to him, to tell him what she felt, yet something checked her. This was not the moment. Afraid to trust her own emo- tion, she tried to smooth it from her tone. "I'm—I'm glad we're together."

Star was never able to fly the craft. To his eyes, to normal human senses, the screen showed only the dust-patched nebular glow, the pulsar's slow, blue beat and a few haloed stars.

Lord Archy had different perceptions. Not so sharp as hers, they were keener than Star's. At times when the dust and gas were not too thick, when no threatening mascon loomed, he could spell her at the consoles.

When Giles Habibula whimpered to be relieved from famine and fatigue, the little robot spelled him too. Driven to the slave rations, he came up from the galley with a pan of yellowish mush for her.

"Horrid slop!" he whined. "A mortal hog would run from it to preserve his precious health, but we must force it down. Aye, lass, we must eat the evil mess to save our blessed lives."

Uncertainly she tried it. The taste was strange, a little bitter, but not much worse than the synthetic protein dehydrates in the Legion space ration. She ate a few more bites and gave the pan back to him. With a wry face, he began spooning at it eagerly.

"Foul swill! But we must stay alive."

Sometimes she needed all her skill to thread them safely through the drift, but there were endless watches when the space ahead seemed almost clear. Without the spur of danger, her own fatigue became a hazard, and she was always glad when Kynan could be with her on the deck.

They talked. She told him more about her grandfather and her childhood at Hawkshead Pass, about the cruel times after Shon Macharn returned, about yawara. He seemed wistfully happy when they recalled their first meetings, back at the Pass.

"Another world." He sighed. "I wish I believed we might someday see it again."

He spoke of his own youth. His father had been lost in space the year he was born. "But not to the flashers." His wan smile showed his feeling for her own loss. "He was racing a one-man starcraft. For a famous trophy the Stars had been winning for three generations."

He had grown up in the homes of aunts and uncles. "All of them Stars. Living in penthouses and villas and mansions. Sportsmen and statesmen and Legion admiral-generals. Cherishing great traditions and enjoying special privilege. Perhaps that sounds like paradise, but the price was high."

"Too steep for me!"

His grin seemed oddly boyish.

"Any Star was expected to be superlative. I never measured up, never really wanted to. Too little muscle for most sports. No talent for music or art. No ambition for distinction in the Hall of Stars. No drive toward the top of my academic classes or genius for high command. Never any brilliant future in the

Legion or outside it. Never many—many friends—"

His low voice had trailed away. Silent for a time, his rueful eyes resting on her, he sighed and shook his head.

"Jil—" His unsteady voice fell lower. "I was married once."

His eyes still clung, dark with an unspoken appeal. "Her name was Keri. She thought I was destined to be another magnificent Star. Both disappointed. She wouldn't live in the nebula and I've never served anywhere else. Ten Legion years since I saw her. She got what's left of my father's estate on old Terra."

He sighed wearily and sadly.

"Jil, I had to tell you this, because you must understand why I can't command us. I never aspired to be a Star. I'm no hero. Just one more man, born no better than the common run. Defeated all my life, because the name kept tossing me into roles too big for me to play."

She saw his jaw twitch beneath the grimy stubble.

"Anyhow, Jil—" Something shook his voice. "That's who I am. Beaten down too long to try a thing that can't—that I know can't be done."

"Thank—" Her own voice quivered. "Thank you, Kynan."

She wanted to take him in her arms, but above her head the conning screen was suddenly lit with a blurred purple-seeming glow that only she could see. She had to turn from him to the wheel.

"Something—something tachyonic!" she whispered. "Coming at us."

She sat his startled glance at the screen, his shrug of dull futility. His thin body sagged. She heard his breath catch, as if he were going to speak. He said nothing, but she saw stark defeat staring dully from his eyes.

Pity for him stabbed her.

She probed the screen, straining her perceptions. Her own eyes could see no more than his. Dark dust and dimly shining gas and the hot, throbbing pulsar. Reaching, she focused and resolved that purple-seeming glow.

"An arrow shape," she told him. "Formed of far-spaced blips. Coming the way this ship did from somewhere closer to the core. I think—I think I can count the blips. Nineteen. All moving together at a trans-Newtonian velocity."

"A flasher fleet." She felt his arm around her. "I'm sorry, Jil."

"They haven't got us yet." She sensed the blips again. "In fact I think they're heading for Ultima, not for our position here. Which would mean they don't yet know we have the ship. They could be stopping there to pick it up."

"But only on their way," he muttered bitterly. "Out toward the channel to hit what's left of the Legion—hit it with geodesic missiles!"

"We'll let them pass us by." She tried to rekindle his dying hope. "Shut down our own drive fields. Let the craft drift like another meteor. And count on the Gyrel luck to lead them on around us."

"Jil!" His hard arm squeezed her to him. "Do you wonder why I love you?"

30

With the drive dead, they floated in free fall.

"Must we lie here, lass?" Giles Habibula shrilled through the intercom. "Hiding like mortal mice from a famished cat? Can't we run?"

"And make a tachyonic wake for them to follow?"

"A mortal wake? Not if they could follow! Hide us, lass! Don't show a sign of precious life."

"I'll check the reactors." Kynan Star swung himself toward the elevator. "To be sure they're fully damped."

"I'll send Lord Archy."

He was below, and she called him on the intercom.

"Affirmative, Miss Three," his gong voice rang back. "We are competent to monitor reactors. We are acting at once."

The ship was still an alien thing, the air still tainted with that cold bog-rot reek. Though she could work the consoles and the conning hood, stranger machines lowered like hostile monsters all around the deck. Worn down by tension long endured, she couldn't help a sense of silent menace, as if the machines were things like the drillers, waiting to take back the craft.

She wanted Star with her.

Yet when she returned to him for human comfort, he looked lonelier than she felt. Hollow-eyed and pale, his face was streaked with grime and long-dried blood, his thin shoulders bent from burdens too heavy, carried too long.

"Better get some sleep," she told him. "I'll wake you if we need—"

The ship had not been equipped for free fall. Turning back from the mike, she reached for a hold-rope that didn't exist and found herself floating off the seat. Snatching for anything, she caught empty air.

"Jil!"

One hand on the console, Star caught her ankle with the other. His chuckle relieved her instant of alarm, and she was laughing at herself as he hauled her toward the deck. Suddenly, his arm tight around her, they were both adrift again.

She clung to him. They spun together very slowly, afloat beside the conning screen. His rough-stubbled chin scratched her face till she found his searching lips. Nothing mattered then, until he pushed her abruptly away.

"Forgive me, Jil!" he whispered. "I never meant—"

"Kynan!" She tugged him toward her. "I love you."

"Jil?" His tired eyes searched her own. "Are you—are you sure?"

She kissed him.

Fulfilled at last, they rested together in the air until she felt a soft collision with a bulkhead. Nudging them toward the conning screen, she searched again for the shadowflasher fleet.

"Still coming," she whispered. "But toward Ultima. Not toward us. We have more time."

Again they swam together, far from pain and danger.

She kissed him and clung while she looked for the fleet.

"Passing us now," she told him. "Nineteen blips, spaced far apart so the fields don't interfere. Nearly a billion kilometers away and flying on toward Ultima. No sign they've seen us."

"Jil, Jil! You can't realize—" Gently he kissed her. "You've made me whole." He held her away from him. Caressing her, his eyes filmed with tears. Wryly, he grinned. "My mind still says we'll never win, but somehow I've caught your hope."

"Anybody!" Giles Habibula's forlorn whine came out of the intercom. "Anybody there? Kynan? Lass? Can't anybody bring a mortal crust to a poor old man before he dies of fearful famine?"

"Giles," Star answered. "You know what's in the galley—"

"Anything!" he wheezed. "Any mortal crumb. Lass! If you're listening, lass, take pity on me. For all the mortal months I've been drifting in this deadly dark, waiting for that fearful fleet to catch us, without a human voice to cheer me or a blessed bite to eat. Even that foul slave swill would be a blessed banquet to me now."

"The fleet is moving on," she assured him. "And Kynan can relieve you."

Star went down to take his place. She stayed to watch the shadowflasher fleet creeping on toward Ultima. Feeling safer as the purple-seeming blips diminished, she asked Star to energize the drive field. At minimum power, they crept on to search for the triple sun.

"A morsel for you, lass." With the internal field still minimal, their feet just brushing the deck, Habibula shuffled very carefully out of the elevator with another pan of mush. "Stinking swill, but we must eat. I know you need it, because I was famished to a bag of mortal bones before that fearful fleet was gone."

"Thank you, Giles."

It tasted better than she expected. The space ahead almost clear again, she let Lord Archy take the console and lay down on the metal deck. The minimal field made it soft enough, and she woke from a dream of swimming with Kynan off a tropical beach her grandfather had spoken fondly of, back on old Terra.

"Information, Miss Three," Lord Archy pealed. "The craft remains on course. We encountered no emergencies, and Pilot Star instructed us not to disturb you."

Oddly, it seemed to her, the alien chronometer ran on Legion time. Ten hours had passed. The last purplish fleck of the enemy fleet was gone when she searched. Back at the console, she pushed up their effective velocity.

Gamma was already lost in the dust behind, and Ultima had become a fading fleck of haze. A crimson-seeming halo had begun to burn around the nebular core. Hard radiation, most of it came from that slow-drumming pulsar, itself the spinning remnant of the most recent supernova.

Its steady flash had grown more and more intense. Though its hot point looked blue to her eyes, the radiation throbbing into the cosmic chaos around it seemed red as waves of blood to her special sense.

"Permission, Miss Three?" Lord Archy came skittering to the deck. "Information, rated significant. We detect increasing gamma radiation from pulsar ahead. Warning, rated urgent. Such radiation rated inimical to human survival. Rated extremely inimical to mutant pilot sense."

"Thank you, Lord Archy."

"Gratitude not required, Miss Three."

"I know the risk," she told him. "I'm trying to steer us around the pulsar, but that triple sun's closer to it than we are now. We'll have to take the radiation, and hope we can all endure it long enough."

"Computing, Miss Three."

He danced on the deck, soundless for a time.

"Reporting, Miss Three." He soared higher. "Referential data on term 'hope' lacks precision required for exact computation. Question, Miss Three. Can you define term 'hope' in present context?"

"I'll try." She reflected, searching for his language. "Hope' refers to direction of action, subject to effect of outside factors. Our direction of action is to find Miss William and stop the shadowflashers. Outside factors include effects of pulsar radiation."

He paused in the air.

"Information, Miss Three. Outside factors rated critical. Computed probable duration of your own useful survival time rated inadequate. Advice, Miss Three. Action should be planned to limit or avoid exposure to gamma radiation."

"I'm afraid it can't be."

"Comment, Miss Three. We compute diminishing probability of successful rescue missioin. We compute increasing probability that pulsar radiation will destroy your ability to pilot the starcraft."

The little image of her head shook slowly in his bright bubble.

"We'll keep hoping."

Silent, he dropped and rose again.

"Continued exposure to pulsar radiation rated inevitable," he pealed at last. "Data held for analysis and possible reference to extended definition of term 'hope.'"

Holding hard to that uncertain term, she kept the starcraft on a long spiral curve around and into the nebular core. Though no normal human sense could detect gamma radiation, she began to feel a vague discomfort. Faint at first, it grew sharper, hotter, until it had become a dull, oppressive pain that seemed somehow inside her head.

She wanted to talk to Star about it. But he was always standing straighter now when he was with her on the deck, his gaunt face grinning easily, his hollowed eyes almost happy. She decided not to shatter his brighter mood.

She found the triple sun.

A close double, both components seeming greenish to her. A fainter single star, distant from the two, blood-red as she perceived it and all but lost in the pulsar's crimson-seeming blaze. Giles Habibula was appalled when she tried to tell him their position and direction.

"Lass, lass! You're flying us to dreadful death. For sweet life's sake, think of me. The medics warned me long ago against the nebula's fearful heart. Their blessed serum can do no good against that mortal radiation. I'll die, lass!

"We'll all die!"

"Perhaps," she told him. "But most of us never even hoped to live forever."

"Jil—" Star came out of the ladder well, bent again and worry-bitten. "Lord Archy says you're hurting from the pulsar radiation."

"I feel it," she told him. "A reddish glow, as I seem to see it. Flashing out of the pulsar."

"Painful?"

"More and more."

His bleak face tightened as if he shared the pain.

"Lord Archy says it will kill my pilot sense," she added. "I can't guess when."

"Jil, I wish—" He checked himself and tried to grin. "At least we have your Gyrel luck! Perhaps, with that, we'll last long enough."

Searching for planets as they neared the triple star, she found none about the close double. The single sun had one.

Power cut, she steered toward it slowly until her eyes could find it on the conning screen, a dim and tiny-seeming disk. It had no moon.

"It's larger than it looks," she told Star. "Though without instruments I can't get specifics. Its rotation is almost locked, its day and year nearly the same. A long day—with no way to measure, I'd guess ten or twelve Legion years."

"No place for life." Star frowned at the faint flicker of its image. "For our sort, anyhow."

As they drew nearer, Habibula came up to squint at the planet.

"A wicked world, by its looks." His wheezy voice turned foreboding. "A fearful problem for us, lass. The whole mortal world to search, and we don't know what we're looking for."

"The laser-maker—"

"Lass!" His bald head shook in sad reproof. "The shadowflashers have the precious laser-maker."

"Not forever." She tried to smile into his dismal gloom. "We can hope a hundred things. Hope she has escaped. Hope her own people have rescued her. Hope they can help us find her. Hope they know some way to fight the flashers."

"Lass, you're lovely!" His yellow face lit briefly. "You've a grand spirit, too." His face faded then, and his head shook again. "But you're too new to the nebula. You ask for mortal miracles."

"If we can make them happen," she said. "With no sign of one just now, I think we have a choice to make. Try for a landing on the planet? Or let Lord Archy try to signal?"

"Signal, lass?" The old man staggered as if she had struck him. "Here in the empire of the fearful flashers? Must we beg them to send another mortal fleet to smash us?"

"How else can we reach Miss William or her people?"

"A fearful risk—"

"We have to take fearful risks. Lord Archy does know their language?"

"He talked to her. Nothing you could hear, most of the time. They both used tach or radio frequencies. Now and then words from a primitive warrior—she rates him a spearman— words mortal hard to understand. She named herself for him."

"I wondered." Jil nodded. "She spoke of an armed rhinoceros—"

"An ancient Terran creature, lass. She asked to see one, but they're long extinct."

Star was standing watch in the generator room when she called for his advice.

"I'd opt for a landing, Jil." His voice seemed wearily grim. "Though neither choice looks good to me. A call from space could set the flashers on us. Down on the planet, Lord Archy can scout it for flashers. If we find none there, we might risk a radio call.

"With minimum power."

"Agreed," she said. "We'll land."

"Don't expect a picnic when we do. A bad world for us. Water will freeze and fall on the night side, piling up in ice kilometers thick. It will boil off again on the sunlight side. Deserts like we never imagined.

"Storms, I imagine, in between.

"A difficult place for organic evolution. Any intelligence evolving there would probably have to be mobile. Migrating around the planet between the desert and the ice. I'd suggest a landing near the sunrise line. The likeliest place to find organic life.

"But no paradise!"

"A wicked bitter thing!" Habibula was wheezing. "If we call, we call the fearful flashers. If we land, we could come down inside a flasher camp. A hard thing, lass, without a mortal drop of anything to brace us for the risk."

"The choice is made," she told him. "Please relieve Kynan and stand by to land us on geodesic power. We're going down to the sunrise line."

31

Jil's space perceptions faded as they slid down into the planet's blinding gravity, until all she could see was the visual display on the conning screen. With a blind spot beneath them, it showed the dimly blazing sky and the whole ice horizon.

"An insane place!" Kynan Star whispered beside her. "We'll need all your Gyrel luck."

She checked their descent at twenty kilometers, cruising toward the sunrise line. With no clouds beneath them here, all they saw was endless ice, broken here and there with a jutting mountain range. Watching for the glow of dawn, she saw a purple flickering far ahead.

"Lightning?" She looked at Star.

"A climate like we've never met." He nodded. "With almost no Coriolis force, we'll have a simple pattern of warm air rising and cold flowing under it. Which would make a permanent storm front just ahead of the sunrise line, crawling around the planet every dozen years."

Worry furrowed his grizzled face.

"If we must risk a landing—"

"I think we must."

The wall of storms rose ahead. Alive with lighting, its cloud towers loomed above their level. She had to climb back to forty kilometers, then to fifty. Even there, its blazing fury boiled up around them. Near thunder rumbled through the hull.

"I don't understand." She frowned at Star. "The storm's coming up to meet us."

"Leakage from our own drive field, I imagine. Lifting the clouds."

Climbing again, into the planet's east, they came out into a sudden dazzle of sunlight. Night and ice lay behind. To north and south, the storm wall ran as far as they could see, white towers blazing. Through broken clouds below, they saw Miss William's world.

Oddly streaked.

A broad zone of rusty red: a jungle of rank leatherweed, Star decided, fed with meltwater. Fading eastward into orange and yellow and brown where floods had stopped and rains had failed. Edged with black where fires had swept.

Farther east, beneath the endless desert day, the hazy horizon was cloudless. The land looked barren. Jagged brown mountains. Vast brown plains slashed with empty canyons. Wide depressions floored with the flat and dazzling white. Lakes and seas, Star said, dried to barren salt.

"No sign of life." He shook his head. "Unless—"

He caught his breath, pointing into the conning screen.

"See that? A long, straight line across the desert. There beyond it, those darker spots. Square-cornered spots, laid in line. They can't be natural features."

"We'll land and look."

Their poorly shielded field caught the ground as they came near. A plume of gravel and broken rock rose to meet them, sank back around the starcraft as it creaked and swayed and came to rest. She heard the muffled crash of stony debris against the hull, and then Star's sigh of relief.

"A neat trick, Jil. I almost wish the Legion had let us try it."

Dense yellow dust had risen all around them. Waiting for it to spread and settle, they searched again for works of the laser-makers.

"A wall?" She pointed. "A double wall?"

It ran across the lifeless, yellow, level plain as far as they could trace it, angled toward the longer wall of storms beneath the eastern sun. Rust-red against the rust-red landscape, it cast a wide black streak of shadow.

"Nothing natural." Star studied it. "Worth a closer look."

"We'll send Lord Archy first."

He was gone for an hour.

"Negative, Miss Three," he reported. "No contact with intelligence. The visible constructions indicate intelligent activity, but not in recent time. We observed no evidence of any life since shockwave passage, except for scattered leather-weed still surviving."

"Is it safe for us to leave the craft?"

"Negative, Miss Three. Environmental hazards rated too severe for human survival. Gravitation nearly twice Terran normal. Radiation intensity rated far beyond human tolerance. Excessive carbon dioxide. Free oxygen near minimum human requirements."

"But nothing to kill us at once?"

"Affirmative, Miss Three."

"How long could we last?"

"Computing, Miss Three." He lay shimmering on the deck. "Results indefinite, Miss Three. Exposure period of one Legion hour rated probably survivable. Exposure period of one Legion day rated probably fatal."

He soared toward her face and fell slowly back.

"Warning, Miss Three. Exposure to radiation causes cumulative damage to mutant pilot sense. We advise against exposure outside the hull."

"We'll keep it brief." She turned to Star. "But I think we must take a look."

"Don't leave us, lass!" Giles Habibula's plaintive wail came out of the intercom. "Trapped in this mortal shadowflasher wreck, down in a fearful alien desert. In air too bad to breathe, under radiation no man could endure.

"If you and Kynan don't come back—"

"We must go," she told him. "You and Lord Archy had better stay aboard. We mustn't risk the secret you share."

"Aye, lass! For the sake of the blessed Legion and the precious secret of AKKA, I'll remain a prisoner on the fearful slaver. And fix myself another mess of that evil swill to save my precious strength and recollection."

She and Star dropped to the lock. A hot wind met them

when it clanged open, edged with the bitter reek of leather-weed. The ground for many meters out was broken stone, lifted when they landed and fallen back to form an accidental barrier.

The heavy gravity caught them. Staggering beneath it, they scrambled out across the boulders to the summit of a barren hillock. Beyond it, flame-yellow dust devils whirled here and there above an endless pain scattered with clumps of dull-red weed. The old wall crossed it half a kilometer ahead.

"Nothing here." Star shrugged. "Shall we go back?"

"Let's look beyond the wall."

They plodded around a long dust dune to a gap in the wall and climbed tumbled stone toward the top. Star paused to scratch with a knife at one shattered brownish block.

"Something artificial. Harder than granite. Weathered here, I couldn't guess how long."

From the top they saw the second wall, parallel, two kilometers away. Both had been ravaged by time and cataclysm. The space between was clogged with broken stone and wind-drifted dust. Shading his eyes, Star squinted along them toward the line of storms.

"An irrigation canal, I imagine. Built to spread meltwater."

Peering along that time-shattered line of stuff harder than stone, Jil tried in vain to picture what sort of things its builders could have been.

"Lord Archy says they weren't mobile," Star was saying. "Which makes their evolution here something of a riddle, because you'd think any kind of life would have to keep up with the sunrise line. However they began, they must have met their symbionts early in the game. Together, they built the irrigation works and carried their culture into space.

"The leatherweed, too!"

He nodded at the dust-drifted thickets.

"I imagine it's native here. Somehow useful to them. Food, maybe, for the symbionts. They scattered it everywhere they went."

"I'd like to know," Jil whispered, "what their world was like. And what finally knocked them out. The shockwave? The flasher attack?"

"Maybe both." He shrugged. "Whatever the story, they're a long time gone."

"But Miss William hoped to find survivors."

She looked at Star.

"Let's try the poles. Mobility might be less essential there."

As they clambered back across the tumbled boulders around the starcraft, she caught a bright-green flash in the rubble their landing had lifted. Pausing to search, she saw the green again, and then a crimson stab.

"A laser-diamond!"

It had vanished before she reached the spot, but she found it when the crimson burned again. An eight-sided crystal a few centimeters long, brightly black and sleek to her touch. She carried it aboard. When Lord Archy skipped to meet them on the command deck, it showered him with sudden laser flashes.

"Is it—living?" she whispered.

"Uncertain, Miss Three. Inquiry rated ambiguous."

"What are the flashes?"

"Signals, Miss Three."

"It's talking?"

"Affirmative, Miss Three. Laser signals rate as communicative speech."

"What is it saying?"

"Correction, Miss Three. He prefers masculine rating. He calls himself Patient Waiting. He states his age in terms we cannot yet translate. He was buried here beneath the ruin of a building which collapsed when the shockwave struck. He expresses gratitude for his liberation."

"Does he know the shadowflashers?"

Lord Archy bounced again, soundlessly.

"Affirmative, Miss Three. He was engaged in the defense of the planet against them until the shockwave demolished all military installations."

"Can he tell us anything about their operations now?"

"Negative, Miss Three. He has been completely isolated."

"Can he help us find his people?"

"Negative, Miss Three. He is uncertain that any survive. He has attempted to call, but his depleted energies limit his range of contact. His attempts have elicited no response."

"Tell him we are searching."

Lord Archy danced.

"He expresses extreme interest in our search, Miss Three. His symbolism rated ambiguous, referred for analysis and possible reference to undefined term 'hope.' He states that existence without his fellows has minimal value to him."

"If he expresses all that," Jil said, "I'll define him as alive. Maybe he can help us. If we come near his people, perhaps he can make contact and guide us to them. Tell him we're going to try the poles.''

They flew the battlecraft south.

A stormy wall of winter met them before they reached the pole, the planet's surface there hidden under cloudy night. Making no attempt to land, they turned back toward the planet's north.

Patient Waiting let them lay him on the console beside the pilot seat, Lord Archy resting near to translate. Laser rays flickered from him now and then, and Jil kept asking what he said.

"Translation uncertain, Miss Three. His signals elicit no response. We have informed him that we now compute only zero point zero four probability of finding other survivors. The symbolism of his response rated ambiguous, filed for analysis and possible reference to term 'despair.' ''

Jil herself was near the same despair. Though her pilot sense was lost here on the planet, the pain of radiation still throbbed in her head. Numb with fatigue after twenty hours on the deck, she asked Star to take the console.

"Please, Jil." He shook his head. "Let's climb back to where you can rest."

"Not with time so short. Kynan, you're a pilot. Down here on the planet, you don't need special instruments or special senses—"

"You don't!" Grinning with a rueful admiration, he shook his head again. "But I was never trained to land an alien ship anywhere.

"Not on geodesic drive!"

"Then I must take us north."

Groggily, dull from that pulsing pain, she lifted them once more above the atmosphere, took them 20,000 kilometers around the salt-mottled curve of the planet's desert face, dropped them back toward the summer pole. The sky there was clear and purple-blue, the low sun cold.

Cautiously, afraid of harm to any survivors, she brought them down to land on a bare granite knob. Before they touched it, the laser-diamond began stabbing green needles toward Lord Archy.

"Information, Miss Three!" He soared high off the deck. "Patient Waiting reports contact."

32

Jil slept.

She knew Star had gone off the starcraft, risking all the planet's hazards to learn what the laser-makers knew. She longed to be with him. But the pulsar's ceaseless stab had grown sharper in her skull. She felt overcome, drained beyond the breaking point.

Wrapped in an evil-odored blanket her father must have used, she slept on the cold steel command deck. Slept through a long and dreadful dream in which she had been trapped in a city of the laser-makers and their strange symbionts when the shockwave struck.

In the hideous chaos of the dream, she thought the shadow-flashers had brought the whole disaster. Rem Brendish was their commander, riding a cliffdriller that came leaping after her like a great black mechanical insect. Above the crash of falling walls, she could hear his nasal whine, mocking her with his satiric ballad of Giles Habibula.

He wanted to plant a parasite in her.

She was searching for Kynan Star. He had gone to the laser-makers to ask for the secret weapon that could kill the flashers. She had to find him, to warn him that the drillers were hiding under cover of the red desert sand, waiting to kill him.

She ran forever through the doomed city, looking for any way out. Brendish was always close behind. Topping towers crashed down around her. The suffocating dust was foul with the evil flasher reek. Ill with that, and with the red agony beating in her brain, she was desperate and all alone.

She never found Kynan Star.

Awake at last, she found her body numb with cold and aching from her hard bed, the radiation pain still throbbing. Yet she gasped with relief to know that Brendish and the shockwave had been a dream.

Stiff and shivering, she sat up on the deck.

"Information, Miss Three," Lord Archy pealed. "The Enside. "Pilot Star is waiting where we found the laser-makers. He asks if you will join him."

"Are they near?"

"Affirmative, Miss Three. The colony is small. Located two point seven kilometers away."

"Will you show me the way?"

"Affirmative, Miss Three."

Habibula was still aboard. When she called, he answered from the galley.

"A haunted planet, lass! Too many things have died here. Aye, a mortal evil world! I've been trying to distill something to dull its wicked fangs, but this foul swill refuses to ferment."

They left him aboard alone, moaning into the intercom.

Lord Archy skipped ahead with seeming eagerness to show the way, and Jil followed him off the barren knob and down along a narrow valley that wound between naked granite bluffs. Fighting the heavy gravity, she was breathing hard and damp with sweat before they came up to star.

"Information, Miss Three," Lord Archy pealed. "The Enduring Ones greet you."

She looked for them. Star was kneeling on dry gravel in a tiny hollow. On the palm of one bruised and grimy hand, he held the small black crystal named Patient Waiting. Searching around him for any other laser-makers, she found only naked slopes of age-worn stone.

"Where?" Bewildered, she turned back to Lord Archy. "I don't see—"

Lord Archy rolled ahead to where Star knelt.

"Here, Miss Three."

Star rose to meet her.

"Jil!" A quick concern shadowed his grin. "Didn't you rest?"

"A hard bed," she told him. "I had bad dreams. But Lord Archy says you've found the laser-makers—"

"Here at our feet."

She saw them then. A tiny cluster of dusty dome shapes, clinging to the granite and blending into its dull-gray color. Hardly half a meter wide, they were wrinkled with low ridges that carried blunt black spines.

She shook her head, astonished.

"Surprised me, too." He grinned. "I'd expected more laser crystals or something like Miss William's said to be. But Lord Archy tells me she's a child. The adults have to fix themselves to something solid before they lose mobility."

"They look"—she shook her head, staring blankly down at them—"look like plants."

"Comment, Miss Three." Shimmering in the wintry sunlight, Lord Archy sailed out above them. "Term 'plant' rated nondenotative except in reference to Terran organisms. This planet, which Elder Wisdom calls Birth World, evolved unusual vehicles for intelligence."

"Intelligence?" She frowned. "How can these things have brains?"

"Comment, Miss Three. Term 'brain' rated nondenotative here. Definitions of intelligence refer to function, not to structure."

"Evolved early," Star added. "We've been getting a little of their history. Life was old here, Elder Wisdom tells us, long before the triple sun drifted into the nebular cloud. Survival here was never easy. Most higher forms migrated with the sunrise to stay alive.

"The Enduring Ones endured. Adapted. Unable to move themselves, they found mobile symbionts. With nothing like the human brain, they evolved the diamond lasers as more compact and permanent analogues. Evolved their cycle of transformations.

"Three stages of life."

"Some slight mobility when they are young. Miss William is what they call a young bud—youthful on their scale of time.

Reproduction by something like budding. Nothing parallel to human sex, but Lord Archy refers to all the young as female.

"The adults call themselves male—I don't know why. They're what we see here. All mobility lost. Almost immortal when they had the symbionts. Nearly defenseless now, even against flood and fire.

"The diamonds are a third stage. Grown in the adults—that must take geologic ages. Vehicles for mind and organs of communication. Surviving even after the adult stage dies. As nearly eternal as anything can be in our universe.

"Here's Elder Wisdom, and his third stage growing."

He knelt again to point into the crown of the largest clinging thing. Bending, she found a black spike projecting from a little pit between the radiating rows of spines. A red flash darted from it toward the black crystal in his hand.

"I was asking when the shockwave hit, but Lord Archy can't yet translate their terms for time—"

He paused to watch sudden green laser arrows flashing back and forth between that emerging crystal point and the crystal in his hand. Lord Archy hovered closer, and their final needles stabbed his silvery curve.

"What's this?" she whispered. "Are they attacking—"

"Negative, Miss Three. Eternal Wisdom is requesting data on Miss William. She is his descendant. We translate his term for her as bud-child's bud-child.

"He informs us that she was lost somewhere beyond the nebular core, when her symbiont died from shockwave radiation. She had been on a mission to observe the flashers and plan defenses against them. He wishes to know how Dr. One came to find her, and why she was chosen to share the supreme secret of our own defense."

She nodded, feeling strange.

"Tell him what you can."

Green needles burned again.

"Elder Wisdom is expressing gratitude, Miss Three, for the rescue of Miss William. We have informed him that gratitude is not required."

Jil was recalling the magic crystal she had treasured once, and all the others like it. Baffling riddles to human science. Most of them finally exported to Terra for women to wear as novelty pendants. Gratitude, she thought, had never been required.

Lord Archy had dropped to alight on the spiny crown of Elder Wisdom's nearest neighbor. Enduring the crushing drag of gravity, the icy air that failed to fill her lungs, the thrusting pain in her head, she knelt to watch the play of silent light between him and the crystals.

"Symbiosis!"

Star's awed face looked boyish, as if wonder had swept all trouble away.

"Alone, the laser-makers were almost bodiless. The symbionts nearly brainless. Together, they were whole. Adapting to each other, they came to dominate the planet. Invented technology. Spread their culture across the cluster.

"Before the shockwave drove the flashers out of the nebular core. They'd evolved in space, in molecular clouds, not on any planet. Became parasites as the nebula condensed and the plasma clouds got too hot for their young. In flight themselves because the shockwave was killing their own organic hosts.

"Elder Wisdom says his people found no defense against the flashers. The symbionts were easy victims, and their inter-stellar culture was already collapsing when the shockwave got here.

"It finished the symbionts—but also paralyzed the flashers. Their adults are still immune to radiation. But, lacking hosts, they couldn't breed. Not till Ben Gyrel opened up the nebula, and they learned to lay their eggs in men.

"The Enduring Ones themselves weren't hurt by radiation. Yet, without the symbionts, they're crippled terribly. Even here on Birth World, they're dying out. Half a dozen other colonies scattered around this pole. None at the other. Their budding has stopped. Only three or four, like Elder Wisdom, growing into the diamond phase.

"Elder Wisdom says they're done for."

Jil had knelt beside him. Shivering in the windless chill, she leaned to look closer at the tiny, spiny dome shapes. They looked a little like the cactus plant her mother had set out one spring, trying to bring a bit of Terran life to the hard clay yard at Hawkshead Pass. Even before the nebular winter, it had withered and died.

A solemn pity touched her, to think that these hapless things were the last remnant of a race so old and once so great, rulers once of worlds all around the nebula, but disabled now, de-fenseless and doomed.

As mankind would be—

Stiffly she staggered erect. Her lungs had to toil too hard for oxygen, and the radiation pain kept throbbing until she longed to reach inside her head and tear it out. A sense of gray futility dragged at her, as heavy as the savage gravity.

She set her jaws against it.

"Can they help us?" Swaying, her whole body aching, she whispered that appeal to Star. "Is there anything—"

"Maybe." He bent to frown at the crystal in his hand. "We've been asking two questions. Can they make contact with Miss William? Do they have any weapon or defense against the shadowflashers? The answers are tantalizing."

She dropped back beside him to listen.

"Miss William did reach them while the *Purple Empress* was passing near. A tach contact, poor and soon broken. But she was able to tell them that the flashers were headed toward a planet she calls Opal Globe. Once a major center of the lost empire. Now apparently a flasher strong point."

"What did she say?"

"Not much. Her vital resources were too nearly gone. She was still a prisoner. Under torture and totally desperate. We're trying now to reach her again. No luck yet."

"Their weapon?"

"They have no weapon. Never did. It would have to be tach, Elder Wisdom says. Because nothing Newtonian can hurt the flashers. Evolved out of those space clouds, they're more energy than matter. The Enduring Ones were working on a tachyonic amplifier, meant to be a weapon, when the shockwave stopped everything."

"If the weapon never existed"—she felt her body sagging to the pitiless gravity—"how can they help us?"

Star shook his head, his awed elation fading.

"I don't know. We're still asking—"

33

They waited.

The low sun hung motionless. No wind stirred. No sound came from the dusty cactus shapes or the silver robot floating over them. Shivering, recalling Lord Archy's computation that one Legion day here could kill her, Jil reflected that a human lifetime would be a very brief instant to the Eternal Ones.

"Information, Miss Three."

Lord Archy was lifting in a burst of laser needles.

"The Eternal Ones report analysis of published data on AKKA. With certainty undefined, they rate it a tachyonic instrumentality."

"Can it—could it kill the flashers?"

"Data lacking, Miss Three. Elder Wisdom uses untranslated terms filed for comparison to undefined term 'hope.'"

"What does he hope?"

"Terms uncertain, Miss Three. Indicated reference to uncomputed probability that AKKA might trigger a lethal increase in unstable tach force components in all shadowflashers within range."

"What would be the range?"

"Data unavailable, Miss Three."

"Room for hope." She looked at Star. "A non-Newtonian effect could have enormous range."

"Hope!" Star muttered the word with a bleak irony that surprised her.

"We've been exposed too long. Let's get back aboard."

"We should be here," she said. "If they do reach Miss William."

He leaned to lay Patient Waiting on a granite jut near Elder Wisdom. They sat on a hard stone ledge. And time seemed suspended, until laser lances exploded from Patient Waiting. Answers stabbed from Elder Wisdom.

"Information, Miss Three." Lord Archy lifted. "Reporting contact with Miss William."

"So she's alive!" Jil whispered. "Can she tell us where?"

"Affirmative, Miss Three. The Killer Things have carried her to the old city called Shining Light on the planet Opal Globe."

"Can she—can she possibly escape?"

"Negative, Miss Three. Though she has endured everything, her vital resources are depleted. She can do no more."

"So we must try to reach her." She looked at Star and flinched from his bone-deep exhaustion. "What can she tell us about her situation now?"

"Her jailor is a man. She says he has most traitorously corrupted the Legion of the realm. He is holding her in an ancient fortress built by the Enduring Ones, when Shining Light was the central metropolis of their interstellar culture. The Killer Things have reclaimed it, to make it the capital of their slave empire."

"What do they want?"

"The secret of AKKA. They fear the weapon and hope to find a defense against it."

"Tell her we're on our way to try to save her."

"Impossible, Miss Three. The contact was very brief. Her tach capacity has been gravely weakened, and the Enduring Ones estimate zero probability that they can reach her again."

"At least"—her voice shook when she looked back into Star's worn and hopeless face—"we'll die trying."

"Literally—" He caught himself, with a wry little grin. "Sorry, Jil. I'll be with you to the end."

"Additional data, Miss Three. Miss William informed us

that Mr. Brendish was mocking her with news that we tried to follow on their wrecked battlecraft."

"So they know?" Star's grizzled face turned bleaker. "They'll have our welcome ready."

"Affirmative, Pilot Star. We compute high probability that flashers are anticipating our arrival. Similar data, less precisely computed, caused Miss William to expect her own early termination. As the contact concluded, she expressed farewell. She begged us not to fear for her, seeing that death, a necessary end, will come when it will come."

"Tell the Enduring Ones we'll try to get there before that end does come."

Silent for a moment, Lord Archy sank again toward the black-spined domes. Red and green blazed again.

"Message continues, Miss Three. Addressed to you and Pilot Star in terms suggesting those of human emotion. Elder Wisdom speaks of Miss William as his last surviving bud descendant. However—"

The gong voice broke off abruptly. Jil watched the silver bubble dive toward that flashing diamond point, climb back toward her.

"Advice, Miss Three. Rated urgent. Elder Wisdom advises against any rescue effort. Although his desire for her safe release is rated intense, the Enduring Ones have concluded that the chance of saving her is far smaller than the chance that we will be destroyed."

"Thank them," she said, "for their concern. But tell them we're going to try. Ask him how we can reach Opal Globe. How we can locate the city and the fortress. How we can reach Miss William."

Lord Archy sank back to the rock, and the laser needles flickered again.

"Data lacking, Miss Three," he pealed at last. "The Eternal Ones question our ability to reach Opal Globe. They question our ability to locate the prison or Miss William."

"Ask them to assume we can. Request every fact they know what might be useful to us."

"Request transmitted, Miss Three."

No answer flashed.

Waiting, Jil wished for some yawara move against the savage gravity. Her breasts ached from it. The icy air had stirred a little, sharp with bitter scents of dust and leatherweed, but still she couldn't breathe deeply enough. Giddy for a moment when she turned her head to look behind them, she shuddered to an eerie awareness of overwhelming strangeness.

A world never meant for men. The shadowflasher battle-craft, looming like a huge black balloon above the old gray cliffs behind them. The empty sky, purple-black and oddly peaceful. The few dusty black-spined cactus shapes clinging to the timeworn stone.

"Let's get to the ship." Star caught her numb hand. "While we can."

"Not yet."

She watched Lord Archy. Silent, he rested delicately on his granite perch, quivering silver skin reflecting the sun in a dancing point. Needles flickered between the Eternal Ones, seldom to him.

"What are they saying?"

"Translation difficult, Miss Three. Patient Waiting informs us that they are engaged in an ancient ceremonial ritual of farewell which honors one no longer able to endure. If we wish to respect the memory of Miss William, we ought not to interrupt it."

"Does that mean she's dead?"

"Comment, Miss Three. We report translation difficulty with term 'death.' The Enduring Ones discover no acceptable semantic equivalent. They prefer another term, which we translate as third-stage withdrawal."

"What does that mean?"

"Definition uncertain, Miss Three. We have requested clarification. Elder Wisdom states that condition of third-stage withdrawal is undefined, because those forced into it so seldom return."

"We need facts," she told him. "Any facts to help us reach her."

"Need them now," Star muttered. "We've been here too long."

Lord Archy lay silent until the lasers flashed again.

"Ritual completed," he pealed, "but the Eternal Ones report no data useful to us. Miss William was forced to with-draw before she had transmitted precise location of her place of confinement."

"But you can identify the planet?"

"Affirmative, Miss Three."

"Can you find how to get there?"

"Elder Wisdom informs us that Opal Globes orbits the nearest star in the direction of the pulsar. It is the third planet of seven. It has three major continents. Two at the poles are unsuitable for human life. The place called Shining Light is at the summit of a large extinct volcano on the third continent. The location is on the equator, near the west coast."

"Thank them," she whispered. "Tell them we must try to set Miss William free."

He skipped back to the Enduring Ones.

"They are not surprised, Miss Three. They respect our decision as much as they deplore the heavy odds against us. They urge us to leave Birth World before we suffer further harm, and they wish us well."

"Come!" Star muttered. "We've suffered enough."

Jil stood a moment longer, her blue hand lifted in farewell to the Enduring Ones in their dusty little cluster. Forlorn, doomed, strange in shape and mind, yet somehow kin. When a green ray lanced from Patient Waiting toward her heart, she wondered if they had understood her gesture.

34

Less than three kilometers, the climb took forever.

"Lass, you stayed too mortal long!"

Giles Habibula was waiting in the lock when they toiled up the last granite ridge. Panting for his own breath, he hauled her into the warmth of the starcraft and the shelter of its internal field.

"We've located Miss William," she told him. "On a flasher planet, in toward the pulsar—"

"For sweet life's sake!" His wheezy gasp cut her off. "We're already in too mortal far, with the wicked radiation boiling our blood and the black vampires swarming all around us. Lass, there's got to be a limit—"

"We aren't there yet."

They climbed back to space.

Her pilot sense returned, and Lord Archy helped her identify the shadowflasher sun. Haloed in yellow-red dust, hanging just above the slow-blinking pulsar, it beckoned them toward the crimson-seeming glow of the nebular core.

"For precious sake, don't drive us too fast!" Habibula's

moan came over the intercom when she asked for added thrust. "Or too mortal slow! We must let the fearful flashers take us for another of themselves."

"A problem, Giles," she told him. "We don't know the flasher traffic rules. A bigger problem, when we get there: finding Miss William.

"We must make a normal approach to the planet," she told Kynan. "If we can guess what the flasher flight rules would call for. Land if we can on or near that dead volcano where the fortress is.

"By night, I should think."

"But always with hope!" A slow grin warmed his worn face. "Jil—Jil!" His breathless whisper quivered. "I love your gift for hope."

She felt her eyes fill with tears.

"A gift I lost too long ago." He reached to stroke her hair, and she felt the tremor of his hand. "You're so splendid, Jil. Too fine to toss your life away."

Wordlessly, she kissed him.

They flew on into the nebula.

The pulsar winked dead ahead. A hot blue point on the conning screen, but ringed with spreading waves of crimson to her mutant sense of space. Waves of pain inside her skull. Always stronger, redder, harder to endure, and still she pushed them on.

She kept to the command deck. Lord Archy took the console when the space ahead seemed open enough, but that was seldom. She was worn and heavy-eyed from endless duty before they came near enough to let her find Opal Globe.

The third of seven major planets swimming through the sun's yellow dust halo. She watched it turn as they approached, spinning nearly twice in a Terran day. The polar continents showed only a featureless glare of ice. A broad equatorial cloud belt was unbroken, except for a single high volcanic summit.

Shining Light.

She wondered why the laser-makers had called it that, because the dead crater was a wide black disk against dazzling cloud. Descending on a long spiral as the planet spun, she followed the caldera down into the darkness.

Star stood beside her. Feeling him before she saw or heard him, she wondered for an instant if emotion had somehow tuned her special senses to him. Her breath came faster, but she had time for only a glance.

"Jil!" His whisper startled her. "See that?"

His vision now as keen as her own, he was pointing at a long dim glow beneath the cloud belt. It ran north and south from near the old volcano, reaching toward both poles as far as she could follow.

"Let's ask Lord Archy what it is."

The silver robot wheeled beneath the conning screen.

"Data, Miss Three. We detect a powerful energy flux covering an extended spectrum. Analysis indicates light, heat, harder radiation, sonic vibration."

"What's the source?"

"Unknown, Miss Three."

"Can you guess?"

"Filed definitions of term 'guess' rated inadequate, Miss Three. Attempting to compute nature of the source, we find zero point eight nine probability that it is industrial production."

"Their military base." Star nodded, tired eyes narrowed. "Where their slaves are building the battlecraft and the weapons to enslave—"

Alarms had exploded. Red lights flashed at the signal center. A voice—a dreadful voice—barked out of the speakers. More animal than human, it seemed as strangely hollow and flat as Shon Macharn's had been when he first came out of the nebula, and it gobbled sounds she had never heard.

"Miss Three!" Lord Archy bounded toward the signal station. "We are receiving a beamed tachyonic signal."

"Can you translate it?"

"Negative, Miss Three. Do you wish to acknowledge?"

"Negative," she told him. "I suppose they're asking for identification. We can only hope they don't decide to fire."

"Comment, Miss Three. We confirm high probability that shadowflasher space control is requesting flight information. Our definitions of term 'hope' are rated inadequate, but we confirm high probability that the shadowflasher battlecraft is armed with non-Newtonian missiles."

"We'll ignore the signal," she said. "Please stop it."

He stilled that uncanny gobble, and they dropped as fast as she dared toward the night-veiled caldera. As her space perceptions dimmed, she tried to map the summit in her mind. The age-crumbled ring wall, a hundred kilometers across. On the level plain inside, a pattern of wide rectangles.

"Kynan, the city!"

She glanced aside at Star and felt distressed to see him look so stooped and worn, so old, so unsure of himself and their venture and the chances of humanity. She ached to comfort him, as if he had been a frightened child, but this was no time for tenderness.

"I never—never imagined!" She tried to steady her uncertain voice. "It's gigantic! Avenues a kilometer wide. Buildings still higher. It fills the whole crater."

Hollowed eyes on the conning screen, he said nothing for a moment. She heard him catch his breath, saw his lean frame draw straighter, felt his weary effort to recover himself.

"Too big for us." He grinned bleakly at her and frowned again at the screen. "The Enduring Ones had quite an empire, if this was their metropolis. If we have to search it for Miss William, I was hoping for something smaller."

At first only a vague dark spot on the screen, the caldera gained size and detail as they dropped, until at last the cliff-ringed city grid began to emerge from the greenish nebular glow, the slopes of the old volcano slanting down toward the clouds all around it.

"It is too large to search." She nodded at Star. "Shall we try to call?"

"I think we must."

"Lord Archy, please try to reach Miss William by radio. Beam your signal toward the central city. Use no more power than you must."

"Command accepted, Miss Three."

Soundless, he bounced on the deck for a time that seemed endless, then rolled slowly toward her.

"No response, Miss Three."

"No surprise!" Star shrugged, his body wearily bent. "There may never be."

"So we must land—"

"If the flashers let us!"

The city grid had spread beneath them, wide avenues drawn straight from cliff to cliff across it. The buildings were vast looming masses, shapeless in the dimness.

"Lights!" He pointed. "There!"

The dark plain swelled higher toward the center of the old

caldera, where the dying volcano must have piled up an inner peak. The immense central building was a many-sided polygon, with lower domes spaced around it. The whole complex was ringed with a pale-gray glow, with scattered brighter glints moving on it.

"A street, do you think? Traffic on it?"

"Perhaps." He nodded. "What would that be?"

She followed his arm to the great, central peak. Flecks of light crept there, and among them she began to make out tall, black balloon shapes, two drifting slowly upward.

"Starcraft!"

"Taking off now," he muttered. "Coming up to inquire—"

"Permission, Miss Three." Lord Archy soared off the deck. "Reporting a radio signal beamed from the starport below us. Not, however, from Miss William."

"May we hear it?"

"Affirmative, Miss Three."

He produced a gabble of hoots and croaks and clucks that left her shuddering.

"Can you translate?"

"Negative, Miss Three."

"But the voice is human?"

"Affirmative, Miss Three. The language, however, resembles none we know. Its sounds appear unsuited for human organs of speech."

"Let's get down." She looked at Star. "Where?"

He frowned into the conning screen.

"Most of the city is dark. Ruins, I'd guess, that the flashers haven't occupied. Maybe places where we might hide—"

"Information, Miss Three," Lord Archy broke in. "Receiving signals beamed from two shadowflasher craft rising from starport and now accelerating toward us."

"Let's get down," Jil whispered. "If we can!"

35

Jil dived the battlecraft into the dark caldera.

Star stood near her on the deck. Glancing at him, she found his haggard eyes fixed blankly on the conning screen, his grizzled face drawn taut with desperation.

Aware of her look, he shrugged and tried to grin. She heard him catch his breath as if to speak, but all he did was shake his head.

"I know it's a pretty grim gamble," she told him. "All we can do is play the best game we can."

She turned back to the dimmed conning screen. The shadowy squares beneath were swelling fast. Vague shapes had begun to swim out of the pale nebular glow. Shattered towers, broken walls, vast piles of time-crumbled masonry. Columned avenues clogged with mountainous ruin.

"Played by rules we have to guess." Eyes and mind on those emerging mysteries, she spoke half absently. "Our first guess is where they hold Miss William."

"She was in a fortress when her people made that last contact. One built before the shockwave hit. Where?" He scowled at the screen. "With no better clue, we might pick that building with their starport on the roof."

She opened the intercom.

"Giles, we're coming down. Fast! Landing likely rough. Enemy craft closing in. We'll have to get out of the ship before they take us. Man the geodynes till we're on the ground, then meet us at the air lock."

"For life's sake, lass! Think of my mortal age! You can't ask me to play fearful games of cat and mouse with man-eating monsters in a demon-haunted world murdered a million years ago—"

"Sorry, Giles. Stand by."

She turned to Star.

"We'll need supplies."

"If we live that long." He gave her a wan, wry grin. "I'll collect what I can carry and join you at the lock."

She had lost the flasher craft. When she found them again, faint dark points on the screen, they were both high above her, separating. One swung as if to circle her. The other drove straight in.

"A radio signal, Miss Three." Lord Archy skipped toward her. "From the approaching ship."

"Can you understand it?"

"Affirmative, Miss Three. We replicate the signal." His pealing voice became hoarsely human, shouting toneless words. "Base Command to rebel slaves aboard Type Nine battle transport. Be advised that rebellion is always brief and always results in the termination of the rebel through maximal penalty stimulation.

"Be advised that no rebel slave has ever been able to injure his master guest. If you wish to escape terminal torture, you will enter normal traffic pattern, land as ordered and leave the transport. Base Command orders you to signal immediate compliance—"

"That's enough," Jil broke in.

The bell tone returned.

"Agreed, Miss Three. We compute no advantage from compliance."

She veered away from the diving flasher craft toward the long slope of that central elevation. Shadow-clotted ruin rushed to meet them. She picked a dark cross street for the landing, lost it again as it slid into the blind spot beneath them.

They came down blind. Dark masses of age-shattered masonry, swelling into the screen, were erased again by clouds of dust and debris lifted by their own unshielded field. With every sense blocked, she had to let them fall. Panic clutched her for an instant, until she felt the deck rock and shudder.

"Down!" Star whispered. "Now the game begins."

She cut their braking thrust.

"Lass, lass!" She heard Habibula gasping over the intercom. "You're smashing us to mortal whey—"

Roaring boulders drowned his voice, raining back against the hull. Strained metal rang. The whole craft tilted, quivered to a stop, settled again.

Stillness fell.

"Giles, we're down," she called. "Kill propulsion fields."

"Aye, lass! I know we're down. In a nest of frightful vipers—"

"Meet us at the lock."

She dropped down the ladder well. Lord Archy came an instant later, a flash of spilled quicksilver. Star followed, wearing a tight backpack, a water bag slung from his shoulder. They had to wait for Habibula, who emerged at last from the elevator, stumbling under an enormous bale too hastily tied and spilling flasher ration bricks. They waited again for the lock to cycle.

"They're taking us for rebel slaves," Jil whispered. "Briefly free the way my father was. They're assuming that the master guests—the larval things—will soon regain control. With luck, that error could give us a few more minutes.

"Time to get away from the craft."

The valve clanged open.

"Air breathable, Miss Three." Lord Archy rolled ahead. "Gravity point nine Terran standard—"

Jil jumped after him, Star close behind. A cold wind struck her, laden with the dusty bitterness of leatherweed and faintly tainted with the flasher stink. Flung off balance by the different gravity, she reeled into the shattered debris pulled up and dropped again by their geodesic field.

"Jil?" Star caught her arm. "Hurt?"

"Not yet. But we must move."

"Dear life, lass!"

They helped Habibula out of the lock.

"I'm too mortal old—"

They stumbled off into the tangle of broken stone. The ship loomed behind them, a huge black balloon against the dusky nebular glow. Ahead a dark wall rose almost to the gloomy zenith.

"Better duck!" Star gasped.

A vast black shadow slid over the wall. It covered the narrow streak of sky. A howling storm came behind it. Suddenly they were weightless, drifting, clutching at nothing. She saw Habibula's bundle lifted from his back. It came apart, spilling in the air.

In another moment they were falling back into choking dust. The roaring wind was already subsiding, but strange thunder still rumbled among the dark towers around them, receding into the sky. Habibula was on his knees, wheezing for breath and scrabbling for his scattered ration bricks.

"Lord of space, what was that?"

"The flasher starcraft." Star mopped sand off his face. "Buzzing us. The field drag picked us up."

"Help me lass, for sweet life's sake," Habibula begged. "All our precious food lost in these mortal rocks. We'll die of mortal hunger—"

"We've got nearer dangers, Giles." Star helped her pull him upright. "Let's look for cover while we can."

They stumbled toward the wall. Even away from the wreck, the going was hardly easier. Shattered and upheaved by unmeasured ages, the ancient pavement was drifted high with bare dust dunes, deltaed with dry mud from long-gone floods and blocked with fallen ruin.

"Take pity, lass!" Habibula gasped. "Take pity on a luckless victim of evil mischance, too mortal old—"

Thunder drummed again in the dully glowing sky. Closer, something crashed. Blue light exploded above, abrupt and blinding.

"Freeze!" Star whispered.

They stopped where they were. Blinking and squinting against that cruel blue glare, Jil looked ahead. The ruin-walled avenue marched on until darkness swallowed it. Towering steep-stepped pyramids. Looming shapes she had no name for, all crumbling, toppled, shattered. She shivered, as if a killing wind out of time had blown on the nape of her neck.

What kind of beings had the symbiotic builders been? Things mightier than men? What mystic kinship had linked them to that tiny cluster of black-spined things clinging to the walls of their bare granite hollow on Birth World? The contrast stunned her, the term "symbiosis" too abstract to illuminate its mystery.

"Lass!" Habibula gripped her arm, voice and fingers trembling. "A blessed door! A precious refuge from our fearful hunters."

That savage glare was abruptly gone. The blackness left her blind. When shapes returned in the nebular gloom, she found the door. A dark archway in the wall ahead. They clambered toward it, up a delta of hard clay and broken stone scattered with stunted leatherweed.

It was farther than she thought, taller than it had seemed, the work of time-drowned giants. Stumbling over the rubble banks that clogged it, they pushed on into silent blackness until Habibula gasped: "Mercy, lass! I'm falling on my mortal face. Let Lord Archy give us a spark of precious light."

"Miss Three, do you require light?"

"If you can make it. Just enough to show our way."

Suddenly glowing, he climbed enough to illuminate the walls around them. Walls of an arched, enormous hall. Water had run down it, carving a winding channel through banks of red mud, dry now and mixed with glittering shards like broken glass. Scrambling up the channel, they came out into a black cavern, too vast for the robot's glow to reveal any limits.

"I wonder—" Star whispered. "What were they? The builders of all this?"

"I can't imagine"—Jil had stopped, shivering—"what they were. Or how they died."

Frowning at her through the gloom, Star shook his head. "If they could build all this, they should have had a chance."

"The flashers must have struck by stealth," she whispered. "And the shockwave must have come too fast—"

She peered into the shadows.

"This building? What could it have been?"

Star shrugged. They pushed on. Lord Archy climbed higher, lighting more of the dusty rubble. It covered the enormous floor as far as they could see. Here most of it was brittle, diamond-glinting stuff, crunching under their boots like breaking glass.

Far across it, they reached a curving line of great, black rectangular blocks that stood a dozen meters apart. They were taller than Jil's head, but she could see mounds of rubble glittering on them.

Crystal fragments—but of what?

"It's all too old," Habibula moaned. "Too mortal old!"

Calling to Lord Archy for more light, she led them through an alley between two huge blocks.

"Far enough!"

From where they stood, the floor sloped into a sudden funnel. Rows of the great blocks ringed it, stepping steeply down. Crystal rubble piled them, with never a hint of what it had been. At the center, a hundred meters below their level, a black pit yawned.

Circular, vast, bottomless.

"What is it, lass?"

She shook her head.

"Miss Three!" Lord Archy had dimmed, dropping swiftly toward them. "Data rated urgent. We detect location of Miss William."

"Where is she?"

"Ahead, Miss Three. Inside the building on the mountain summit."

"Can she tell us how to reach and help her?"

"Negative, Miss Three. She remains in third-stage withdrawal."

"How did you find her?"

"Information, Miss Three. We detect extremely weak tachyonic echo from her inactivated mind. It reveals her location and the stage of her withdrawal. Nothing further."

"But you can guide us toward her?"

"Conditional affirmative, Miss Three. Tachyonic echo feeble and irregular."

"Can you wake her?" Star rasped. "If we do get there?

"Negative, Pilot Star. Probability of success, computed from all known data, rated zero."

36

Habibula said he was hungry.

Sitting on something like shattered glass piled against a great black block that might have been an altar to some dead god, they shared hard fragments of a flasher ration brick and icy water from the bag Star had brought.

"Trapped," Star muttered. "We can't go back. The ruins behind us must be crawling with them now—"

"Permission, Miss Three." Lord Archy bounded higher. "We report a source of daylight."

With a lift from Star, Jil scrambled to the top of the block and found a tiny fleck of light near their level, far beyond that black, yawning pit.

"A way out?"

"A way we can try."

Crunching over that brittle crystal stuff, groping through gloomy alleys between the empty altar stones—if perhaps the place had been a temple—they got safely past the pit. The gray fleck became a long slope of shattered debris, dimly lit from above and beyond. Climbing, they came through a jagged hole in the building wall, out at last into dazzling day.

They stood on the gravel of a dry stream, which must have broken long ago through the wall into the building. A jungle of rust-red leatherweed fringed its banks, sloping steeply for several kilometers up to a ragged line of ruined walls and towers.

"The mountain." Star shaded his eyes to study the summit. "The flasher fortress—"

"Information, Miss Three." Lord Archy dropped out of the air. "Craft coming overhead."

Crouching back into the passage, they watched the searching ship. A great, black teardrop shape, it came silently but fast, flying low along the jungle edge. Jil swayed to the sudden haul and fall of its propulsion field. It left her giddy and confused, battered by its sonic crash, her sense of direction blurred.

"Hunting us down!" Habibula gasped. "Like mortal rats."

She staggered on the rubble, fighting to recover.

"Still hunting!" she gasped. "They haven't got us yet."

They climbed out of the dry ravine and into the bitter-scented leatherweed, freezing under its cover when the flasher craft came over them again. The long climb kept them weak and breathless, and the rapid sun had passed its zenith before they reached the crest.

The old battlements stopped them there.

"Lass!" Habibula puffed. "Do you take us for mortal—mortal supermen?"

"Only for the last human hope."

They clambered around the mountain in the shadow of a frowning overhang for most of the rest of the day, scrambling back down the slope for cover when patrol craft passed. The cold sun was low before they reached a break, a jagged gap fifty meters wide.

"Maybe knocked out by a meteorite."

They climbed through the gap into a ranker belt of leatherweed. Beyond that, they came at last to the edge of the vast avenue they had seen from space, circling the central citadel. Any damage here had been repaired. The wide pavement was glassy smooth and glaring white. Creeping as near as they dared under the last fringe of dusty leatherweed, they saw traffic moving.

"The blessed Legion!" Habibula whispered. "Here in time to save us!"

Jil stared. For men, in fact, were moving on the pavement. Men in Legion green, driving Legion fighting machines. She saw a Legion missile launcher. A Legion laser gun, splotched with camouflage that made it seem to leap and change. Legion staff triphibians. Armored Legion troop transports. They came and went through wide doorways under the white domes beyond the white roadway. She blinked at them and shook her head.

"Slaves," she said. "Flasher slaves."

"In captured equipment," Star muttered. "Maybe moving now into positions against us—"

"Don't say that!" Habibula groaned. "I've grown too mortal old to take such frightful shocks."

"We've come a long way, Giles." Trying to smile, she raised herself to point across the pavement. "Here's the flasher capital. The circle of domes. The old fortress inside it, with the starport on the roof—"

"Not really on the roof." Star shook his head, pointing at a black balloon shape lifting above another line of low, black cliffs beyond the white shining domes and the frowning inner walls. "Though it looked that way from space. The starport's on the central peak."

"A lot of kilometers around it." Jil turned to the robot. "Lord Archy, will you try to contact Miss William again?"

"Attempting contact, Miss Three." He lay silent, a quicksilver shimmer on the bitter-odored carpet of fallen yellow fronds. "No contact, Miss Three. No tachyonic echo detectable now."

"Can you tell us where she was when you made the last contact?"

"Affirmative, Miss Three."

"Where?"

"Straight ahead, Miss Three. Three point eight kilometers from us. Zero point four kilometers beyond the nearest gate in the fortress wall. Two hundred forty-seven meters below our level."

"Guide us there."

"Comment, Miss Three. We accept your order, but available data indicates probability of reaching her location too small for computation—"

"Spare us, lass!" Habibula was gasping. "Spare a poor old man who has lived too mortal long and endured too mortal much—"

"Our problem now—" She looked at Star. "To get across the road."

"Hear me, lass!" He shrilled louder. "For life's precious sake, remember who I am. Aye, lass, a noble hero once. But I was younger then, and we had a mortal chance to win. Now—now we're already done for. We can't do it, lass! Not with all the frightful odds against us. Not with the evil creatures swarming to sting their gnawing worms into our precious flesh. You might as mortal well expect three miserable mosquitoes to take a Legion fort."

"They might." She grinned at him. "If they carried the right microbes."

"Aye, lass." He rolled his eyes and sighed. "That's all we are. Lost among the ghosts of giants dead a billion years ago and the fearful vampires seeking to make shrieking ghosts of us.

"Mortal microbes—"

"Information, Miss Three." Lord Archy dived to her side. "Flasher starcraft approaching."

A great black teardrop. Flying low and fast above the ancient battlements, it passed behind them, gone before the thunder of its passage shook the leatherweed around them. They watched till it had sunk behind the black loom of the citadel.

The starport on the central peak was too high for them to survey, but black starcraft moved now and then across the blue-black sky above the cliffs, toylike with distance. Searching for any hint of a way inside the citadel, Jil felt overwhelmed by a sense of its frowning power.

She wondered what kind of enemy had occasioned the building of it. Creatures savagely hostile and themselves gigantic, if they had been a threat to those vanished symbionts. Like the barrier behind them, the walls were blocks of dark basalt, larger blocks than men had often moved.

She tried to grasp the dimensions of that enormous, ring-shaped pile. Its sheer outer wall loomed a full kilometer high. Counting and guessing, she thought it must have thirteen sides. Thirteen blunt angles, each just touching one of the lower domes around it.

She found no entrance.

"A fearful prison!" Habibula shivered, blinking at it. "Those wicked walls have stood a blessed billion years. Look at them, lass! It's mortal folly to think of breaking through."

"I'm looking, Giles. And now—" Her breath caught. "Now I think I've found the doors! Don't you see the dark niches, one at the center of each wall, down at ground level?

"They must be gates—"

"Locked and guarded, if they are! Dear life, lass, this is no baby game, played for precious paper stars to stick on our chins. You're asking us to throw away our last mortal chance on an idiot move—"

"You can open locks," she reminded him. "You got us into the slaver."

"Lass, you hope too much." Dolefully he sighed. "Hope can't teach a mortal stone to fly."

"But a small boy can!"

"For precious mercy's sake. Life—life—life—" Hard sobs shook him. "Life's gone, lass. Even if some mortal miracle comes to snatch us from these closing jaws of frightful doom, I'll never be a blessed boy again."

The sun dropped. In the sudden frosty dusk, the white pavement shone with its own cold light. Shivering on their hard carpet, they waited for a chance to cross the roadway. Lord Archy soared above the leatherweed, his own light quenched, scouting for them.

"Information, Miss Three." Lord Archy dropped back at last. "No starcraft now in view. Observing occasional surface vehicles now in motion, we compute zero point seven nine probability that none will reach this point within two point four minutes, which is our estimate of the time you will require to cross—"

"Let's go!"

Stiff with cold, they ran clumsily. Soon they were breathless. Gasping for air, Jil wondered how vehicles found traction on the glassy pavement. Habibula slipped and fell, moaning for help. They lifted him and stumbled on. Motors were already whining behind when they staggered off the glowing roadway into scattered leatherweed.

They fell flat.

Jil heard the traffic drumming again behind them, but no alarm. The leatherweed was thinner here, pushing up through breaks in the ancient pavement, and they crawled a long way through it on hands and knees before they dared stand again.

Stiff now with cold, they staggered at last into the niche. An arched recess, reaching deep into the fortress wall. The only light within it came from the green-glowing scrap of nebular sky behind them. Crouching to keep below the level of the last ragged weeds, they came at last to the doorway. The gate within it was massive metal, wide and high, weathered dull and greenish in the gloom.

It was shut.

"I told you, lass!" Habibula shrugged at her dismally. "No way in. If the fearful thing was ever open, it must have been a mortal million years ago. If the flashers ever used it now, they'd cut the leatherweed—"

"Giles, there's the lock!" Star pointed. "Looks like the one you worked to get us into the slaver—"

"Too many mortal meters up!" He backed away, blinking at the hinged access plate high above them. "Do you take me for another blessed giant—"

"We'll lift you, Giles."

They lifted him.

The metal plate clattered.

He squirmed and wheezed and moaned.

"No mortal use!" he gasped at last. "All the mortal tumblers frozen with a blessed billion years of dust and rust. Fused, more likely, when the fearful shockwave passed. The thing has not been open since the giants died, and it won't open now.

"Lass, you can't ask a dying man—"

His wheezing changed into a croaking scream. As if abruptly lifeless, he collapsed into their arms. Staggered, they lowered him to the pavement. Jil heard boots behind them, and her stomach knotted from a nauseous bog-rot stench.

"Well, Jil." The high, mocking whine stabbed her like a blade. "You've come a long way since we met, and I won't stop you now. Never mind the rusty lock. You're a welcome caller, and we'll escort you in."

37

Jil woke in the dungeon.

Twenty meters square, twenty tall, built like all the old citadel of black volcanic rock sawn into blocks as large as common rooms, it had been designed to hold something more savage than she could imagine.

The door was a grille of some age-grayed but uneroded metal, itself ten meters tall, the great square bars closely set and strong enough to stop a Legion battletank. Blue light burned through them to paint long black stripes on bare black stone.

She lay naked on the floor, numb and shuddering. Her whole body ached. Her head throbbed and her stomach churned when she tried to rise. Sinking back, she shut her eyes against the glaring light and tried to remember.

All she recalled was a broken blur.

That bog-rot reek. The voice of Rem Brendish, shrill with gloating triumph. The flash and crack of Star's projectile gun. A brighter flash and a cruel stab of cold. Lord Archy darting beneath her, trying to soften her fall. Brendish laughing, his nasal whine calling orders.

Her stomach heaved when she recalled it.

Gasping and quivering with the effort, she sat up and hugged her icy knees against her breasts. Radiation pain exploded in her skull when she moved, a pulsing flame she couldn't reach or quench. Teeth clenched, she fought for breath. Her nose was dripping from the cold, and she had to wipe it on her hair. She rubbed her arms when she could, slapped her shuddering body. At last, weak and reeling, she was on her feet.

Boots!

Boots on bare stone. She peered through the bars. All she saw at first was that second barrier, which was cunningly angled to hide everything beyond. The boots grated nearer. Silently, that second grille slid up. She saw a third beyond and two men.

Rem Brendish—and another.

Brendish strutting jauntily in trim-fitted purple and gold. Tight purple trousers with gold-braided seams. A long purple jacket, with a bright gold crown embroidered on the breast. Cocky mockery on his yellow-bearded rat face.

Though both looked small on the scale of the dungeon, on the human scale the other was a giant. Naked to the waist, dark hair kinked and thick on chest and arms, head and beard dyed a dingy orange-red. Crouched a little forward, great black-haired hands hanging empty, he strode first.

Behind him, Brendish was a malevolent pygmy.

That second barrier dropped silently behind them. They came on across the basalt vault toward her cell. The inner grille lifted. They marched inside. With surprising soundless speed, the great gray bars slid back to lock them in with her.

Naked, she faced them.

"Jil Gyrel." Brendish murmured her name, smiling a little, his bold eyes consuming her. "An odd thing, babe." He chuckled. "I'd just been thinking of you. Recalling the rebel waif you were on that occasion so long ago in the Quasar Club when your impulsive grandfather threw his wine glass at me. Dreaming of the long-legged doll you bloomed into on Alpha III. Reliving my delight when I saw you on the *Purple Empress*. Of course you were untouchable then, but things are different now."

"Where's my mother?"

"One thing, babe." His shrill tone turned mockingly disdainful. "Though things between us won't be all that formal, I must ask for a certain respect. I'm proud to say the masters have allowed me to assume the title of your dear stepfather since his unfortunate termination. Under their supreme authority, I am now Emperor of Men. You will be required to recognize my new status. You will address me properly. As sir. Or, more formally, as Your Interstellar Eminence."

"I see—sir!" She couldn't help the shudder in her voice. "Shon Macharn—is he dead?"

"His master matured—I suppose you noticed his physical condition on the *Purple Empress*. Control was interrupted at a most unlucky moment. Just when we were coming into landing orbit here.

"Free long enough, he got to the pilot. A stupid oaf named Greb." His quick little eyes swept her body again, bright with malicious anticipation. "Together, they put the ship on a collision course toward a big munitions center the masters had built down on the coast. Wrecked the controls before we could stop them.

"Doing his best to send me down with the ship, but I conned the pilot." Brendish grinned in elation with himself, yellowed teeth flashing through the straggling beard. "He thought your poor mother was human. We got him to put her and me off in a life pod before he went down with Macharn and his craft."

"So my mother's safe?"

"If you want to call it safe." He grinned wider. "She's a host, of course. Or would you say hostess? My own consort since Macharn was terminated." His narrow nostrils twitched. "If I could take her stink!"

Quivering, she made herself stand fast.

"Sir—" Her whisper was a broken rasp. "Where are the men—the men with me?"

"Well secured." With a self-pleased grimace, he gestured at the basaltic walls and the great gray bars. "I've just come from a visit with old Habibula.

"A rare character!"

Brendish chuckled happily.

"Amazing, how bitter he was when I crooned the chorus of my ballad about him. His chief claim to fame in our time, but he still has to learn a decent gratitude."

Again he came closer, until he could have reached her. His avid hands rose slowly. Filthy hands, the nails black and broken.

She felt her body trembling, but she refused to cower back.

"So, doll baby!" His grin grew hungrier, and she quivered from the sardonic mockery in his whine. "Here we are among the masters. I'm totally delighted with your arrival, and I have their permission to make you an offer you'd be stupid to refuse.

"For all their powers, they're poor company. I'm not even sure they should be called intelligent. Not, at least, in any sense that we can understand. I believe they originated here in the nebula, in some condensing gas cloud. The adults can still live in space, feeding on energies that would be fatal to anything organic.

"Don't ask about the old ones. Such questions often get unpleasant answers. Most of them don't hang around after metamorphosis. Go back to space, I understand. Back to their ancestral plasma. Anyhow, babe, that's what you'll need to know. Except—"

His filthy finger prodded her left breast.

"Except one thing, babe. A point you'd better keep in mind. Every one of them is fertile—though they have nothing we would understand as sex. Any one of them, young or adult, can reproduce itself at any time. Whenever a suitable organic creature is available."

Grinning wide, he licked his lips.

"Baby doll, you're available!"

In spite of herself, she cringed from his yellow teeth and his sadistic voice and his prodding black-nailed finger.

His avid stare dwelt on her.

"Babe, here it is. I'm offering you your darling mother's place. That's a high one. I'm Emperor, remember. A place I've earned because I understood the masters and agreed to play their game. Played it pretty shrewdly."

He chuckled, prodding harder.

"A fact you must admit, even if you can't quite admire me. I made them see they needed me. Because of that mental gap between themselves and men. Even though they think through human brains, their thought processes are often hard to follow. Early on, they ran into communication problems.

"I made them see they had to have an untouched human agent."

"You—" She recoiled in spite of herself. "You knew what they were?"

"Early on." He grinned at the giant. "Back before you were born."

"And joined them?" She blinked in stunned disbelief. "Spied for them?"

"I sized them up. Picked them to win."

"Helped them?"

"Babe, we made a bargain. I explained human ways, advised them on strategy, found how to pull the fangs of old Habibula." He nodded at the giant. "I doubt you'll ever learn to like the odor, but at least I've found them honest. Maybe too naive to lie. And they've promised me a lot.

"Including you, baby doll!"

Chilled and quivering, she shook her head.

"Think about it, babe!" His dirty finger pinched her nipple. "Consort to the Emperor. You'll get imported food, not the synthetics they make for the masses. The service of all the hosts you need—if you can stand the stink. Whatever luxuries you care to ask for. Your last chance, babe, for life."

"Life?" she breathed. "I'd rather die."

"Not an option, babe." His broken yellow teeth gleamed through a yellow-bearded grimace. "When you know what the real options are, I think you'll say yes. I hope you do. Because your little mother has got too much like a walking skeleton to fit my taste, and you smell better.

"But if you really must refuse—"

"Baby doll, meet my free-styler friend Mad Bull Marbok."

Shambling one step toward him, the giant uttered an animal grunt.

"A professional name, of course." He beckoned the giant back toward her. "My own coinage. I'd always admired his style in the pit. When I came to terms with the masters, I arranged to have them give him a special implant. One ordered neither to damage his magnificent physique nor impair his fighting skills.

"So here's your option, babe.

"You can become my loving consort, with special privileges very few human beings will be allowed to enjoy. Or—the Bull." His rat eyes leered. "I've seen him in the pit with yawara masters, and they never delayed him long.

"I must warn you, too, that he has a master in him.

"A somewhat better weapon than your yawara tricks. What

you get from him will be more than human sperm." His hard fingers tweaked her nipple. "Babe, he'll plant a new master in you—under orders to make you mine.

"You'll smile, babe!"

He snickered in her face.

"You'll smile and squirm and do your best to please me. If I can stand the stink." He grimaced at the giant and grinned expectantly at her. "So how about it?"

She stepped a little back, dropping into a yawara crouch.

"Not quite yet." He waved to check the crouching giant. "I want to offer one more inducement. Your two friends. Star and old Habibula. When I spoke to them, they showed a keen concern for you. If you happen to care as much for them, consider this last concession. I can't preserve their lives—even as Emperor, I must respect certain limits. However, as a fitting gift to my adoring consort, I can promise them a quick and painless termination.

"So how now, baby doll?"

Afterward, Jil wondered.

She loved Kynan Star. Even for old Habibula she had found a deep affection. Yet, in that dark instant, she took no time to weigh the threat to them.

Reeling with illness from the ache in her brain and the stench of the giant, already tortured far beyond any limits of logic or pity, she slid away from his avid eagerness and his cruel fingers on her nipple.

She crouched to face the crouching giant. Loosed by a hiss from Brendish, he was stalking her, staring eyes and crimson nostrils wide, hairy hands grasping.

Almost before she knew it, her body was flowing into the mode of the quaking plain. Head down, she twisted. His clutching arms went safely past her, but his nude torso felt like iron when her shoulder reached it.

Jarred and numbly aching from the impact, she sprawled on the bare basalt.

The giant was falling on her.

Rolling aside took all her will and too much time. She felt his fingers on her ankle, a steel trap closing. Nerved with stark desperation, she coiled back on him in the mode of the striking snake, chopping for his throat.

Too cold, too slow.

He countered with his great head butting. All she struck was his heavy-haired skull. Paralyzing pain came up her arm. Flung off balance, limp and ill, she saw his hobnailed boot flying into her face.

The form of the sinking sand. Her mind heard Kita Kano's quavering command, but her numb limbs were deaf. The boot grazed her chin, the shock of it blinding. Her slow body folded, and she could not escape the falling giant.

The impact of his black-haired torso crushed her against the cold basalt. He lay gasping on her. His evil breath was overwhelming nausea, and her own breath was gone. She felt his knotted arm around her neck, saw stiff fingers jabbing for her eyes.

"Don't you love him, baby doll?"

A great wave of crimson pain had broken in her skull, clouding everything. Yet she caught a fainter voice, calling through the drumming dimness. Old Kita Kano's, breathing out of her memory to name the modes she needed. The mode of the snapping twig, the mode of the rising wind, the mode of the stabbing blade. She heard the names, but she found no force to make the moves.

"Won't you love your own baby master, growing in your precious flesh and sucking up your blood? While it eats you, think of me, baby doll!"

That far mockery touched some unsuspected trigger. Her body acted, almost without her will. The mode of the snapping twig broke the arm around her neck. The mode of the rising wind flung the heavy torso from her. The mode of the stabbing blade reached its lethal target.

The giant's breath rattled out, a long-drawn snore. A fouler cloud filled the air as his bladder and bowels let go. When she could, she rolled away and reeled to her feet. Flesh crawling, she recoiled from his unmoving mass.

Dead. But—his master?

The silent parasite was surely still alive, maybe more deadly than ever. She backed farther, blankly staring. Could its evil seed somehow reach her yet? Could the creature itself somehow leap from a dead host to a living one? Ill and shivering, she didn't even want to know.

Groping for nerve, she turned to face Brendish. He was

gone. She heard the far-off thudding of his boots and saw the gray-barred gates sliding down behind him to lock her in again.

She gasped and ran.

The first barrier was half shut before she reached it. The second grazed her head. The third was too far down, a ruthless metal jaw smashing down against hard black rock. With too little time, she dived into the mode of the flying arrow.

Her head slid through the closing crack. Cold metal scraping her ribs and her hips, she doubled into the mode of the rolling ball to pull her feet farther. The grille crashed down. The floor quivered under it.

She lay there, drained of oxygen, gasping air too thin to fill her lungs, drenched and shivering from a nervous sweat. Without strength or will, she didn't even wonder whether her numb limbs had been caught between those closing jaws.

Something was pounding. Her own rapid heart? It kept fading, and at last she knew it had been Brendish's retreating feet. The great metal gate lay cold against her hip, but it let her roll away. She reeled unsteadily upright.

In stifling midnight.

The blue glare filtering through the bars made a pool of light around her on the wide stone floor. Black stone loomed ahead and around the gate behind her, walling a broad tunnel that reached off into the dark. Far away along it, she found another tiny island of light. Beyond that, yet another.

Lighted cells?

Kynan and Habibula perhaps locked in them? Stiffly, weak and reeling, she limped down that immense and endless-seeming corridor toward the flecks of light. When she stopped to hold her breath and listen, the footfalls were gone. Brendish with them. She staggered on as fast as she could drive herself.

He would be back.

Not, however, with the gigantic free-styler. A spark of elation flickered within her, and then a solemn sense that was almost regret. She had killed. Killed a man. Since her first falls on the yawara mats, she had wondered if she could kill. Knowing now, she shook off that brief compunction.

She limped faster, trying to think. Brendish would be armed when he returned. Escorted, no doubt, by armed flasher slaves. Nude and weaponless, lost among these unknown dungeons, what could she hope to do?

Habibula and Star?

If those faint flecks of light ahead really showed where they were, could she hope to reach them? Somehow set them free? Not likely. Even if she reached their cells, she lacked Habibula's famous way with locks.

Cruel reality came to dim her first elation. The ancient tunnel seemed to stretch ahead forever, colder than her own cell had been, its musty air so thin she was panting fast. The faint patter of her bare feet rustled back from its unseen walls, their whisper a haunting reminder that these great black stones had been laid to contain things powerful and dangerous beyond nightmare.

How could she hope?

"Because—"

Gasping the word, gasping it again, she clung hard to the vanishing wisps of her triumph and staggered on toward that first pool of light.

The entrance to another cell, when she came reeling to it. Strangely, the outer grille was lifted. When she peered around the corner into the angled passage beyond, the second gate was also lifted.

Listening eagerly for Star's voice or Habibula's wheezy whine, she crept into the passage. Pausing to listen again, she trembled in terror of whatever might emerge to meet her. Shadows shifted as she moved, changing into shapes as monstrous as those unknown things the dungeons had been designed to hold.

A voice!

Elation raised her for an instant, let her fall again. It was neither Habibula's nor Star's. Heart pounding, she crept on. From beneath the lifted grille, she could see into the dungeon.

Huge as her own had been, now in use as a laboratory. Cold blue light glinted on the metal and crystal of devices strange to her, arrayed all around the lofty walls. With no pause to wonder what they were, she peered at two snowballs.

These lay on a long workbench at the center of the room. White fog hung around them, draining in wispy streamers toward the floor. Two people bent over the bench.

Brendish—and her mother!

She saw them in harsh-lit profile. Brendish flushed and panting. Her mother pinched and ashen, tiny-seeming on the cell's huge scale, looking cold in a black fur jacket too large for her. One thin hand held a thick-tubed weapon pointed at the white-smoking workbench.

Brendish was rasping. "If you want my opinion, I don't think the little monster will ever tell us anything. I've always said we ought to kill it by any means we can. I've just had one nasty jolt, and I don't want another."

He glanced uneasily behind him.

"Hit it again—"

He must have seen Jil.

"A human spy!" Darting behind the bench, he turned to point at her. "That naked bitch sneaking in the door. Freeze her! Quick!"

Her mother spun, the black tube lifting.

"Think you're chilly, baby doll?" His nasal taunt echoed against the great stone blocks. "Take a taste of total cold!"

38

The snowballs smoked.

Brendish was a scraggy-bearded demon, leering through white fog. His sardonic jeer rang and died against the basalt walls. Naked, chilling, waiting, Jil had time to study her mother's face.

An enigmatic mask, nearly fleshless, made up heavily, smiling vacantly above the black-barreled weapon. More skeletal than human, empty of all emotion, that empty smile ordained by the cruel parasite within.

Jil had time to regret all her old resentments. Time to understand her mother's second marriage. Time to recall her dismayed bewilderment at all the dreadful changes since. Time for wrenching pity. For this thing about to kill her was not her mother really, but a painted machine.

The thick black tube had come level in the frail-seeming, blue-veined hand. Jil shivered, looking into its dark hollow. Something clicked, and a cold blue glow began to flicker there.

Tired of waiting, she suddenly wanted the weapon to flash. Total cold, she thought, would erase her being instantly. No master parasite would ever feed upon her—

The weapon was wavering, the blue glow gone.

Her mother's face had changed into another sort of mask. A grimace of utter tragedy, quivering and contorted. The mindless smile drew into a snarl of hopeless hate. The dead eyes came alive again, black with stark despair, yet ablaze with overwhelming rage.

"Baby—doll—"

The sound through the red-painted snarl was a sobbing moan. The skeletal body slackened for an instant in the too-large coat, like a puppet with strings cut loose. Alive again, shaking violently, it swung the weapon from Jil to Brendish.

He cowered down into the ice fog.

"Rara!" He screamed that old pet name. "Freeze the snooping bitch! The masters command it—"

"The monsters—don't command—don't command me now." A hoarse and oddly broken whisper, as if her mother had to grope for speech. "I—I'm free—"

"No, you aren't!" Narrowed eyes darting from the weapon to Jil and back again, he dragged himself defiantly straighter. "Not for long, Rara. The masters may lose their grip for a moment, but they always come back. And they'll make you suffer—and teach you how to love—"

"Love?" Her mother's fleshless body jerked in the loose black fur as if she had been a puppet worked on wires of agony. "We won't—be loving—loving you—"

Brendish shrieked.

Suddenly steady, the black weapon clicked. Blue light flashed. The kneeling man shone for a moment, luminous and blue in the swirling fog, a blue halo around him. The blue went out. His rigid body turned crystal white with sudden frost. It toppled very slowly backward to the black stone floor and shattered there like fragile white glass.

Jil shrank back, arms against her breasts, shivering from a flash of searing cold. Stunned, staring, she watched the glittering crystals growing over the shards of what had been Rem Brendish. She heard their dry crackle, watched a new pool of fog that formed around them, flowing away into vanishing streamers.

Her mother stood motionless a long time, staring down into that tiny cloud, seemingly not even breathing. At last, with a long sigh, she shook her wasted head, leaned to lay her weapon on the bench and turned unsteadily. Dilated and empty at first, her eyes came slowly into focus.

"Jil?" Her whisper seemed strangely tentative and faint. "You are my Jil?"

"Mother!" Her own shaken voice was no stronger. "I am Jil."

"Don't hate me, Jil!" her mother begged. "Please say you don't."

Choked and voiceless, eyes welling, Jil could only shake her head.

"Through all that hell, I thought you did. And never—never blamed you for it. Because I did neglect you so." Her mother hugged her harder. "I thought—grieved because I thought I'd never get to tell you—tell you that I loved you."

Clinging, she sobbed again.

"Grieved because I couldn't—couldn't tell you I really loved your father. As much as I did Shon. Oh, Jil! I never understood. Never really tried to see what the nebula was to them or why you always loved it so. I hope—hope you can forgive—"

"Mother!" Jil found a quavery little voice. "There's nothing—nothing to forgive—"

"Thank you, baby—baby doll!"

"I did hate the way you called me that." Jil squeezed the frail-seeming frame against her. "Till now."

"I never knew." A little calmer, her mother paused to shake that fleshless, death-white head. "Jil! Jil! I was such a fool. I guess because of what my people taught me. Because they named me Tsara and brought me up to be an Ulnar princess. Because I caught their crazy dream.

"Rem used that to trap me.

"My silly pride. My old love for Shon. He made me believe there would be a cure for Shon—life with him was dreadful, but they let me believe they were arming people in the nebula to lead a revolution—I thought it would be a human revolution—to restore the Empire.

"When I was on the *Purple Empress*." The lifeless whisper sank. "When Shon's parasite had put the creature into me. Then I knew what they were and what they'd done. It's dreadful—dreadful, Jil—the way they use you.

"I hope—hope you never know."

Her mother shuddered in her arms.

"I saw—saw you, Jil. On the *Purple Empress*. Saw you serving them in what they called the throne room. I tried—tried so hard to speak. But of course they wouldn't let me make a sign. I knew they meant to plant a creature in you. I was glad—so glad when I thought you'd escaped.

"But now—you never should have come here." The stick-thin figure sagged into her arms, a puppet with all strings cut. "Because you'll never get away. Nobody will. Except—"

The skull face jerked toward the weapon on the bench.

"Except with the cold-gun. They can't bring us back from that—"

Jil shrank from it.

"We can't just kill ourselves. Not while we have any sort of chance—"

"Not we." Bleakly forlorn, the gaunt head shook. "Not me."

"But"—dismay shook her voice—"you've escaped."

"Not for long." The dark-shadowed eyes stared into the thin white blanket spreading away from what had been Brendish. "I could kill Rem, because he was still human—in his dreadful way. It's the creatures that can't be beaten.

"Not by anything organic. Because they aren't organic. Rem had studied them. He used to taunt me with what they are. He said they would always rule us—what is left of us—because they don't die."

"Tell me, mother!" Jil implored her. "All you know."

"You'll never understand, baby doll. Not until—unless—you have a master in you."

"Please! I've got to know."

"If I can find the words—" The whisper halted, the skull face still. "They aren't anything—anything that can be touched. Fighting them, Rem used to say, would be like fighting starlight. Because, he said, they aren't matter.

"Their molecules evolved in the nebular clouds. Very tiny particles, linked only by fields of force. Magnetic, electric, partly tachyonic. They lived in space—if what they are is really life—till they made what Rem called their evolutionary leap."

"Can't they be killed?" Jil whispered. "Can't we keep you free?"

"Never. When they seize the body they damage its own functions. They keep it going with their own controls so long as they possess it. When they're gone—"

The death's-head shook.

"The body stops."

"But you—" Jil stared. "You aren't stopped."

"Because the thing—the thing in me—is still alive." The ragged whisper had grown almost too faint to hear. "I can feel it now. Reaching—fighting—to take me back and make me hurt —hurt—"

Too stricken for speech, Jil could only hug her. For a long time, she didn't move or speak or even seem to breathe, but then the spidery body jerked and straightened.

"Till it comes—" The shuddery voice came stronger. "If I could help—"

"The men—" Jil's breath caught. "The men who came with me?"

"Locked up. Farther down the corridor."

"Can you help me get them out?"

"No time for that. No use to try. I've seen the creatures work the locks. They sense the motion of the bolts inside. With senses no human being has."

"We were looking—" Jil peered around the high-walled dungeon in search of any shard of hope. "We came looking for a little creature we call a laser-maker—"

"Here she is—" Her mother nodded at the snowballs on the workbench. "Dead, I think."

"Dead?" Jil stared at the balls of frost. "Did—did Brendish—"

"Rem and the creatures. The one in me. Trying to make her talk. They thought she knew some secret. Something about AKKA. They tried every sort of torture but they couldn't invade and control her the way they do us, because she is not organic.

"She never—"

She felt her mother tense and shudder.

"Jil!" Fainter, faster, that breathless whisper rushed ahead. "So much to say, so little time—"

The haunted eyes fixed on that thinning pool of fog.

"The laser-maker never talked. They kept her alive a long time, looking for new ways to cause her pain. But she always beat them. Escaping into something close to death. Always closer.

"Just now—"

The whisper changed again, as if something tried to choke it off.

"Just now Rem—Rem rushed in. Shouting that she had to be killed."

"The creature in me was going to make me kill her, because they're so terribly afraid—afraid of AKKA. They think it's tachyonic. They're vulnerable to tachyons.

"That's why they fear the robot—"

"Lord Archy?"

"The robot they caught with you." That skeletal arm jerked at the nearer snowball. "It can generate weak tach pulses. Rem was using the cold-gun, trying to torture both of them. He thought he could make the robot read her mind.

"The master in me was here to watch—watch and hold the gun—because they'd never entirely trusted Rem. It kept my body back from the robot, but I guess not far enough. Because the robot helped me escape—

"Till—now—"

Her voice rose on that last word, jagged with agony, an endless keening scream. The glazed eyes stared from her painted skull face, mute and unbearable. One stick arm gestured, jerked and flung as if on a hidden wire.

"Back—" A voiceless shriek. "Quick—"

39

Jil stood breathless, terror-frozen.

Her mother was moaning, shaken with a strange convulsion. Agony contorted the made-up face. Brighter blood smeared the scarlet mouth. The bare-boned frame jerked and tossed. A puppet hung on tangled strings, it snatched the cold-gun off the bench, flung it to the floor, dived to recover it.

Writhing there, kicking, gasping, it fought itself. Insane hands flailed at the weapon, trying first to fling it away, then clinging grimly. The thick tube twisted as if itself alive. Once it came toward Jil. She saw the blue glow inside the tube, felt a glow of cold.

But then the muzzle swung down.

The mechanism clicked.

A hard blue flash swept that tortured form. All motion stopped. The contorted stick thing glowed blue for a moment, till crackling frost turned it to an epic of agony, done in pure and instant white.

Jil stood where she was, staring down into the fog forming around it. Her eyes ached, and dry sobs of pain and gratitude convulsed her. That final scream dying in her mind, she heard her mother's voice from long ago.

Crooning loving lullabies when she could first remember. Scolding her for tracking the red mud of Hawkshead Pass on the fresh-mopped floors of her grandfather's house. Yelling in the icy nebular night to call her inside from the white-streaking meteors and the hot-sulphur scent of the wild storms she loved.

The air was good again, somehow cleansed by that blue flash. Breathing deep, she remembered wondering how her mother could hate the clean, dry bitterness of leatherweed on the wind at Hawkshead Pass, or how she could like the stale perfumes that clung to her decaying Ulnar relics.

Swiftly, the ice fog hid that image of agony.

Its stark tragedy was still unbearable. But at least—at last—the terror had passed.

Her mother was free.

She listened. The crackle of frost had ceased. In the dead stillness of the dungeon, all she could hear was her own quick heart, but it became a drum of marching danger.

Danger here from the horror that had owned her mother.

Danger all around her, from the swarming parasites, surely now alarmed and closing in to take her.

Danger the Gyrel luck had all run out.

Trembling, reeling from too many blows, drained empty by too much emotion, longing for time, she stared again at the great black blocks of the dungeon wall—

Legion green!

Star's cosmonalls, rolled into a bundle on the end of a shelf. Habibula's. Her own. Their space boots tossed beside them.

Alive again, breathing fast, she slid into her torn yellow suit. The boots stiff and cold to her numb feet, she stumbled to the doorway with the other bundles and turned there to glance back at the smoking snowballs.

Lord Archy and Miss William—dead?

Crusted deep with frost, they were still too cold for her to touch, lying too near the ice fog writhing around the dreadful shape that had been her mother.

She spun, ran clumsily.

Caution checked her at the third barrier. Peering out into the corridor, she found its darkness soundless and unbroken except for two tiny lights. The far blue glow from the cell where she had fought the gigantic free-styler.

The other light—Star and Habibula?

She ran for it.

Too far. Her breath was too soon gone, and her footfalls rang too loud on the wall she couldn't see. Slowly, too slowly, the dot grew into a dim-blue pool, black-streaked with shadows from great gray bars. Lungs aching, she tried to hold her breath long enough to listen.

A wheezy groan?

"Giles?"

"Lass?" His moan came faintly through the grille. "For life's sake, lass, we're dying. Dying in this mortal dungeon. Of fearful cold and famine, lass! Mortal soon, unless you let us out—"

"Giles, I can't."

"Open the mortal door—"

"I've no key."

"You need no key." His voice came louder. "I conned that stinking rat when they were dragging us in. Stripped and shivering and left to perish without one precious morsel—"

"How, Giles? How?"

"I let the yellow-bellied bastard think he had me senseless, but I could hear the way he worked the mortal lock. Listen, lass! You'll find a gold-colored plate set deep in the mortal stone by the door, about as high as you can reach. Hit it three times. Quick and hard. Count ten, slow. Hit it twice. Count fifteen. Hit it four times, slow."

She found the plate. On tiptoe, she struck it with her doubled fist and counted, struck it and counted, finished and waited.

"Try, lass!" Habibula was gasping. "Try the mortal lock, before we're dead—"

Finally, silently, the great gate lifted. Thirty meters beyond, a second barrier stopped her. Habibula called another code that raised it. Beyond the angle, she came to the third, Star and Habibula standing in black silhouette against the great bars.

"Jill!" Star breathed. "I never thought—never dared hope—"

Habibula was wheezing the code. She strained to reach and strike the sensor plate. Panting, swaying again to the cruel crimson pulse beating forever in her skull, she waited. Habibula wheezed and tried to shake the gate.

"Hit the mortal thing again! Hit it mortal hard. To save our mortal souls—"

The barrier rose.

Star caught her in his trembling arms.

"Dress!" She kissed him, sobbed and clung, pushed the bundle at him. "Lord Archy and the laser-maker are in another cell, back along the corridor. Frozen with a flasher cold-gun. Maybe dead, I don't know. In whatever time we have, we must try to wake them."

"Aye, lass! Before the fearful flashers come—"

Habibula got into his garb with magic-seeming speed, but he fell behind, puffing and moaning, as they ran back toward the dungeon where her mother had died. At the angle beneath the second grille, Lord Archy skipped to meet them.

"Miss Three!" His pulsing sphere was quicksilver bright once more. Though the bell tones reflected no emotion, she imagined delight in the way he soared toward her head. "We offer service—"

"Miss William?" she whispered. "Is Miss William alive?"

"Affirmative, Miss Three. When you stopped the heat drain from the shadowflasher weapon, we were able to restore our own dead circuits and reactivate Miss William's mind. She has returned from third-stage withdrawal."

Giles Habibula had overtaken them.

"Giles—now—" Her throat was suddenly dry. "Can you use AKKA? To stop the flashers—"

She saw him shake his head.

"Not I, lass."

"Lord Archy?"

"Nor Miss William. We're all forbidden, lass, by the Legion High Command. Because of our own special missions, and because the Keeper's fearful burden would be too heavy for any one of us. Ah, lass, I've known too many blessed Keepers. Mortal martyrs, torn away from all the precious joys of life to wait and age and die in some secret fortress like the one around us now—"

"Can't we do—anything?"

"You can, lass." His mud-colored eyes blinked sadly at her. "I've spoken to Kynan, and he agrees that he's too mortal old." His wheezy tones turned solemn. "Lass, the dreadful duty must fall to you."

She shivered.

"Do you—do you mean—"

"A heavy thing. Too heavy for one so young and mortal

lovely—" He had to gasp for breath. "A wicked burden for you, lass. But we have no mortal choice except to make you Queen of the Legion and Keeper of the Peace."

Heart racing, she swayed as if dark dungeon walls had rocked around her.

"First, lass, you must swear the Keeper's oath. For life's sweet sake, answer me fast. Before our time runs out. Will you swear—"

"I will."

"Lass, you must kneel—" A wind in her mind swept his creaky voice away. "—repeat after me—"

Kneeling, she tried to echo his wheezy hush of words. Undertaking the sacred trust of AKKA, she would shield the secret with her life, sharing it only as instructed by the Legion High Command, employing it only as the weapon of last, most desperate resort to defend the Hall of Stars and all mankind—

"I do so swear."

"Information, Miss Three!" Before she could rise, Lord Archy was darting to her. "Information rated urgent. We perceive an elevator opening on this level. Armed guards are emerging—"

She scrambled upright.

"We need the weapon, Giles. Now!"

He blinked at her, gloomily shaking his head.

"Giles, we've no time—" She gripped his pudgy arm. "How does the weapon work?"

"None of us knows." He sighed. "No more than a mortal morsel of the secret. I have one tiny bit. Lord Archy has one. Miss William another. But we're forbidden to share the bits we know with any being whatever, save the sworn and chosen Keeper—"

He squatted on the floor. His fat hands swifter than his plaintive whine, he had produced several small and simple-seeming objects from inside his clothing. Two little disks of some bright metal. A rust-colored rod that looked like a plain iron nail. A bit of twisted copper wire.

"The instrument, lass." Wide and sad, his eyes rolled toward her. "How it works, I never knew or wanted to." Swift and sure, his thick fingers fitted the tiny parts together. "It's harmless, lass, as I hand it to you. Harmless as a mortal toy, till you hear Lord Archy and Miss William."

She took it in trembling fingers. Lord Archy skittered ahead of her back into the blue-lit tunnel. She crouched with the tiny device on the cold stone floor, and he chimed very softly what she had to know about its setting.

"Information, Miss Three!" His tolling was suddenly louder. "We perceive twenty prison guards marching from the elevator toward us. Advice, Miss Three. Rated imperative. We urge action now—"

"Jil!" Star's hoarse whisper came from the dungeon doorway. "Here's Miss William."

The laser-maker lay on his open hand. A fluff of silver-colored fibers, shining brighter than it had been aboard the *Purple Empress*. When she held out her own palm, it flew silently to settle there, weightless, slightly warm.

He withdrew toward the main corridor, where Habibula wheezed and waited. Lord Archy moved back into the dungeon, soaring slowly, slowly sinking. Breathless, trapped between hope and unbelieving dread, she shivered again to the soundless cold.

"Thou art Miss Jil?" Miss William's voice was almost soundless too, a lilting vibration more felt than heard. "Beloved of the noble Kynan Star?"

"I'm Jil Gyrel."

"O brave new age that has such beings in it! My dear kinsmen on Early World have foretold your coming to end the revels of our common enemy and so to let their insubstantial pageant fade, leaving not a rack behind."

"Just tell me what to do."

"Make haste, Miss Jil, the better foot before. Delay have dangerous ends." The singing tones changed to another voice, a woman's, low-pitched and pleasant, yet gravely concerned and crisply precise. "To the newly sworn Keeper of the Peace. I am Vivi Star, Keeper as I speak, these words to be communicated only in the event of unpredictable emergency, only in the event of my own disability or death.

"This message is recorded to complete the conveyance of an ultimate trust, the secret of the weapon known by its symbolic acronym, AKKA. In obedience to the oath you have sworn, you will shield it as supremely secret and use it only as a last desperate necessity.

"To use it, you must understand it.

"In the first two stages of instruction, you have received an assembled and adjusted instrument. This third stage will instruct you in its use. The instrument has been called a fulcrum—"

"Warning, Miss Three!" The gong voice startled her. "Rated imperative. We perceive a living shadowflasher in the dungeon cell behind us, emerging from your mother's frozen body to search for a second host."

"Please!" Jil bent toward the bright fluff in her hand. "We have so little time—"

"In peace and honor rest, Miss Jil. For now the whirligig of time brings us our revenge." Again the voice had sung, and again it changed. "The instrument is a tachyonic amplifier—"

"Tell me how to use it."

"Your friends declare you young and fair, Miss Three." The voice lilted louder. "In your own brain, you have the gift to know and use the force of temporal power. Your native Gyrel talent. We have seen more devils than vast hell can hold, but they are more tachyonic than we are. As most spotted lilies shall they pass into nothingness, and no world shall mourn them—"

"Lass!" A stifled croak. "Behind you!"

She whirled to look.

All she saw at first was a white fog wisp, crawling like a snake from inside the dungeon. In silent flight from it, Lord Archy skimmed past her. She saw it recoil, as if it had sensed some danger in her. The tip of it thickened, lifted, paused as if exploring.

She saw it change.

It took her dead mother's shape. Almost luminous in the light from behind, shining white, its mist limbs writhed in a dreadful mockery of her mother's dying agony.

Darting at her, it struck like a snake.

40

Terror held her paralyzed.

The thing in the mist came at her silently, riding the flying motes of ice. But moving them only as momentary tools. It had ruled and used her mother, and she felt its savage hunger now for her own body and her reeling brain.

"Hit it, lass!" Habibula was yammering. "Mortal hard!" With the Keeper's secret power.

She knew what he meant, but she couldn't move, couldn't breathe, couldn't think. Her aching fingers were too numb to feel the tiny device they clutched, and still she hadn't learned the way to work it. Even here, deep beneath the old basalt battlements, the pulsar radiation kept surging through her skull, blurring everything with pounding pain.

Transfixed, she watched the thing recoil and rear again.

Watched bright ice fangs forming, distorting that mockery of her mother's last agony into a mask of dreadful terror.

Watched them driving at her heart.

Far away, rustling like the wind in dead leatherweed, she heard the voice of her old yawara master, whispering what she needed.

"The mode of the playing kitten."

The breath of the ice thing struck her face, a freezing bog-rot reek. It shone with its own cold glow. Its bright fangs would stab through her in an instant, and she knew nothing human could harm it.

Yet she tried—

Time and motion ceased. That shining horror-shape was stopped, like something glimpsed by a lightning flash. Nothing moved anywhere, except her own awareness. A strange illumination blazed within her, shining out, and her whole being expanded with it into everything around her. She felt Habibula's terror and Star's despair, somehow shared Lord Archy's steady readiness and Miss William's cool serenity.

That blinding brilliance shone through the old stone walls, through all the ancient fortress, out across the dark caldera, on across the clouded continent. It let her awestruck brain embrace the planet and its sun. As if the Gyrel gift had been immensely multiplied, she knew the whole nebula again, all its violence stilled, its hot core frozen, its racing shockwave checked.

And even on beyond the nebula—

Her being grew out into the cosmos, until she felt the human worlds as near as her own hand, until she was alive in the little drift of stars that made the home galactic arm, until the whole wide spiral of the galaxy dwelt inside her mind, until she had grasped its entire galactic cluster, still on and on until she held within herself the cluster of its clusters, all their spins suspended.

Grasping for the mode of the playing kitten, she searched for the shadowflashers.

"Bow, my child." Kita Kano's whisper, rustling through that arrested vastness. "Pride must be felt only in the ancient art itself, never in its humble instrument. Your only feeling should be sorrow for the fools you must erase."

She found the flashers, and they became her own shameful flaw. She knew and shared the burning needs that drove them and ached with pity for the wrongness in their manner of survival. Sadly, their cruelties had grown beyond all sufferance. With a haunting grief, because they now belonged to her, she knew they had to be erased. She erased them.

Time returned.

"Aye, lass!" Habibula's elated quaver came from far away,

meaningless at first. "You killed—killed the mortal terror!"

Face down, she lay sprawled on the cold basalt. Her breath was gone. Sickness knotted her stomach. Chill sweat drenched her. Her temple ached where she had scraped it on the stone. Trembling, she felt too weak to move, but Star was lifting her upright.

Standing unsteadily, she looked for that bright-glowing shadow shape. Its ice fangs were gone, with all its dreadful life and purpose. Broken into tattered wisps of common fog, it was dissolving fast.

The air was clean again.

"Data, Miss Three."

Lord Archy came soaring to poise himself in the air before her.

"We perceived your creation of a far-reaching tachyonic impulse, which Miss William rates a Roman thought."

Everything around her shone with a new reality. The burning brightness of his quicksilver bubble was almost painful. Star gripped her arm too hard, trembling with his joy. Habibula's wheezy breathing was a roaring storm.

"What—" Star seemed to shout in her ear. "What's a Roman thought?"

She felt no need to know. Everything seemed strangely near, yet strangely far. She breathed sharper clammy dankness of long decay, sharper than it had ever been, and felt the cold stone floor quivered briefly to a tiny seismic quiver, too slight for common senses, but nothing really mattered except that halted instant when she had been the Keeper of the Peace.

The moment was gone, with all its dazing wonder. The suspension of time, the cosmic awareness, the fleeting power. Gone as abruptly as it came, like a lightning flash. Longing for it, dazed and lost without it, she clung to all she could recall.

"Term 'Roman thought' undefined." Lord Archy's peal seemed remote yet still too loud. "Except as Miss William defines it. She informs us that the flashers, towering in their pride of place, were by a mousing owl hawked at and killed."

"Killed?" Star seemed to shout, as if from far away. "More—more than one?"

"Affirmative, Pilot Star."

"Additional data, Miss Three."

Lord Archy hovered close above her, shimmering in the chill blue light.

"Miss William has spoken to her home on Early World, that better place where her fathers lie. She informs us that they have looked into the seeds of space and time and found no surviving foes within the limits of their detection. Our own computations support her conclusion that all the flasher parasites within the nebula were swept to dusty death."

Still living in that lost instant, Jil felt numb to everything since, even when her senses pressed events upon her with a newly blazing vividness. She knew when they came out of the dungeon and found the human hosts who had been marching down to kill her, all fallen where they had been when she erased the parasites. She knew when they came up into an ice sunrise on the ancient battlements, into more still fields of the newly dead.

"A mortal blessing, lass," she heard Habibula whispering. "Not a one but died rejoicing."

Picking her way among those sprawling forms, she hardly felt their horror. Nothing else she thought could ever be as real as that vanished instant of supreme control when she had seemed to grasp all the cosmos.

Emptiness ached in her now, because it was over.

They found her father's starcraft, the ancient *Iron Argo*. The mirrored hull dulled and scarred from too many years too deep in the nebula, it stood at the edge of that peak-top field inside the fortress ring, where he and Shon Macharn must have landed it after they were taken.

Giles Habibula cycled them through the lock and waddled eagerly to lead them aboard. In the galley, he found the supplies gone stale as rat-bait, but still better than the flashers' slave-ration bricks. Sampling the full case of Nebulon wine that Jil discovered in her father's locker, he found that it had aged mortal well.

They climbed back to space.

Jil knew all that, sharing Habibula's uneasy haste and Star's weary triumph, but only absently. Still she lived in that ended instant, treasuring her fading shreds of that infinite vision, recalling old Kita Kano's rustling whisper and the mode of the playing kitten, striving to understand all she had commanded.

Lord Archy flew the craft when they took off, but she stood beside him under the conning screen. The throb in her head had eased, and she tried to hope that the mystic power of AKKA had made her immune to radiation.

Hoped until she looked up into the screen.

It showed the pulsar, behind them now and only a hard blue point. It still winked slowly, but she could no longer see its blood-colored pulse rippling out into the clotted dust. The nebular core around it shone blue now, with merely visible light. She had gone blind to its lethal radiation. Out of the planet's gravity well, she reached again to feel the spinning masses of the nebula, tried to trace its tangled forces. They were gone. What the screen showed was all she could perceive.

Her mutant sense was dead.

"The art is all." Old Kita Kano's warning, whispering in her memory. "The artist is only a tool, used and thrown away."

She had been thrown away.

"Question, Miss Three." Lord Archy danced nearer in the air. "Does evident radiation damage to your special sense perception result in interior malfunction defined as pain?"

"Yes—" She hesitated, because the power she had known so long was gone. "But not enough to matter." Peering into his bright spheroid, she felt a surge of gratitude for his concern. "If we can fly the ship without it."

Unless her command of AKKA required it. She shivered to a chilling dread of that, because it must have helped expand her senses to find the shadowflashers. Without it—

"Data, Miss Three." The soft bell notes were chiming cheerily. "Your mutant skills no longer rated essential to our survival. Inspection shows no damage to interstellar navigation gear. We have already computed a safe flight path back to Miss William's Birth World."

The Gyrel gift had been well spent. AKKA was something vastly greater. If she could recover it, to live again in that suspended instant that had brought her so near divinity. She yearned to rekindle its lost illumination. Yet—

Would that require some new peril? As grave, perhaps, as another flasher invasion? Hoping that would never come, she tried to quiet her longing. The flashers were gone. Star had not been harmed. Or old Habibula. She loved them both, and smaller moments could still be good.

With Lord Archy on watch, they bathed and slept. They found clean green cosmonalls. Star shaved his gray stubble. She washed her hair. Habibula was humming the Legion march when she found him waddling out of the galley to retune the geodynes.

She had been Keeper of the Peace.

The words had a wonderful ring, even since that instant had ended, and she set out to learn if she still possessed the Keeper's power. With time enough now, she claimed the narrow cabin that had been her father's and called upon Habibula and Lord Archy and Miss William one by one to tutor her again in their separate shares of the secret.

Bit by bit, its awesome mysteries dissolved into awesome revelations. The physics of the geodesic drive helped her see how tachyonic energy could deform the coordinates of Newtonian spacetime. In the dazing geometry of AKKA, dimensions scarcely mattered. Whole planets, the virus-like micromolecules of the flasher parasites, any sort of target could be displaced with equal ease out of Newtonian reality.

Alone in the austere little cabin, she worked very cautiously from theory into practice. Trembling at her own daring, yet calmed again by a dawning serenity that astonished her, she displaced grains of sand—crystal grains she found in her boots, which must have come from the ruins where they had hidden. She displaced an empty ration sealer. Vanishing with a startling crack, as air closed into the sudden vacuum, it filled her with a dazed elation.

Edged at first with terror.

Could she trust herself? If duty called her again to strike at some great enemy, could she recover that cosmic awareness, recall that fearful power? The Keeper's burden lay heavy on her until in the middle of one sleepless night she heard old Kita Kano's faint singsong.

"Forget yourself," his squeaky quaver urged her. "Your art is everything. Used with trust and love, it will serve you truly."

Comforted, she slept.

Awake again, certain now that she was really still the Keeper, she went back to the command deck to take her turns on watch along with Star and Lord Archy. Forgetful of herself, she no longer really minded that they were better pilots now than she was. Free of pain again, with warmth and strength and nerve returning, she still loved the cosmic chaos of the nebula, as splendid as it had ever been. Even the pulsar's terrible power had become thrilling wonder.

"A danger we defied," she whispered to Star. "And got away alive!"

Off duty, they explored the old starcraft together. In her

father's cabin, they found small things that brought him closer than he had ever been. Drama record crystals. A few antique paper books he must have brought from Terra. His journal. Her mother in a holo made before the wedding, proudly posing as an Ulnar princess. Her own holo at five, gap-toothed and shyly smiling.

When she read the journal, mixed emotions choked her.

"I used to wonder," she told Star. "But the journal says he always knew. How much Shon and my mother loved each other. He offered more than once to set them free. Shon declined. He had loved her first, back on Terra, but quarreled with her bitterly. He despised her Ulnar pretensions. Wanted no part of the Ulnar schemes to rebuild the Purple Empire.

"As for my father—"

When she remembered the dreadful puppet she had found on the ice cap of Ultima I, an ache in her throat cut off her voice, but she knew her father had loved them both.

As for Kynan Star—

He saw her pain and moved to touch her. When he drew abruptly back, she saw and understood the gnawing pain in him.

"You loved me," she whispered. "When we were flying into the nebula."

"We're bound for Terra now. You're Queen of the Legion and Keeper of the Peace."

"If you thought that could matter—"

She pulled down the folded berth.

They were together when Lord Archy called from the command deck to report that the *Iron Argo* was emerging from trans-Newtonian flight into polar orbit around Early World. Slipping out of the cabin without waking Star, she went to the deck.

"Message, Miss Three."

Lord Archy floated from the map-tank console to meet her. "Message from Miss William."

Miss William had lain on the console in second-stage withdrawal through most of the flight, healing from her injuries. She was returning from it as they neared her home world, but she still preferred to speak through her soundless communion with Lord Archy. Waiting for the message, Jil smiled fondly at them. Two silvery balls, a liquid-seeming bubble and a puff of shining fibers, both grown nearly human to her now.

"Comment, Miss Three." Lord Archy perched on the console. "Miss William employs terms she learned from the songs of the savage spearman. Since our data banks contain inadequate definitions, we transmit them without translation.

"She addresses you as a most unspotted lily. She states that all Early World shall mourn the loss of your mutant gift. It lies beyond the understanding of her people, and they cannot restore it.

"She adds, however, that the Eternal Ones can offer us some small reward for her rescue. Before the shockwave came, they were working to preserve their symbionts from harmful radiation. She believes that the same tachyonic power you have learned to control so well can be used to shield you and those around you from radiation harm, at least here outside the nebular core."

"Thank her for me. For all of us."

His bell tones became a woman's voice. An echoed voice, Jil imagined, from the classic record crystals where Miss William had picked up the idioms of that ancient spearman.

"The Eternal Ones do highly value and return your gratitude. Words pay no debts. Yet they praise the valor of the Legion, both in feasting and in fighting, that has brought them out of death endured forever, back to life in the eye and prospect of time. I myself thank heaven, fasting, for my own return to my good progenitors and future heirs, who wear such precious jewels in their heads. For this relief much thanks, dear Jil Gyrel. 'Twas a long and bitter exile, that left me sick at heart.

"When you fly up again, I will remain below—"

"You mean—" Jil looked at Lord Archy. "She wants to stay."

"Affirmative, Miss Three."

The bell notes returned.

"Comment, Miss Three. Miss William wishes you to understand her decision. Her people suffered a sad sea-change when the shockwave passed, and the comfort of their children left them. She wishes to remain with them, at least for a period that we compute as several Terran centuries. She says we should select another to carry her share of the saving secret."

"I'd wondered," Jil said. "I know her people need her. Tell her that Kynan Star will take her place beside you and Giles."

"He will be instructed." She saw the silver fluff move

slightly on the console, heard the woman's voice again. "We love you, Miss Jil! And honor with our soul. Though we may stay behind, our friendship goes with you forever. True friendship, that needs no ceremony. Though we are rooted here forever, we beg you to return."

"We will," Jil promised. "We and the Eternal Ones—I think we need each other."

She turned to Lord Archy.

"Before we land," she added, "there's something else I'd like to know. Miss William spoke about an armed rhinoceros. I'm still wondering what she meant."

"Data requested, Miss Three."

For a time he lay silent.

"Data received," he pealed at last. "But rated inadequate for useful computation. Miss William defines term 'armed rhinoceros' as poetic metaphor. Search of memory banks reveals definition of rhinoceros as extinct horned Terran animal, rated dangerous, but no definition for term 'poetic metaphor.'"

"The data's good enough," Jil told him. "I think she was speaking of Brendish and his friends."

Miss William imparted her share of the secret to Star, and they left her with her people, those tiny black-spined dome-shapes clinging to the worn granite walls of the dusty polar hollow where they had endured so much.

They left the nebula through Gyrel Pass. Avoiding Devil's Creep, they took the main channel. Touching down at Gamma II, Beta I, and Alpha IV, they found human survivors of the flasher war, a few haggard people shattered by baffling disaster and more bold souls eager to risk the nebula again and probe the farther stars beyond it, but no parasites or hosts or parasites. They found no flashers waiting on Terra.

Nor any hero's welcome.

Instead, they met something nearer chaos. The Legion had been left leaderless by unexplained catastrophe. All its highest officers, wherever they were, in planetary command centers or orbital forts or aboard battlecraft in space or anywhere else, all had fallen suddenly and strangely dead, felled by some dire new malady the space medics had not yet been able to identify.

The Hall of Stars had adjourned to wild disorder, all its most influential leaders swept away by the same appalling pandemic at the same fatal instant. The Church of the Oversoul had lost its exarchs. The Cosmic Harmony Party had abruptly splintered into furious factions, its surviving seekers of universal peace turning to the virtues of private meditation.

The remaining Legion leaders were still disorganized, bitterly suspicious of one another and what was left of civilian authority, engaged in desperate random efforts to explain the inexplicable. Star tried to make reports to a dozen conflicting groups and antagonistic individuals before he found believers.

He and Jil and old Habibula were all interrogated, locked up and again interrogated, until at last, reluctantly, Jil coaxed the skeptics to a weapons-testing range for a wary display of AKKA. Even then, the new High Command vetoed any public recognition of their victory in the nebula.

"A wicked wrong!"

Habibula howled about it.

"When we've shed our blessed blood—aye, and risked the sting of fearful parasites into our mortal bones to save the human race!"

He glared at the nervous new commanders convened to sit in judgment on them.

"Can't you see we're mortal heroes? If you want to rob us of the precious little morsel of glory we toiled and fought like mortal gods to earn—" He sniffed in wheezy contempt. "Better we should have let the fearful demons come, to feast on the loon-livered fools you are—"

A banging gavel cut him off.

"Contain yourself, corporal."

The senior admiral-general was a pale, perspiring little man who looked too young for his grade.

"We're considering—considering everything." Uncertainly, he looked for support from the uneasy aides seated beside him before he scowled again at Star. "Personally, I find your story hard to swallow. However, Miss Gyrel's demonstration did impress my staff. We'll get back to you when we have reports in hand from further investigations still in progress."

He wet his lips and frowned at Jil.

"We do find ourselves all agreed on one paramount point. Whatever happened in the nebula, it's not for the public. Not yet. Not until order has been restored and our space perimeters secured—"

"Lord of space!" Habibula gasped. "If you're too mortal blind—"

The gavel banged.

"Provisionally, Miss Gyrel—" He shuffled documents before him. "Yielding to the initial conclusions of my staff, I am accepting you as the new custodian of AKKA. For the time being. Since the robot claims to be your personal property, you may keep it with you. Pilot-Major Star and Corporal Habibula will be assigned to temporary duty on your guard detail. A secret and secure place of residence will be established—"

"It better be mortal secure!" Habibula wheezed. "Ask him, lass! For something warmer than that frigid jail on Alpha V. Ask for cellars full of wine. Ask for every blessed gift—"

Again the gavel.

"At the moment, Miss Gyrel, until my staff can get back to the matter, your quarters will be—"

"General, we've already chosen our fortress." Jil smiled at Kynan Star, and he reached to take her hand. "It will be the nebula."

"Impossible." The admiral-general goggled at her. "The Legion has withdrawn—"

"Better listen, sir." Habibula squinted shrewdly at him. "Better listen blessed well. I'm just a mortal corporal. A precious small reward for all the mortal generations I've served the blessed Legion. But Jil's the Keeper now. She had mortal well better get every little thing she asks for."

Jil shook her head to silence him.

"Really, Miss Gyrel—"

"We're going home to the nebula." Her firm tone stopped him. "We've friends there, and we'll be secure enough."

Returning through shockwave under new cloaks of security, Jil Gyrel slips out of history into myth, her life recorded in the honored annals of the Legion along with the legend of Nowhere Near and the epic of the lone Legionnaire who had to battle the Basilisk and all his own companions. Most of what is known has been related here, much of it revealed in defiance of security by old Habibula himself. Incomplete, it is yet enough to let her story stand beside John Star's odyssey across the Medusae's nightmare planet and the heroic saga of Bob Star against the Cometeers.